Harri Nykänen, born in Helsinki in ~~crime~~ journalist before turning to fic~~tion~~ ish crime writing award "The Clue" in fiction exposes the local underworld criminal, the terrorist and, most recently, from the point of view of an eccentric Helsinki police inspector.

NIGHTS OF AWE

Harri Nykänen

Translated by Kristian London

BITTER LEMON PRESS
LONDON

BITTER LEMON PRESS

First published in the United Kingdom in 2012 by
Bitter Lemon Press, 37 Arundel Gardens, London W11 2LW

www.bitterlemonpress.com

First published in Finnish as *Ariel*
by Werner Söderström Ltd (WSOY), Helsinki, 2004

Bitter Lemon Press gratefully acknowledges the financial assistance
of the Arts Council of England and the WSOY Literary Foundation

© Harri Nykänen 2004
English translation © Kristian London, 2012
Published by arrangement
with Werner Söderström Ltd (WSOY), Helsinki

A CIP record for this book is available from the British Library
ISBN 978–1–904738–923

Typeset by Tetragon
Printed and bound by CPI Group (UK) Ltd, Croydon, CR0 4YY

1

Men are born, they live, and they die. Few leave any permanent trace of their sojourn. For most, the only memory remains in the photo album gathering dust in the bookcase's bottom cabinet. For some, it's impossible to come up with any reason for their lives, even with a touch of goodwill.

Pehkonen belonged to this latter caste.

If I had been the contemplative type, I would have doubtless dedicated more time to pondering the meaning of his seemingly pointless existence. God alone knew where and why this gadfly had drifted around the earth in the period between his birth and his death, in other words approximately fifty years. I knew a piece here and a fragment there, but as a policeman I just wanted an answer to one question: who killed him?

The late Mr Pehkonen was lying in a recycling dumpster, yesterday's news covering him like a quilt. The early autumn night had been cool, around forty degrees, and a blanket of newspapers was warmer than nothing.

On his head, the deceased wore a bizarre fake-fur hat that looked more like a waterlogged raccoon dog that had been flattened in rush-hour traffic than a piece of headgear. A dark-brown wool scarf had eroded into a rope-like rag around his grimy neck.

There was a deep contusion at his temple, and next to his head sprawled a square-sided cobblestone, a clunker that weighed at least ten pounds. The newspapers mounded into a pillow beneath his head had soaked up the blood that had drained from the wound. The combined odour of printing ink and urine wafted out from the dumpster. As a parting gesture, Pehkonen had done it in his pants.

When I saw the body, the first thing that came to mind was that next morning there would be a newspaper in that exact same paper container reporting about a man who had been found dead in a newspaper container.

Pehkonen's death was as meaningless and insignificant as his life, unless you consider it an achievement to end up a one-column story buried in the inside pages of the national paper and a two-column story in the tabloids. I was sure that somewhere nearby that same day we'd find the guy, who, in a bout of drunken insanity or to assert ownership over a bottle of booze nursed by Pehkonen, had bashed the life out of his pal with a cobblestone. The investigation and the autopsy would be routine in the truest sense of the word. Cremation, an urn paid for by social services chucked into the ground, a couple of handfuls of dirt on top, end of story. What happened to Pehkonen after that was no longer the concern of a detective from the Helsinki police force's Violent Crimes Unit.

The lieutenant on duty had called me about the body, which had been discovered by a paper deliverer, only because he knew I lived right next to where it had been found. The wake-up had come at four-thirty, and I hadn't had time for my morning coffee yet, so I went back to my place. Around eight I headed into town. I always took the same route: Fredrikinkatu to Iso Roobertinkatu, and once I hit Erottaja I headed past the Swedish Theatre down Keskuskatu to Aleksi, where I jumped on a tram.

I was usually able to walk to work in peace, but this time I only made it as far as Fredrikinkatu before being stopped.

I don't know where the Rabbi came from, but there he was, suddenly standing right in front of me.

"Shalom, Ariel!"

"Shalom, Rabbi Liebstein," I responded. I took a step back, but Liebstein pursued.

I glanced around and understood that the Rabbi's materialization hadn't been a genuine miracle after all.

There was a van parked at the edge of the pavement: the congregation's van, which I should have recognized and spotted before it was too late. Peering out from behind the van's cargo windows was Roni Kordienski, the congregation's combined super, handyman and driver. Liebstein and Kordienski had been carrying an old ornamental cabinet from the nearby antique shop out to the vehicle, and just at that moment my mobile phone had started to ring, causing my vigilance to flag.

"Nice cabinet."

"The congregation received it as a donation."

"Excuse me," I said, raising my phone to my ear with an apologetic look.

"Detective Kafka."

The caller was my immediate superior at Violent Crime, Chief Detective Huovinen.

"Bad time?"

I glanced into the Rabbi's expectant eyes.

"Kind of."

"We need you pretty fast."

"What is it?"

"Two bodies at Linnunlaulu. One of them in the rail yard. Two tracks are closed, it's holding up the trains. The deceased are most likely foreigners."

"Anyone there yet?"

"Simolin headed out fifteen minutes ago… and a patrolman has cordoned off the area. Forensics is probably already there by now, too."

"I'm on it."

"Call me when you're en route and I'll fill you in."

You wouldn't have taken Liebstein for a rabbi, not by how he dressed anyway. He was wearing a stylish black wool over-coat, a burgundy silk scarf knotted in an almost bohemian fashion, and gleaming black shoes. Still, at least a fellow Jew would peg him unmistakably for a Jew. He had the broad, furrowed brow of a thinker, and it was easy to imagine him, head tilted, reading the Torah at the synagogue or preaching on the Sabbath. The bridge of his ponderous eyeglasses had chafed tender red gouges into the sides of his nose. The aura of good-natured clumsiness he radiated was, however, an illusion, and I didn't let it fool me. Liebstein dug his nails into his victims with the tenacity of a debt collector.

I didn't have anything against him; he was an amiable and intelligent man. But right now I didn't feel like talking, even amiably and intelligently.

"How are things going at the congregation?"

Good eyesight and quick reflexes had kept me out of the Rabbi's path for over six months. Now some courteous resolve was called for. Otherwise I knew that before I realized it, I'd have made half- or two-thirds promises that I had no intention of keeping.

"Ariel Isaac Kafka," the Rabbi repeated, this time stressing each name. "If you dropped by the synagogue slightly more often to pray, you'd know how things are going there. Can you tell me why you delight me and the other members of the congregation so infrequently with your presence? I saw your uncle just yesterday and we discussed the matter."

Liebstein spoke with an accent, the origin of which was difficult to pinpoint. And that was no wonder, if you knew his background. He was born in Germany, fled from there to Sweden to escape the Nazis, and then moved to Denmark in the 1950s.

"It's the police work... I'm always busy. As a matter of fact, I was just called to a crime scene. Two bodies."

The Rabbi nodded sympathetically.

"I understand, Ariel, don't think that I don't, even though I was born into a slower age. Everyone is busy these days. The whole world is like an enormous clock whose spring has been wound too tight. I'm afraid that before long its gears are going to start flying off."

My phone rang again, this time in my pocket. I fiddled with it blindly and managed to silence it.

"And the mobile phone. It was meant to be a servant, but it has become the master. It has taken over everywhere, it orders and the servant obeys, he runs and runs until he's out of breath and collapses to the ground…"

"It's just that my work…"

The Rabbi raised his forefinger to his lips.

"I understand, I understand," he continued. "You do important work. All of us in the congregation are proud of you. If only we had more frequent opportunities to tell you how proud."

The Rabbi lowered a hand onto my shoulder. His touch felt heavy, almost disapproving, although the expression on his face remained gentle.

"I saw your picture in the paper last week and I told your aunt that, once again, you had solved a serious crime. We consider you a blessing to our congregation and to our small community, which has seen such hardship."

Liebstein was exaggerating. The serious crime was an everyday assault that had led to manslaughter, and the perpetrator had been apprehended thanks to a surveillance-camera photo published in the tabloids, not me.

The Rabbi smiled and hoisted his rimless glasses farther up his nose. The chafed spots itched, and he rubbed them between his thumb and forefinger.

"Your aunt said that you wanted to be a policeman even before you had your bar mitzvah. Is that true?"

I shrugged. Even the Rabbi didn't need to know everything.

He bent over towards me and whispered as if he were divulging a secret.

"I've always liked detective novels."

I instinctively furrowed my brows.

"You're a police officer and Satan will ensure that your work will never end. Evil will always walk at your side. And that's exactly why I've been waiting for you to pay us a visit, to reflect and withdraw even for a moment from all the blackness you encounter in your profession. The soul requires rest, otherwise a person becomes as frail as the ashes of burnt silk paper, and eventually crumbles into the tiniest motes of dust."

"I'll try to come… I'll come as soon as I can."

"We haven't been able to put together a *minyan* for three days. Yesterday morning only two members showed up for synagogue."

I nodded.

You needed ten male congregants thirteen years or older for a *minyan*. Women were not accepted, but this was a topic I didn't feel like delving into. I would have proposed the best and easiest solution to the problem: accept women into the *minyan* in Finland, as had already been done elsewhere.

I could sense my gaze wandering towards my destination and my feet taking surreptitious steps.

"Rabbi Liebstein," Kordienski interrupted apologetically. "They're waiting for you."

The Rabbi didn't respond, he just looked at me. My mobile began to ring again. Liebstein shook his head and smiled, albeit wanly.

"Have to go, busy busy busy… some day the spring will snap and all the little gears will ricochet off and people will go mad and start killing one another… Yamim Noraim. Remember Yom Kippur, Ariel…"

Liebstein was right: I had to remember. Being born a Jew brought along with it certain responsibilities other than refusing to eat pork. It was almost impossible to skip out on celebrating the Jewish New Year altogether. It began with ten days of repentance, the last of which, Yom Kippur, was the most important. It was then that the entire congregation prayed together and asked for forgiveness for all of their conceivable sins, starting from masturbating and malicious talk.

The Rabbi spread out his hands to illustrate all of the whirling, twirling gears, springs and wheels in the universe being hurled outwards into eternity, and then he followed Kordienski into the shop.

I gave a sigh of relief, and as I passed the van, I checked my reflection in the tinted side window. Short hair, slightly thinning at the crown, sideburns that reached halfway down my ears, a narrow, introverted face and a high, domed forehead.

I hiked up the collar of my brass-buttoned pea coat and took a few hurried steps to ensure my getaway before calling Huovinen.

"Where are you, Ari?"

"Downtown, on my way to Linnunlaulu."

"By car?"

"No, but I'll get there just as fast by tram."

"You know that bridge that crosses the railway tracks?"

I conceded that I did.

"You'll find two very lifeless bodies there. Kind of an unusual case, you'll see what I mean. One of them is in the rail yard beneath the bridge. Just kick things into gear and inform me as soon as something comes up. You can bet the media's going to have a field day with this one… That bad timing: were you at one of your people's celebrations where we pagans aren't allowed?"

I told him I'd been investigating a corpse that had been found in a recycling dumpster.

"Someone else can take that. Shalom!" Huovinen said, ending the call.

I knew Huovinen so well that I found it impossible to be offended. We had graduated from the academy at the same time. Huovinen had been the best in the class, and I was only the fourth best, which had aroused a general sense of bewilderment among my relatives. Everyone remembered how my brother Eli had been number one in his class and had been accepted to study law on his first try and how my sister Hanna's matriculation papers had been the best in the history of our school.

At that time, the burden that Einstein and Oppenheimer had left for less brilliant Jews like myself had weighed heavily on me.

The bridge was cordoned off with police tape, but the officers who were patrolling the site, radios crackling, recognized me and let me through.

I stopped in the middle of the span and gazed towards downtown.

Beyond the rock face, a maze of train tracks immediately began; it looked like a bunch of ladders had been toppled over in the same direction, stopping at the wall of stone and glass formed by the station and a few other buildings. Above the tracks ran a confusing jumble of electric wires; here and there you could see bright-red warning lights.

A large, ornamental pink wooden villa teetered perilously close to the edge of the high rock face.

A double-height express train approached from downtown; its roof swept past only a couple of yards beneath my feet. I could feel the bridge sway from the mass of the carriages.

On the other side of the bridge's railing hung a six-foot-wide flange of corrugated metal. Yellow danger signs had been attached to it. I glanced over the edge of the railing and saw several uniformed policemen on the tracks. A tent had been erected over the rails, so that the tender morning sensibilities of the commuters on passing trains wouldn't be offended by the sight of the body.

"Kaf… Ari!"

Detective Mika Simolin was approaching the crime scene from the direction of the Linnunlaulu villas.

"I went and had a look down below."

Simolin was ten years younger than me. He had only been in Violent Crime for six months and still treated me with a respect that bordered on bashfulness.

"The shooting took place here," Simolin said, indicating a bloodstain on the ground. "Afterwards the killer shoved the body down the slope and jumped or fell from the bridge onto the roof of a train and died instantaneously. I mean the presumed killer," Simolin corrected himself.

The body lay on the slope that descended from the bridge, almost up against the steel mesh fence running above the rails. A green tarp had been draped from the fence to block the view. A CSI named Manner in white overalls was standing next to the body.

"All right if I come over there yet?" I asked.

Manner glanced up.

"Be my guest."

I climbed down with Simolin at my heels and positioned myself a little awkwardly next to the fence. The body was lying on its back, partially hidden in the tall grass. It took a second before I understood what had happened to it. The face was like a mutilated stump from some pagan sacrifice: its nose and ears had been sliced off, and what was left was covered in blood.

2

From day one as a rookie cop, I had prepared myself for my first encounter with a corpse. I learnt how to look in such a way that I skipped over the most disgusting details. I also learnt how to breathe through my mouth. Relying on these techniques, I made it through my visits to the pathology department and the cabinet of horrors that was the police crime museum.

My first body was, nevertheless, an easy case. It was New Year's Eve, and the evening had started out with a hard freeze. Later that night it had started to warm up and lightly snow. The body was found by a late-night partygoer, and the desk officer ordered me and my partner to the scene.

The deceased, a man of about forty, was lying under a large oak. He was blanketed by driven snow, as if he had pulled a freshly laundered comforter over himself and dozed off to the rustle of the wind in the branches. His eyelids and hair were dusted with powder.

The sight was almost beautiful.

Later I came across much uglier corpses, but I learnt to accept death as part of my job, and violence as part of death.

Although the face of the body lying on the embankment was mutilated, you could still tell that the man it belonged to was young and foreign. He had on black jeans, grey running shoes and a black leather jacket. The Adidas ski-cap he was wearing had hiked up far enough to reveal three small holes in his forehead, a few centimetres apart from each other. The blood trickling from them had converged with the gory mess that was his face.

Simolin pulled on a pair of disposable gloves and squatted next to the body. He pointed at the bullet holes.

"Twenty-two?"

"That's what it looks like," Manner nodded. "What about this?" He opened the leather jacket, revealing two stab wounds in the upper torso. "Plus one more bullet hole here in the chest. Someone wasn't taking any chances."

That's exactly what I was thinking.

"When did the call come?"

"Eight-fifteen," Simolin said. "First they said something about a man jumping under a train; they thought it was a routine suicide. Then we got the call about the second victim. There was only five minutes between calls. The first one was from a woman out walking her dog; she noticed a human ear in her pooch's mouth. At almost exactly the same moment, the body was spotted from a passing train."

"You check the pockets yet?" I asked Manner.

"Yup. Nothing."

"Take another look."

Manner searched the pockets of the tight jeans, front and back. The leather jacket had side pockets plus two more pockets inside. Nothing in them either.

"A whole lot of empty," Manner said.

"You'd think there'd be some keys at least."

"But it's still clear it wasn't a robbery."

"Everyone carries something on them… keys, mobile phone, bus pass, money."

"If you shoot someone three times in the head and then stab them twice in the chest, you're going for the kill. If you're just robbing them, intimidation or a blow to the back of the head will do the trick."

"What's the deal with cutting off the nose and the ears?" I asked, looking at Simolin questioningly.

I knew perfectly well that Simolin already had a theory, as did I. All I had to do was tease it out of him. Besides, a wise superior always listens to his subordinates first.

"They did it to make identification difficult. *Gorky Park*," he deduced. "The victim's face was slashed so that the victim wouldn't be identified."

"Pretty risky business, giving your victim a nip-tuck in a spot like this," I said.

"It wasn't fully light yet," Manner reminded me. "And it wouldn't have taken more than a few seconds... the nose and ears were cut with a sharp knife or shears."

"Have the other ear and nose been found?"

"Not yet."

"But one of the ears got left behind up there, why?"

"Maybe the killer was in a rush and dropped it. It was still semi-dark, and in a situation like that, you're not going to be very eager to start poking around, even though the perpetrator must have pretty steady nerves. Ice in the veins, as my father-in-law would say."

"So where are the shells then? He probably wouldn't have had time to gather them up."

"Maybe the shooter used a revolver. Or else they just haven't been found. We haven't gone over the embankment with a metal detector yet. A twenty-two shell would be pretty hard to spot in terrain like this."

A red-and-white Pendolino clacked northwards under the bridge. On the next track over, a local train approached from the opposite direction. I waited for the noise to die down.

"What else do we have?"

Manner glanced over his shoulder.

"The victim was coming from Töölönlahti Bay, in other words he was headed towards Kallio."

"How do you know?" Simolin enquired. He was an avid student and eager to learn all the tricks of the trade.

"There's no sand in the treads of the victim's running shoes. On the Kallio side, the path is covered in crushed rock, which has sand in it, while on this side of the bridge, it's paved. If you came from Kallio, take a look at your shoes. Now, the guy who was hit by the train approached from the opposite direction. There was crushed rock and sand from the path in the soles of his shoes."

"How do you know?" Simolin repeated.

"Ever heard of a mobile phone? Siimes is over examining the train body, but we just consulted each other. Amazing what technology can do, isn't it?"

"Has the other victim been identified?"

"No, he wasn't carrying any papers either, just a map of Helsinki and a mobile."

I bent my right knee to take a look at the bottom of my shoe. Manner was right. There was grit in the sole. There were also a few bigger chunks of crushed rock between the grooves.

"Any sign of a third person?"

"Not yet, but the bridge and the path haven't been examined yet. I'm not sure we'll find much; it's going to be tough, or at least time-consuming. Hundreds of people go through here every day."

"But why here, in this exact spot?" I wondered. "If the point was to kill this guy, you'd think there'd be better places to do it."

"Maybe a jealous spat between two gay guys," Manner suggested. "Those cases can get bloody, and all rational thinking flies out of the window. The suicide also fits that scenario."

"But the mutilation doesn't."

Manner considered for a moment. "It could be some sort of revenge ritual, an ex-lover... or the desecrating of an enemy's body. That would fit the foreigner aspect. On the other hand, one thing I've learnt over thirty years is that you never know with crazy people, the motivation can be just about anything, like orders from God or some little green man... I called in a medical examiner just to be sure. Hand me that case?" Manner asked Simolin.

I sought a firmer stance with my left leg.

"Send the fingerprints to be checked as soon as possible. I'll go see how things look down below."

I left Manner to examine the body and went to see if I could find the easiest way down. Simolin watched Manner work for a moment but then followed me. I stopped at the bridge and waited for him to catch up.

"Call in as many patrols as can be freed up to scour the terrain on both sides of the bridge. We also need to search the tracks; something might have been carried along with the train. I'll call Stenman and Oksanen."

Vuorio, the medical examiner, was huffing as he climbed the path to the bridge. He was overweight, and the exertion was a strain. He nodded at me but didn't acknowledge Simolin.

"These are going to be the last cases of the year for me. I'm headed to Canada day after tomorrow for some further training."

Vuorio was an enthusiastic fisherman and hunter, so enthusiastic that he had been to Africa to hunt big game. He couldn't hope for a better destination for an educational exchange.

"Good for you."

"Over there?" Vuorio asked, looking across the slope.

"Over there."

"The places they make an old man root around."

Vuorio shook his head but nevertheless started his laborious descent, muttering to himself.

I called my two other subordinates and ordered them to the scene. Simolin was also on the horn; he stood at the railing, scanning around. After wrapping things up, he walked over to me.

"They promised three more patrols to start with…" Simolin looked like he was about to pop, so I asked:

"What are you thinking about?"

"Why the killer struck here, in this spot. What if he had no choice?"

My interest encouraged Simolin to continue.

"The victim was on his way to do something that the killer wanted to prevent, to report something to the police or to meet someone. If the victim was headed towards Kallio, this is one of the last places he could be stopped without taking too much of a risk, and…"

"It's possible."

Simolin's theory was precisely the kind that was useless at this point. At the beginning of an investigation, there's no point sacrificing time to developing too many theories of equal weight. It made more sense to wait for one to have more pull than the others. Simolin knew it himself and shut up.

I looked around for a way I could access the tracks.

"How did you get down?"

"Over by the rail-traffic control centre. It's that square glass building over there. There's a gate."

"Go talk to the residents of nearby buildings while I'm down there. I'll send Stenman and Oksanen to help out as soon as they arrive. Someone must have at least heard the shots, unless the killer used a silencer."

Simolin looked like he still had something to say. Apparently it wasn't very important, because he turned and left.

Getting down to the tracks required a walk of at least three hundred yards along the shore path and across the lot of the traffic-control building. In addition to the crime-scene investigator, three patrol officers and a few men in State Railways overalls were standing on the tracks. I went over to the nearest officer and was told that nothing out of the ordinary had been found.

The man who had fallen or jumped from the bridge had incurred surprisingly few injuries from his collision with the train. The only contusions were on his face, which would significantly hamper identification. Still, I could tell that the victim was about forty years old, dark-haired, and looked Arab. He had on a black leather jacket, grey trousers and a pair of black loafers. You could see a black shirt and a silver-grey tie beneath the jacket; he was also wearing black leather gloves.

A train approached from the north and Siimes covered the body with a paper sheet.

"What'd you find?" I asked, even though I knew that the majority of the forensic results wouldn't be ready until a battery of tests and exams had been conducted. But Siimes knew what I was after.

"Nothing surprising. The guy hit the roof of an A train from Leppävaara, ricocheted from there to the ground head-first. You don't have to be a doctor to be able to tell that his neck was broken. Other than that, minor injuries, because the trains tend to brake at this point, they're going maybe thirty miles an hour, tops. The deceased isn't carrying any ID, but you can see as well as I can. He looks like a foreigner. These were found in his jacket pocket."

Siimes held out two plastic bags. One contained a mobile phone and the other a folded map of Helsinki bearing a Hertz logo.

"He may have a car rented from Hertz. They give you a map with the car and this one's brand new. No marks on it."

"What about a weapon?"

"Hasn't turned up, either the pistol or the knife, but he may have chucked them or they may have been carried away by the train. The train was driven to the Ilmala rail yard as soon as the passengers were unloaded, and it still needs to be inspected. Of course I've taken gunpowder-gas tests just in case our buddy here is the shooter."

"Anything to indicate that he isn't?"

"Nothing except the fact that neither the weapons nor the missing ear and nose were found on him. There's blood on his hands, and some splatters on the lower part of his jacket."

I showed him the mobile phone.

"Can I play around with this?"

"Knock yourself out."

The phone wasn't on. I pressed the power button but nothing happened. I didn't know what else to do, so I removed the battery and SIM card, wiped them against my sleeve, and pressed them back into place. The phone started up and asked for a PIN code. I swore. Siimes glanced at me.

"It's asking for a PIN code."

"Try one two three four."

I tried, but nothing happened. I entered the same series of numbers backwards.

"No good."

"Then try four zeros."

I entered four zeros and four ones. No good. The minimal skills at my disposal had been exhausted. I was lousy with tech stuff, even though my dad had been an engineer. One of the guys in overalls walked up to me.

"You're in charge of the investigation?"

I said I was.

"Our chief of security, Repo, asked when you'll be able to question the engineer of the train that was involved in the collision. Apparently he wants to get home as soon as possible to rest. So if it's all right with you..."

"Where is he?"

"At the Ilmala rail yard. They'll tell you where to find him."

"You can let him know I'll be there soon."

"And that means?"

"Ten minutes."

I told Siimes: "If our guys show up, I'm questioning the locomotive engineer. Three more patrols are coming to help scour the terrain. As soon as this area is searched, close up shop. We need to get rail traffic back to normal as fast as possible."

"Done."

A gust of air from a passing train caused the paper sheet that covered the body to billow.

Just as I reached the bridge, a white Ford Mondeo started climbing towards it. I could see that Stenman was driving and Oksanen sat in the passenger seat.

Despite the surname, Senior Constable Stenman was a woman, first name Arja. Senior Constable Jari Oksanen was the same age as his partner. He was a key player in the police-guild rally club, which is precisely why Stenman didn't let him drive.

I gave them a quick rundown of what I knew.

"Simolin is out questioning the residents of nearby buildings. You two check everywhere else. There's a dog park at the other end of the bridge. Talk to anyone who might have seen something. Find out if there are security cameras in the area and confiscate the tapes. Three patrols will be showing up here soon. Have them scour the slope and along the tracks. At least a pistol, a knife, a nose and one ear are missing."

"A nose and an ear?" Stenman wondered.

"Nose and ears were cut from the deceased."

I held out my hand.

"Keys. I'm borrowing your car. I need to go over to Ilmala and have a chat with the locomotive engineer."

Stenman slapped the keys into my palm.

Vuorio had finished his work and was clambering back up the slope. I waited for a second for his breathing to even out.

"I must admit, you have an interesting case here. It even piques the interest of an old-timer like me."

I let him continue at his own pace. I knew from experience that rushing him was pointless.

"Two weapons? I'd suspect that there must have been two perpetrators. First, one stabbed him in the chest twice; either blow appears fatal. Then three shots to the head and two to the chest."

"He was shot five times?"

"Correct. One bullet hit one of the stab wounds so slyly that the entrance wound is difficult to notice. Based on it, though, I can still conclude that the knife was used first and the pistol afterwards. The man was killed deliberately and extremely thoroughly."

I took a moment to consider what Vuorio had told me.

"Two perpetrators would explain why we haven't found either weapon or the nose or one of the ears. Is there anything else?"

"The nose and ears were sliced off pretty handily," Vuorio continued.

"What does handily mean?"

"It means that both ears were sliced off with a clean stroke. That takes a determined hand. Nine people out of ten would blanch and be forced to use multiple strokes. Our butcher was the cold-blooded type. He knew someone might show up and acted quickly and efficiently."

Manner had said the same thing. Ice in the veins. If that ended up being the case, it wasn't going to be an easy investigation.

"There's one more item of interest," Vuorio said. "The deceased was a drug addict. He had used drugs intravenously for years. Some of the needle marks are very fresh, in other words he may have been under the influence when he died. We'll know once the forensic chemist finishes her tests."

Repo, the head of security for the State Railways, was waiting outside, looking cold. The weather was chilly, and he was blowing his runny nose. Usually the heads of security at large corporations were former cops or ex-military. Repo didn't look like either.

"The driver is still in a state of shock because of what happened. I hope you'll take that into consideration."

Before stepping inside, I looked around.

"Where's the train that was involved in the accident?"

"Behind the building, on the maintenance track."

"Has it been examined?"

"It's being examined as we speak."

"Our CSIs will take a look at it… Something may have fallen from the man who was hit…"

"If we find anything, we'll let you know."

The locomotive engineer was waiting in the break room, looking out into the rail yard. I sat down across from him. His hands were trembling.

"Coffee?" Repo asked.

"Please. Black."

Repo took a fire-engine-red mug that read *I Love NY* from the draining board and filled it for me.

The locomotive engineer stared out of the window a moment longer before looking at me. He was a thin man on the far side of fifty. His face was etched with the grooves of a hard life. He wore bifocals, the only hair he had left was at the back of his neck and on his ears – and now this.

"Who was he?" he asked.

"We don't know yet."

"I've done this job for over twenty years and no one has ever jumped in front of me."

The man turned to look out of the window again. I could barely hear his words: "Did he jump?"

"I was hoping you could tell me that."

The engineer shook his head.

"I'm not sure… I was about fifty yards from the bridge when I saw them…"

"What do you mean, them? Was there someone else on the bridge?"

"At least three of them, all men. First they were walking side by side towards the City Theatre, so from the direction I was coming from, from right to left. Then one of them ran to the railing and jumped over it onto the lip of the bridge and began crawling towards the edge…"

The man rubbed his temples uneasily.

"I could see his face when he turned and fell. I could hear him slam into the roof… And then I caught a glimpse in the mirror of him just lying there next to the track."

"What about the other two men? What were they doing?"

"I didn't see them after that."

"I mean, what where they doing when the man climbed over the railing? Did they try to stop him, for instance?"

"I've been thinking about that this whole time. At first I thought that they were trying to help him, to keep him from jumping…"

The driver looked at Repo as if he were entering sensitive territory and needed his approval. Repo nodded.

"Then when I heard what had happened at the bridge, I started thinking harder about it —"

"Wait a minute," I interrupted. "What did you hear?"

"That a murdered man had been found there."

"Continue."

"Afterwards I began thinking about the whole thing from a different angle, and it seems to me that the guy who fell was afraid… afraid and was trying to get away from those other two men because he was afraid. I saw his face right before he fell, and I'm pretty sure that he was a lot more afraid of them than he was of falling."

3

"I have a theory," Oksanen said. He was sitting next to me in the police van, holding a to-go cup of coffee like all the rest of us except Simolin, who only drank tea, preferably green. I also had a doughnut covered with so much sugar it was impossible to keep from showering it all over the place.

Oksanen's parka was emblazoned with the logo of a German car manufacturer. I knew that he also had a motor-oil company pen, a tyre-company key ring, a car-parts-chain pocketknife and an insurance-company fleece. Stenman and Simolin were sitting across from us.

"Or a couple of theories, actually."

Oksanen sniffed his coffee, which Stenman had picked up for us from the Neste station at Eläintarha.

It was eleven-thirty in the morning and they had earned their combined coffee break and warm-up. A freezing wind was blowing outside; I was shivering myself.

"The first thing that comes to mind is drugs. Maybe this is a territorial war between drug gangs or something like that. No one heard the shots. Why not? Because the gun was equipped with a silencer. And right off that means we're looking at the tool of a professional killer."

"So where are the shells, then?" Simolin asked. "Five shots and a silencer. The shooter must have used a semi."

"Maybe he picked them up from the ground."

"What about the other theory?" Stenman prodded. She had opened her green oilskin coat, revealing a high-collared

Norwegian fisherman's sweater. She managed to blend the freshness of a country girl with the class of a sophisticated woman who frequented Café Ekberg. The combination had its charms, I had to admit.

"The victim was in the wrong place at the wrong time and saw something that meant he had to be killed."

Oksanen's theories were so obvious that I had already considered them. Like Simolin's, though, they were nothing more than theories, and I wouldn't promote any of them above the others until I saw a solid reason to do so. On the other hand, playing around with theories occasionally generated valuable ideas.

"If it was a coincidence, then why did they need to chop off the nose and ears? Plus, the victim would have been shot from behind as he was running away. I doubt he would have hung around waiting to be shot," I said, before going on: "We know that there was a total of three men on the bridge, one of whom evidently fell when he was trying to escape from the other two. And yet the hands of the man who fell to the track were bloody. Based on that, it seems as if he stabbed the man on the bridge, got off a few shots just to make sure, cut off the ears and nose. What were the other two men doing on the bridge, and where are they now?"

When no one answered, I continued: "At first I thought those two unknown men showed up by accident. When they saw what was happening, they apprehended the knifeman, but he got away and fell from the bridge. Afterwards, for whatever reason, the unknown men decided not to get in touch with the police. It's possible that... unless..."

I glanced at my subordinates.

Simolin was the first to figure it out: "A twenty-two, a knife, a nose and an ear."

"Right. Where are they?"

The coffee cup paused on its way to Oksanen's mouth as he stopped to consider my question.

"I have a better theory," Stenman said. "What if we switched up roles and the chain of events a little. Two unknown men knife a third, who is waiting for his friend on the bridge, shoot him with a twenty-two, and cut off his nose and ears to desecrate the body."

I knew where Stenman was headed before she even finished and was annoyed that I hadn't thought of such an obvious idea myself.

"The dead guy's buddy shows up, sees what's happened, and rushes over to help. As he's helping his friend, he gets covered in his blood. The killers notice him, go back and grab him. The rest goes the way Ari suggested. The motive might be simple, too. Both victims are foreigners. It might be a racist attack, skinheads or neo-Nazi retaliation."

"That sounds a lot more realistic," I admitted. "But according to the locomotive engineer, the men were walking together towards Kallio. Why didn't they kill the other guy right away, and where were they taking him?"

"Maybe someone was approaching from Töölönlahti Bay and they had to keep moving."

"In any case, by far the best theory we have. But it might be smartest to let the theories be for now. There are still too many alternatives."

I remembered the phone.

"This was found on the guy who jumped, but I can't get into it. It's giving me error messages because I don't know the PIN code."

"Show me?" Simolin asked, taking the phone. He nimbly fingered it open, removed the SIM card, and examined it.

"Prepaid SIM. Tough to trace."

Simolin took his own phone and switched the SIM card into the other phone. Then he powered it up and, when prompted, entered his PIN.

"At least it works."

Simolin examined the phone from all sides.

"Brand-new, protective plastic still on the screen. In other words, it was probably bought in Finland."

"Can you get into it?"

"Not me, but I can take it to a friend who can. After that, the phone's memory will at least tell us the calls that were made and received."

"Do it. I have a hunch that at minimum we'll get the identity from the phone, maybe more."

"Right now, you mean?"

"If it's possible."

Simolin looked up a number on his phone and called.

"Hey. Where are you?… Good, we need to crack a mobile PIN code… as soon as possible… OK, I'll be right there."

Simolin ended the call.

"We're good to go."

Oksanen was doubtful. "Don't we need authorization for that?"

He was right, but I didn't let it bother me.

"Take that phone to your friend and see what's in it. Call me as soon as you know. Arja will take care of the photos… Make plenty of copies of both, for us as well as for the media, just in case – but we won't be releasing the pictures for distribution yet. And while you're at it, bring me a list of nearby security cameras."

A State Railways van pulled up next to the cordoned area. A man in overalls said something to one of the police officers. The latter pointed in our direction. The man in overalls headed over to our van carrying a bundle of paper. I opened the door.

"This is for you," he said, handing me the wadded-up newspaper.

It felt heavy. I unrolled a few layers of yesterday's news and caught a glimpse of blue-black metal.

"The gun had got caught on a really weird spot on the current-collector and didn't fall off because the train was going so slow," he explained.

"The current-collector?"

"It's on the roof. The train uses it to draw the current from the contact wires. No one has touched it without gloves."

Everyone looked at the weapon, intrigued. It was a barely used nine-millimetre Beretta. There were threads on the barrel for attaching a silencer. I sniffed the mouth of the barrel, but all I got was a whiff of gun oil.

"It hasn't been fired."

"Besides, it's a nine-mil, not a twenty-two," Oksanen noted. "The guy didn't have a holster, so he was carrying it in a pocket or under his belt, which is probably why he dropped it."

"Either that, or he pulled it out in self-defence," Simolin added.

I reflected on how the discovery of the weapon changed things. At least it fitted with Stenman's theory. Plus, it also said something about the guy carrying it. No normal person in Finland goes around packing a gun. The guy was either a criminal, a cop… or afraid of something.

I handed the wad of paper to Stenman.

"Take it in for testing."

Stenman stepped out of the van. I watched her, still holding my empty coffee cup. For a second I wondered where I should put it. I couldn't come up with anything better, so I just left it on the floor. Oksanen wasn't as conscientious; he crumpled his up and tossed it under the van.

"Arja!"

Stenman stopped about ten yards away.

"How are things going at home?" Stenman's husband had spent the past two weeks in a National Bureau of Investigation holding cell on suspicion of harbouring stolen goods. He owned a construction-equipment rental business and about twenty power tools that had been reported missing

had been found there. The tax authorities were also investigating the matter.

I had a bad conscience for not having offered her much
support as her boss, even though I knew she was taking the
whole thing pretty heavily.

"Hessu got out yesterday."

"You need some more time off?"

"No… thanks. I think the worst is over."

"If there's anything I can do, let me know."

Stenman gave a faint smile.

"I will. Thanks."

I went back to the van. I still didn't feel like a good boss.

Oksanen was leaning against the van, twirling the keys
around his forefinger. The key ring had a miniature car tyre
attached to it. I pulled the plastic bag containing the Hertz
map from my pocket.

"Check what this will get us. It was found on the guy who
jumped."

Oksanen eyed the map.

"You get one of these when you rent a car from Hertz.
Luckily I have a friend there who can help."

"Good. I'm going to do one more round of knocking on
doors."

I was already about to head for the bridge when Simolin
stopped me with a touch to my shoulder.

"Based on what the locomotive engineer told you, you
got the impression that they were taking him somewhere,
in other words they wanted him alive. They must have
had a car somewhere pretty close; you can't force a
struggling man very far. And those shells. The weapon
could have been in a bag when it was fired. A gym bag
slung over a shoulder wouldn't arouse any suspicion,
and it'd be easy enough to shoot through one, or use
it for cover."

"Good hypotheses, both of them, really good," I said.

Simolin self-consciously hurried off. I watched my lanky subordinate retreat for a moment. For some reason I was pretty sure that Simolin was right about both of his deductions.

I crossed the bridge and glanced down. The bodies had already been conveyed to the medical examiner's office in Ruskeasuo, and the section of track that had been closed all morning had been reopened to traffic. The bridge, on the other hand, remained closed, and the area cordoned off, because the terrain searches were still under way. A couple of journalists and photographers were doggedly hanging around on the other side of the tape at the Linnunlaulu end of the bridge. They had tried to grill me for information on the killings, but I had told them to call Huovinen. He was a natural at dealing with journalists.

I stopped for a minute to collect my thoughts. The fact that one of the men was being taken somewhere meant that they wanted something from him. It couldn't have been drugs or some other item, because they would have just taken that from him. So what they wanted from him was something else: information, for instance. And he knew what would happen to him, and was so afraid that he attempted the suicidal escape from the bridge. You don't pull a stunt like that unless you know your life is at stake. The fact that he was carrying a weapon implied that he had been prepared for trouble, but he had still been caught off guard.

The dog park was at the end of the bridge and to the right. There were two dogs inside the fenced area, a dirty-brown mutt that was racing around rambunctiously and a small black poodle that stuck timidly to the feet of its sixty-year-old mistress. I walked up to the owner of the poodle and introduced myself.

"Were you here with your dog this morning?"

"Yes, I was."

"What time?"

"Eight o'clock. I always come at the same time."

"Did you see anything out of the ordinary on the bridge?"

The woman eyed me crossly.

"Young man. If you'd be so kind as to start by telling me what occurred on the bridge, I would find it easier to decide what you mean by out of the ordinary."

I felt like a pupil being interrogated by a stern schoolmistress. I've always been intimidated by loud old women. Maybe it was because of my mother. She always felt she had some eternal right, bestowed by her maternal status, to treat men like mischievous little boys.

"I'm sure you're capable of making that distinction regardless."

My secretiveness was met with a disapproving look.

"Should I have heard something, for instance gunshots?"

"Did you?"

"No."

"You didn't hear any shots or anything else, such as yelling?"

"I never said that. A man did yell, but I was incapable of making it out. It wasn't Finnish, it was some language related to Arabic."

"What did he yell? One word or more?"

"There was more than one word, at least two, if not three."

The man in a tracksuit and ski-cap who was out exercising his mutt came closer.

"Are you a police officer?"

"Yes. Could I have a word with you in a minute?"

"I didn't see anything, I wasn't even here then."

The man retreated slightly, and I returned my attention to the woman.

"Do you remember any of the words?"

"Remembering something like that would be impossible; it's all Greek to me. Metaphorically speaking, of course."

"What happened next? Did you go see who was yelling?"

"Heavens, no. I don't interfere in such matters."

"What matters?"

"Altercations between foreigners."

"What do you mean by altercations?"

"Well, I don't suppose the man was yelling at himself…"

"What happened next? Did you see anyone right after the yelling? Anyone who might have been involved in what happened?"

The owner of the mutt edged furtively closer. The woman gave him an angry look. He had clearly violated her territorial bounds.

"Two men came from the bridge. That's when I was certain that they had been the ones arguing and yelling… they looked foreign."

"Can you describe them in more detail?"

"Dark… dark-skinned."

The woman gave me the once-over.

"Like yourself. Both of them were wearing coats, with the hoods pulled up over their heads… and gloves, both of them. Between thirty and forty, moved lithely, like athletes."

"Try to remember any details about their appearance or clothes. I'm certain you have excellent powers of observation."

My flattery paid off.

"Dark-blue sweatshirts and black sweatpants and running shoes. That's all I can say. They walked a little way, then one of them started running…"

The woman paused and frowned.

"Then a woman screamed."

"Screamed what?"

"Or more like shrieked. There were no words."

"But you didn't see who screamed?"

"No. It only lasted a moment."

"Was there anyone here in the dog park besides you?"

"At least two people, maybe three, but the only one I remember is that actress from the City Theatre, a young woman who lives somewhere nearby, because I've seen her on many occasions. She has a Jack Russell terrier. Her picture is in the case out in front of the Theatre. Brunette, slim, short hair."

I waited for fifteen minutes, freezing the whole time, and chatted up every dog owner I ran into. No one had seen or heard anything. And so I cut across the park to the City Theatre.

The display cases were in front of the main door. Vivica Mattsson. Brown hair, slim, short hair, just like the poodle lady said.

She was one of the stars of a musical that was about to premiere.

The porter hung up the phone as I entered. I showed her my police ID.

"Is Vivica Mattsson here?"

"She's in rehearsal."

"Would you ask her to come out here, please. It's important police business."

She hesitated, but went off to find Mattsson. It took four minutes.

Evidently it was a dress rehearsal, because Mattsson was in costume. She had on a Fifties hoop skirt with red polka dots and a shirt with a white collar. She looked as innocent as a girl who was about to be confirmed, but that was highly unlikely.

"I was told you're a detective. What's going on? I've been in rehearsals all morning."

I told her what happened at the bridge without going into details. I didn't want to read them in the tabloids.

"You were apparently out walking your dog next to the bridge at that time."

"That's true. It was about eight o'clock, but I don't remember seeing or hearing anything out of the ordinary."

"The killers most likely passed the dog park as they left: two dark-skinned guys in hoodies and sneakers. At least one of them may have been carrying a gym bag."

"Do you mean dark or black?"

"Dark, like me."

She gave me an evaluative look.

"I'm Jewish."

"So some of you are cops?"

"At least one of us."

It wasn't the first time I had been asked this question. People seemed to have a strong belief that Jews have some secret, Old Testament-based motive for not joining the police force. In reality, there was only one reason: the lousy pay.

Vivica Mattsson sat down in one of the armchairs in the lobby and tossed one leg across the other. I eyed her tanned thigh. Despite the warnings of dermatologists everywhere, Mattsson clearly enjoyed sunbathing. It was easy picturing her in a string bikini on the rocks outside a seaside villa inherited from her grandpapa.

I decided it would be more natural if I also sat. Mattsson frowned; it looked as if she were remembering something.

"So Arabs, maybe?"

"Maybe."

"I didn't see, but I might have heard. Do you speak Arabic?"

"No."

"Someone angrily shouted something from the bridge in Arabic, or at least that's what it sounded like. A train went past right then and after that I didn't hear anything else."

"We know those two men probably headed this way at about the same time. But you didn't notice them?"

"I think this one dog owner came over right then to talk, and I was focused on that."

"The woman with a small black poodle?"

"Right."

"Do you remember who else was in the dog park?"

"No. It was a late night last night, and I was pretty groggy this morning, I still am. I can't wait to get some rest... I didn't feel like talking, but she's such a chatterbox... Did you need anything else from me? It's opening night tomorrow..."

"Call me if you remember anything more."

I gave her my card. She looked at it for a minute and started to smile.

She was beautiful, so beautiful that I couldn't help taking a quick backwards glance from the vestibule. But she was already gone.

4

Oksanen was sitting in the back of the van, talking into his mobile phone. There was no sign of Stenman. Oksanen hung up as soon as he saw me. From the haste of his movements I knew it wasn't a work-related call, most likely arrangements related to the next police-guild rally.

"We're making progress," Oksanen told me, waving the plastic bag containing the Hertz map.

"How so?"

"This edition of the map only came out a couple of weeks ago, and it's meant to be left in the car. My buddy at Hertz promised to get his team to find out how many maps have been snagged from vehicles. Then he'll go into the computers and dig up the personal info on the customers who rented those cars and give it to me."

"Sounds good."

"I was thinking, during rush hour, trains would have been going through here pretty often, and some locomotive engineer might have seen something on the bridge. We can get a single message out to all the engineers through the control centre."

"Also a good idea."

Huovinen's metallic green VW Passat was climbing the hill, behind it a black Opel Vectra.

"Here comes Huovinen," Oksanen said.

You could tell from Oksanen's voice that he didn't care for Huovinen, and presumably the feeling was mutual. Huovinen had lectured Oksanen pretty harshly a couple of times about time on the clock going to his rally pursuits.

Huovinen was accompanied by a man of about forty, wearing a light-green poplin coat and dress trousers. He had intense, almost black eyes.

I was sure that I had met him before somewhere, but I couldn't remember where. Still, I guessed what he was doing with my boss.

"Let's have a little powwow. Where are Stenman and Simolin?"

I told him.

"We don't have time to wait."

Huovinen nodded at his visitor.

"This is Inspector Sillanpää from the Security Police. I'll let him explain why he's here."

Sillanpää had the hard look of a punched-up boxer.

"There are quite a few things about this case that interest us. Two foreigners, facial mutilation, the method of killing, the scene of the crime, which is Finland's busiest and perhaps most important section of railway track. I also understood that the deceased haven't been identified yet, and we'd like to assist in identification so we can do background checks on them. If they have a record, maybe we can piece together some kind of scenario for what happened. And of course the case also interests us as a possible hate crime."

"Do you have any suspicions about what this is all about?"

"No more than you do."

If Sillanpää was lying, he was used to it.

"What was found on the bodies?" Sillanpää asked.

"On one of them, nothing; on the other, a map of Helsinki and a gun. Or actually, the gun had fallen onto the roof of the train. It was found later at the rail yard."

"No mobile phone?"

"And a mobile," I was forced to admit.

"We want the phone. We'll immediately deliver you everything we recover from it."

"The phone is critical for the investigation at this stage."

"You'll get the call data as soon as we retrieve it. This has already been agreed on with the deputy police chief."

I glanced at Huovinen. I could tell he was irritated by this news.

"One of our detectives has the phone at the moment."

"Where is he?"

"Probably already on his way back here."

"Let him know we want the phone immediately."

Typical SUPO talk, I thought. Sillanpää spoke as if the entire Security Police, right up to the chief inspector, stood behind his wishes.

"I'll try to get in touch with him."

I walked a little way off and called Simolin.

"How's it going?"

"We're just about done."

"There's a guy from SUPO here, he wants the phone."

"You want us to quit?"

"Nah. How long will it take?"

"Ten minutes, max."

"Make a note of all calls, both received and made, and messages, and write down the security code. The boys from SUPO can crack it for themselves."

I went back to the van.

"He'll be here within half an hour."

Huovinen looked at me thoughtfully. He had a keen nose in matters like these. He handed me a printout that was folded in quarters.

"The official press release that was distributed through the Finnish News Agency, in case you're interested."

I read the release. Huovinen had been unusually succinct. I was sure the journalists wouldn't be satisfied.

"I promised to flesh it out this evening. You have anything to give me?"

For a moment no one spoke. The silence clearly bothered Oksanen the most.

"I'll call Arja and ask about the security cameras. I could go get the tapes."

"Good," said Huovinen. He looked preoccupied.

Huovinen was forty-seven, but he was already greying. He was a handsome man, so handsome that during our time in the police academy he had earned money on the side as a male model for a clothing manufacturer. He was remarried, and wife number two was an Estonian-born cellist.

Huovinen came out of his reverie.

"Don't do anything I wouldn't."

Coming from Huovinen, this meant almost completely free rein. He probably knew how to cut the corners that could slow an investigation better than anyone else at head-quarters.

Sillanpää was also roused from silence.

"I've got other things I could be doing. Where's this detective? I'll go pick up the phone from him myself."

"I didn't think to ask, but he'll be right here."

Sillanpää eyed me with the usual suspicion. He had a clearly exaggerated need for control. Maybe it was part of the job description.

Huovinen buttoned up his charcoal-coloured wool coat. "You gentlemen can manage without me. I'm going to head over to the ministry. If something comes up, call. I'll let you know about the meeting."

He got into his car and drove off.

"Was the phone unlocked?" Sillanpää asked.

"Nope. Apparently it died or broke when the guy hit the roof of the train or the ground. Will you guys be able to unlock it?" I asked innocently.

"I think we can manage that."

"We expect you to deliver all call data as soon as you retrieve it."

"Of course." Once again, Sillanpää's promise seemed so breezily tossed out that I didn't believe it. Luckily, thanks to Simolin, I was a few steps ahead, and I intended to stay there.

"Of course, why wouldn't we?" Sillanpää added, and I trusted him even less.

Oksanen returned, looking busy. One more rally arrangement had been squared away.

"Arja's almost here… Mind if I take my legal lunch break now?"

"What about the security cameras?"

"Arja's bringing a list. I'll go through it right away."

"Don't be long. How are you going to get anywhere? Arja has the car."

"A buddy's coming to pick me up."

Oksanen rushed off to meet his friend. Work matters were clearly interfering with the demands of his busy free-time schedule.

"Someone told me you're Jewish," Sillanpää blurted out.

"Someone was right."

"I heard a Jewish joke yesterday. You want to hear it?"

"Don't let a good opportunity go to waste."

Sillanpää's eyes bored into me.

"Let's leave it for another time. You speak Hebrew?"

I looked at the humourless inspector.

"A little."

"We might be able to use you from time to time. Rumour has it you've practised martial arts and were the best shot in your academy class."

Sillanpää was right. I had started taking tae kwon do at the Maccabi, the Jewish congregation's athletic club, during my first year of high school. When I was younger, I also played table tennis in the club's competitive team.

"Let me guess: someone told you?"

Sillanpää chuckled.

"I'm serious. If you're interested in something a little different, we might be able to use you more than you realize…"

Simolin sped up the hill and shuddered to a stop. I didn't have time to think about what Sillanpää meant.

"Here comes the phone," I remarked.

"Think about what I said."

Sillanpää took off. He grabbed the phone on the fly from Simolin and jumped into his car. As soon as it disappeared from view, Simolin pulled his notebook out of his pocket.

"I wrote down all the calls out, calls in, and messages. As it turns out, the messages are in French. The last three calls out were placed to the same number, two this morning and one yesterday evening. I already checked it: some Ali's Body Shop in Vartiokylä. Three calls were international, two to France, one to Israel, and the rest to one and the same unlisted mobile phone. I called the body shop on my way over, but no one answered."

Simolin saw my expression and explained: "I would have just asked how much a brake job costs. Besides, it would have been the truth; the Renault needs new brake pads, and the tailpipe's leaking too."

I was tired of standing there, so without giving it any further thought, I said: "Let's head over and find out in person how much a brake and tailpipe job would cost for the Renault."

The body shop was off the Eastern Expressway, a couple of miles past Itäkeskus towards Porvoo. A right turn at the Teboil station, and then another immediate right.

The area was a mishmash of small industry housed in buildings of various ages. Some were corrugated-metal prefabs on the verge of falling apart, others were brand-new contemporary industrial structures, the rest somewhere in between. The body shop was located in one wing of an old yellow building; the entrance was at the rear. Out back there were a couple of rusty shipping containers, dented body parts,

45

an ancient, completely rusted-out Mercedes, a newish Volvo hatchback and a relatively old 300-series BMW. At the edge of the property, right under a birch tree, stood a boxy white RV.

Over the door to the shop, it read *A. Hamid, Auto Body & Paint.* The door was locked, but the crossbar that should have been padlocked was dangling.

Simolin groped for his weapon. I instinctively did the same; my gun was right where it was supposed to be.

"Think we should load?" Simolin asked.

I nodded and pulled a round into the chamber, set the safety, and put my gun back into its holster. Simolin held on to his, but concealed his hand under the edge of his coat.

I knocked on the metal-plated door and listened. There was no response. I rattled it a little, but that didn't produce any results either.

"Take a look in the side window," I ordered Simolin. He obeyed, returning a second later.

"Don't see anyone, but the lights are on."

I beat on the door more heavily. It still didn't open.

"Why don't I get some tools from the car?" Simolin suggested.

"Do it."

Simolin bounded off. When he returned, he was carrying a crowbar and a one-pound mallet.

"Go for it."

Simolin pounded the crowbar in between the door and the jamb, right next to the lock. When it had sunk in deep enough, he lowered the mallet to the ground and twisted the crowbar. The door popped open on the first try.

The heavy, gentle scent of motor oil wafted out. Right across from the door there was a car with the hood up. A burning work lamp hung over the engine block. The distributor cap was off and the plug wires were unattached. Problem with the ignition, I figured.

The space was approximately fifteen by thirty feet. Another car was against the long wall. It had been driven onto the lift and raised a couple of yards off the ground. At the far end of the space, there was a little office around thirty square feet with big windows. Across from it was a much larger walled-off space, with double doors big enough for a car. An ad for car paint hung on the wall, next to a shelf full of paint cans. From that and the paint splatters, it was easy to deduce that cars were painted behind the double doors.

I peeked into the office. I didn't notice anything out of the ordinary, unless you count the fact that there wasn't a single girlie calendar on the wall. Customer appointments had been marked in a desk calendar; it looked like A. Hamid had his hands full.

"Not a living soul," Simolin said.

I stopped in front of the double doors and sniffed the pungent fumes coming from the painting chamber. Then I opened them.

A young man in overalls was leaning in a sitting position against a wall covered in splashes of paint. Another, older man dressed in slacks and a checked jacket was sprawled in a recliner sitting in the middle of the floor, both hands tied to the arms of the chair. There were bruises on his face and two bullet holes at his right temple. A fire-engine-red air compressor stood next to the chair, its hose dangling in his lap.

Simolin peered over my shoulder and saw the same thing I did. He said, almost enthusiastically:

"That's four bodies already. Looks like we got the biggest case of the year."

As I looked at the bodies, the Rabbi's words came to mind: Yamim Noraim.

Yamim Noraim, the Days of Awe.

If Rabbi Liebstein was right and the world was falling to pieces, an unpleasant role had been reserved for me. It was my job to gather up all of the gears that were flying off and repair the clock so it would work again.

5

A good thirty minutes later, the crime scene was buzzing. The area was marked off, the medical van had come and gone, and an ambulance had been ordered for the bodies. The same CSIs who had been at Linnunlaulu, Manner and Siimes, were opening their aluminium cases.

I had already called Huovinen and apprised him of the situation.

"Stay there and direct the investigation; I'll send over as many people as I can tear away. Someone's going to regret they ever started making trouble in our territory. Tell everyone no breaks, not even for a second, not even if they see a pair of elephants fucking right in front of their face. I'll be there in half an hour."

I went back inside. I had already communicated our movements to Manner, who was marking them on the floor with chalk. He saved himself from having to take a few shoe prints this way. Siimes was getting some wider shots before moving in to the details. Manner walked over to me.

"A day to remember."

"You can say that again. How does it look?"

"I can already tell you that this was a last-nighter, in other words these two were offed first, before the guys at Linnunlaulu. Based on the samples, I'd say it looks like the same killers were at work."

I had come to the same conclusion, and it hadn't been the least bit hard.

"This guy lounging in the chair here was tortured before he was done in: you notice the compressor and the air hose? The other one was just shot; there's no sign of other external injuries."

Manner squatted and inspected the pockets of the body that was in the chair. In the breast pocket of the sport coat there was a wallet; the side pocket contained two bunches of keys. He opened up the wallet and showed me the driving licence in its plastic sheath.

"Ali Hamid, apparently the owner of this body shop. In addition to the driving licence, a little money, business cards for the shop, photos of the wife and kids, that's it."

He put the wallet away and studied the keys.

"Two normal Abloys: one to a Disklock and the other to a deadbolt. The other bunch is all car keys."

"Check the other body while you're at it."

Manner put the wallet into a plastic bag and tucked the bag into his case. Then, carefully picking each step, he walked over to the other, noticeably younger victim. A black wallet was found in the back pocket of his overalls.

"Wasin Mahmed, born 1979," Manner said. "Judging by his outfit, works here."

Wasin Mahmed's wallet also contained business cards for the shop, plus a photo of him posing with a man about ten years older with bad skin. They had similar features; perhaps they were brothers. There was still sixty-five euros in the wallet, a few coins, and a letter in Arabic that was, judging by its shabbiness, at least several months old.

"Ari!" Simolin called from the doorway.

I handed the wallet back to Manner and went over to Simolin.

"Looks like the employee lived here. We found a back room."

Calling the nook a room was a slight exaggeration. A sofa that seemed to double as a bed, a small table and a chair had

49

been jammed into the tiny space. On the table there was a bag of bread, a bottle of water and a few cans of food. Next to the wall stood a metal locker containing a pair of belted jeans, a sweater and a padded nylon windbreaker.

Two receipts, one for groceries from a nearby store and one from a petrol station, were found in one of the jeans pockets. There was a mobile in the inside pocket of the jacket. I handed it to Simolin.

"Have it checked, although it doesn't look like the most urgent thing. But we need to find out who the loved ones are anyways and let them know what's happened."

Beneath the bed there were two cheap plastic suitcases. I opened them. All they contained was clothes.

Stenman swept in.

"There's someone in that RV out there."

The mobile home was at the edge of the car park, only twenty yards from the body shop. A piece of paper covered in plastic wrap had been taped to the door. It read JÄPPINEN in stick letters.

The door was opened by an elderly man who looked half-asleep and hung-over. His grey hair was sticking out all over the place, and there was some cream-coloured gunk in the corners of his eyes. I could make out the stench of stale booze from a yard off.

He was dressed in old-fashioned polyester trousers and a moth-eaten flannel shirt that spilled out over his waistband. His shoulders were so narrow that his faded grey braces barely stayed up.

"Jäppinen," I guessed.

"What do you want?" he asked crankily, licking his dry lips. His gaze was unsteady.

I showed him my police ID.

"From Criminal Investigations. So's she." I nodded in Stenman's direction. "You live here?"

"A person's gotta live somewhere. It's not a crime to not report your address, is it? Besides, I work here."

"Where here?" Stenman asked.

"Around… As much as a person on disability is allowed to, building maintenance and stuff like that. I fill in over at the body shop if they need me. Had my own for thirty years, but it was too hard on the joints. I've had both knees operated on, and my back —"

I interrupted Jäppinen's recitation of his medical record. "Were you home last night?"

"Home last night? Probably." His gaze brightened. "Yeah, now I remember for sure. I was watching TV."

"You mind if we come in?"

He backed up and sat down on a sofa bed that had seen better days; a tangle of bedclothes was heaped on it. The RV stank of ingrained filth. Scraps of food and empty beer bottles littered the table. Not the slightest hint of a woman's touch to be seen anywhere.

"Did you see anyone visit Hamid's body shop last night?"

"Last night? There's always people running in and out of there. Customers and Hamid's and his helper's friends. There were always folks dropping by."

"Did Hamid work a lot of overtime?"

"Almost every day… Haven't seen him today, though. A couple of customers came by asking for him. Didn't answer his phone. Kinda strange, Ali's a conscientious guy… Did something happen to him, a break-in at the shop?"

"Who did you see enter the shop last night?" Stenman demanded.

"Show me that cop card again. My eyes are just starting to clear up."

He eyeballed my police ID right up close.

"Kafka… Back in the Sixties I bought a good wristwatch from the Kafka pawnshop on Pursimiehenkatu, the good old-fashioned wind-up kind, a steel Zenith Star. Then I left it on at the Harjutori sauna once when I was drunk. Got water inside and that was the end of it," Jäppinen said ruefully. "Related to you, by any chance?"

After about my hundredth enquiry about my relatives, I had come to learn that people from Helsinki only know two Kafkas. One is the author; the other owns a pawnshop.

"No relation. What happened last night?"

"Why don't you ask Ali himself? He's a nice guy for a Muslim. Wouldn't have sold my shop to some prick."

"The body shop used to be yours?"

"Mine all mine. Ali's from Baghdad, from Iraq. Came here to Finland as a refugee and worked for me for years. Seemed like an honest fella to me, so I didn't see any reason not to sell it to him when I went on disability. We agreed that I can keep this RV here."

Jäppinen noticed a beer bottle on the table that still contained a few millimetres of liquid and tossed it back.

"They were working late yesterday… I went down to the Teboil around eight to buy sausages and milk and a little beer. At that point the lights were still on over there."

"Did you go into the shop?" Stenman asked.

"No."

"Did you see Hamid or the other repairman?"

"Wasi? He's from Iraq too. Nope."

"Anyone else?"

"Nope."

"Just a minute ago you said a lot of people were in and out of there, customers and Wasi's friends," Stenman reminded him.

"I meant during the day, not at night… I meant in general a lot of people came by."

"But you didn't see anyone last night, huh?"

"No."

Stenman took a long look at Jäppinen. Jäppinen picked up rolling gear from the table and began rolling a cigarette.

"What about any cars?"

"Ali's Volvo and Wasi's Beemer were there. He just got it a couple of weeks ago. Bought some new doodad for it every day. Had prayer beads hanging from the rear-view mirror and so many dice that he was lucky he could see the road."

"The red BMW?" I offered.

"Yeah."

Both cars were still in the yard. They were being checked at the moment and would soon be moved to police premises for even more thorough examination.

"What kind of man was Wasin Mahmed?" I asked.

"Hard-working, good kid. I gotta hand it to the Muslims, they respect their elders. Always calling me papa: papa this and papa that. Wouldn't get me booze, and believe me, I asked."

"Did you see any other cars?"

Jäppinen's eyes searched around for something else to wet his whistle but came up empty.

"Last night, you mean?"

"Right."

"No, but I was down at the Teboil station for a while."

"How long were you there?"

"As best as I can recall, I had a beer and then came straight home. About half an hour."

"You have the receipt?"

"The receipt?" he repeated, perplexed, but then he fumbled around the table for his glasses, which were missing one arm, stood, and went over to the coat rack near the door. He fished his hand into the side pocket of the old-fashioned leather jacket and carried his catch over to the table. A broken cigarette, a six-millimetre bolt, a couple of small coins and a few slips of paper tumbled from his fist. I picked up the slips and found what I was looking for.

According to the receipt from the petrol station, he had bought sausages, milk, bread and a six-pack of beer. The sale had been made at 8:05 p.m.

Jäppinen looked outside through his teetering, one-armed spectacles and saw the police officers moving around the yard.

"There's cops out thicker than blueberries in a bog. Were those devils dealing drugs or selling stolen goods or something?"

I didn't answer, I just asked: "Do you remember anything else about last night? What did you do when you came back here?"

"I guess I watched the news... and knocked back a few beers. Then I went to bed."

"Do you have a prostate problem?" Stenman asked. I glanced at her, slightly taken aback.

"I'd wager at this age, just about every man does."

"You drank a beer at the Teboil and more when you got back. Where did you do your business?"

"Out back, behind the RV."

"And you didn't see anything then either?"

"I was looking at the stars, it was a clear sky, and the moon, there was a fine moon. And I was a little tipsy, I guess."

The apartment building was one of those well-built ones from the 1950s, four stories of plastered brick. The stairwell smelt of food and floor wax and I knew that the basement smelt of lime wash. These kinds of buildings always make me feel cozy and safe. Maybe it was because I had lived the first ten and happiest years of my life in one. I was positive this had the same kind of chicken-wire walk-ins as in the basement of my childhood home. In one of them, on a foam mattress laid out on the floor, I had done my damnedest to try and get into the pants of Karmela Meyer, my girlfriend who lived in the same building. Although Karmela breathed promisingly in my ear, I had to work at it for almost a year before I succeeded.

I studied the name board in the lower lobby, the same kind where as kids we used to move the letters around to make up new, better names for the residents. Hamid lived on the third floor. There was no elevator.

I had asked Stenman along. I wasn't eager to face the wife and four kids whose husband and father had been killed all alone. Besides, you never knew what you'd find waiting for you in someone's home.

"Who breaks the news?" Stenman asked, when we reached the second floor.

"You do, if you don't mind."

"That's fine. You know if they speak Finnish?"

"Pretty sure. They've lived here eleven years already." I had called HQ from the car and got the stats on Ali Hamid and his family. Aged forty-six, wife and four kids, a girl and three boys. The oldest fourteen, born in Iraq, the youngest five. Hamid and his wife had been granted Finnish citizenship four years ago.

We stopped at the fourth-floor landing. I caught my breath before I rang the doorbell. The door was opened by a boy of about seven.

"Is your mum at home?"

"Who are you?"

The boy's mother came to the door. I showed her my police ID.

"Police, Criminal Investigations. Good afternoon."

Panic flashed in her eyes, but she forced herself to stay calm.

"May we come in?" I asked.

The woman moved aside and allowed us to enter.

"You're married to Ali Hamid?"

The woman ordered the children to their rooms.

I glanced around. The living room was decorated in the Arab style: plump leather chairs, dark wood, sickly-sweet glass and porcelain objects by the dozen, ornately framed photographs and lush cascades of drapes. Actually, it looked like the room hadn't been decorated, like each object had just been set down in the first available spot.

It was only after the most curious child had exited that the woman asked: "What's happened to him?"

"Unfortunately, he's dead," Stenman said.

"When?" the woman asked, as if she hadn't understood the words.

"Last night, apparently."

"He didn't come home last night and I tried to call him... he didn't answer."

Her voice faltered and she turned her head aside.

Stenman went over and placed a hand on her shoulder.

"We're sorry. We need your help to catch the person who did this. Your husband's employee Wasin Mahmed was also killed."

The woman clumsily wiped away her tears with her knuckles and let out a loud sob. The oldest child peeked out from his door, frightened. She immediately snapped: "Out! Go back to your room!"

The boy's head disappeared and the door closed.

"I was always afraid something would happen to him."

"Why?"

"I told him not to get mixed up in anything."

"What did he get mixed up in?"

Stenman guided the woman over to the sofa. She collapsed onto it.

"We need your help, do you understand?"

"Ali was a good man, a good father, why did they do it? He didn't do anything bad to anyone."

The woman pressed her fist to her mouth.

"They made orphans of my children... my four children."

Stenman took the woman's hand between hers.

"Who was he afraid of?"

"I don't know... My husband told me that they came to his work... Someone had given them his name... They asked for help, they said he was a good Muslim and that he should help them... that they were all doing Allah's work."

"Help with what?"

"A car, they needed a car… I begged Ali not to get mixed up in it."

"Did you see them?"

The woman shook her head.

"Why did they do it? They made orphans of my children," the woman repeated in despair.

"Do you know how many of them there were or what their names were?"

Stifled crying began to be heard from the oldest boy's room.

"We need to know everything that your husband told you about them."

"One called here last night, angry, and asked why my husband wasn't answering his phone."

"What was his name?" Stenman demanded.

"He didn't say his name, he just asked why Ali wasn't answering and said that Ali needed to call him as soon as he came home… he spoke English at first and then Arabic."

"Did your husband give them a car?"

"I don't know. I heard him call somewhere and ask about renting one."

"Didn't you ask him anything about it later?"

"I could tell that Ali didn't want to talk about it."

The crying boy rushed out of the room and straight into his mother's arms.

The woman stroked the boy's hair and cradled him in her arms. Then she gently pushed him away.

"Go take care of your little brothers and sister."

He obeyed with a sob.

"What were you afraid of, that something bad would happen to your husband?" Stenman asked.

"He was afraid… He didn't say it, but I know him and I know he was afraid of those men. That they would do something to us…"

She burst into tears.

"We thought we'd be safe here... that we could raise our children without fear here... that we could give them a good, safe childhood... my husband didn't want to get mixed up in anything bad... he was a good man, a good father to our children."

Stenman let the woman vent her anguish for a moment before continuing: "We don't believe that the caller killed your husband. We believe someone else did, someone who wanted information about the caller. We think that the caller is also dead. Do you have any idea about who could have killed the man who your husband was supposed to arrange a car for?"

"No."

"Did your husband have any idea why they asked for his help specifically?"

"Because he was a Muslim and they were Muslims."

"There are a lot of other Muslims here. Why him?"

"I don't know, maybe because he had an auto-body shop."

"Did your husband have any relatives or good friends in Finland?"

"One cousin."

"We'd like the name and address."

"Tagi, he studies at the restaurant school in Helsinki. I think he lives in Kannelmäki, at least he used to."

I glanced at Stenman.

"The photos."

Stenman took the photos of the deceased from one of her inside pockets and showed them to the woman.

"Do you recognize either one?"

The woman's gaze locked in on the victim who had lost his nose and ears. The retouching had been a success. The photo looked almost normal; the eyes of the deceased were open, if slightly drowsy. But it couldn't have been unclear to anyone that the man in the picture was already off in another dimension, well beyond consciousness.

"Tagi... That's my husband's cousin. Is he... also..."

"Unfortunately."

"Was your husband in close contact with his cousin?"

"Tagi moved to Finland last year. At first they met often, because my husband gave him advice on all kinds of things. He even worked for my husband for a while and lived here. Then Tagi got into school, and they didn't meet very often after that."

"What about recently? When did you see Tagi last?" Stenman asked.

"He came here three days ago."

"What did he want?"

"Want? He ate here and then he went with my husband to the mosque to pray. My husband went there three times a week."

"Did anything special happen to him that evening?"

"He didn't mention anything, at least."

"What time did he come home?"

"Nine-thirty, like usual. He went straight to bed."

The woman looked at me, eyes clouded over. I could see that she had reached her limit. Stenman saw it too. She left her card on the table.

"Please call us if you remember anything," I said.

"Would you like us to arrange some company for you before we leave?" Stenman asked.

"Could you please just go now," the woman pleaded.

Four bodies in one day was a lot, so much so that the Violent Crimes Unit was being pushed into overdrive. That meant a total of about ten detectives assigned to the case, only half of whom made it to the evening briefing. Also present were Huovinen, Deputy Police Chief Leivo, Lieutenant Toivakka from narcotics and Inspector Sillanpää from the Security Police.

Huovinen straightened his snazzy Italian tie and stepped over in front of the flipchart.

"It looks like everyone's here, so let's get started."

Huovinen collected his thoughts for a moment or two.

"We're starting from a pretty massive bloodbath, four dead, three killed in cold blood and one who apparently did himself in trying to escape from the killers. All of the deceased appear to be of Arab origin. The identities of three have been confirmed. One is an Iraqi who has been granted Finnish citizenship, one a fellow Iraqi who worked for him, and the third the first man's cousin, a citizen of the UK who has lived in Finland for about a year. None has a criminal record, at least in Finland, but we do have some information on them."

Huovinen indicated Lieutenant Toivakka. "Take it from here, Seppo?"

"We have a couple of tip-offs on the cousin, Tagi Hamid. One of his buddies is a Moroccan citizen who has been convicted of narcotics violations. Hamid's name came up during routine monitoring of the Moroccan. In addition, we have an anonymous tip-off according to which Hamid brought over or had someone else bring over three kilos of hash from Morocco. Since then, we've been in contact with Birmingham, where Hamid has lived for over twenty years. According to the police there, Hamid only has minor convictions, but he's considered a mid-level drug dealer. At this moment, however, we don't have any information indicating that an Arab-led drug gang is operating in Finland. That's it."

"Thank you," said Huovinen. "As far as the killers, we know that there were at least two of them. They were also dark-complexioned, meaning Arabs or southern Europeans, about forty years old and athletic. That's as detailed as the description gets."

"What about the security-cam footage?" Leivo asked.

"We've got some images from the rail-traffic-monitoring camera that most likely are of the suspects, but they don't offer any new information. The shots are so blurry that we won't be able to get anything close to identifying characteristics from them. The only piece of additional information is that the men approached from downtown on the path that goes past Finlandia Hall and heads along the shore of Töölönranta Bay to Linnunlaulu."

"What about the cars?"

"The Vartiokylä Teboil security camera gave us some good footage of cars headed towards and away from the auto-body shop owned by the victim named Ali Hamid. Not all of the vehicles have been identified yet, or their owners contacted, but we believe we've found what we're looking for. One was a white Nissan-make minivan with stolen plates. A similar Nissan has been reported stolen. We suspect Hamid's killers used this vehicle, and an APB has been placed on it."

"How do we know for certain that the Vartiokylä killings are related to the events at Linnunlaulu?" enquired Deputy Chief Leivo. He was clearly annoyed that the majority of the information he currently possessed had come from the media.

Leivo had only himself to blame. He'd been at a seminar in Lahti and unreachable all day. Besides, he was known for not developing interest in a case until the media started asking about it.

"Through the family connection, as I said," Huovinen answered. "In addition, the person who was hit by the train had made numerous calls to the owner of the body shop, so the connection can be considered certain."

I eyed Sillanpää. His dark eyes narrowed. Sillanpää returned my gaze with a piercing look and said: "It would be nice to know how we know about these calls to the body shop. As far as I'm aware, the only way would be accessing the caller's info. But it just so happens that we have the phone, and it's only now being unlocked because there's no PIN code, at least in our possession."

Huovinen didn't let Sillanpää's prickliness bother him. He was much thicker-skinned that he appeared.

"I don't think we ought to be splitting hairs at this point. I'm not interested in where the information came from, the main thing is that we have it and that it's been useful to us."

"Well, we *are* interested, because —"

Leivo started losing his patience and interrupted Sillanpää.

"Split hairs some other time. Do we have any theories as to what this is all about?"

I'd only seen him at work in a suit and tie. Now he was wearing a dark-green sweater and slacks. Apparently he'd dropped by the house on his way in.

Huovinen nodded in my direction.

"Kafka can report on developments in the field. He has by far the most accurate information on everything."

I looked at Leivo's gentle, unlined face. He was exactly what his previous subordinates in central Finland had warned us about: a nice guy, great company and an excellent storyteller, but totally out of place as a cop. Unfortunately, he wasn't the only one of his kind.

Maybe people like him were a blessing to humanity, but they were also a hell of a burden when they wound up in positions not suited to their character. They never wanted to throw the first stone and always discovered mitigating factors, even in places where they didn't exist. Thanks to them, the bad guys were back out on the streets faster than you could spit, realizing their true natures through foul deeds.

It was my belief that the world wasn't ready for nice people yet. Nice people didn't stick their noses in the business of a neighbour who beat his wife and kids; nice heads of state didn't attack a neighbouring country, even if its dictator had butchered millions of its citizens. Avoiding inconvenience was a fundamental trait of nice people. That's why they let unpleasant things happen rather than get involved.

Nice people were in their element as nuns, midwives, nurses, scientists, dentists or activities counsellors, but in the kind of position where you had to be capable of handling pressure and problems, they were in the wrong spot.

"None of the deceased except for Tagi Hamid have a criminal background, and all of them are foreigners from a specific region of the globe. They're also all Muslims, and according to Hamid's wife, the man who called Ali Hamid had stressed that Muslims here have a responsibility to aid their fellow believers. Aid them in what? We could propose a couple of theories, but for now, at least, they're only theories."

"Do any of the theories have anything to do with terrorism?" Leivo demanded.

Most people in the room had already seen this coming for a while. Still, the mention of terrorism silenced the group.

"If it does, I want to know how," Leivo continued. "Everything would also fit with international organized crime and a territorial gang war. Killing and mutilating competitors as a warning, forcing compatriots to aid them. Even though most of the deceased don't have a criminal background in Finland, they might turn out to have one back home."

The deputy chief's aggressive stance surprised me. It was no longer pure self-defence. Nor was it his place to offer already-digested theories to the lead investigator.

"Like Toivakka said, we don't have any hints of organized crime of Iraqi or other Arab background," I said. "For a territorial war, you need a territory."

"So what about the mysterious killers? Who were they, where did they disappear to, and what was their motivation?" Leivo wondered out loud.

"Huovinen said that there were at least two of them, I'd say at least four. We know that Tagi Hamid, who was shot and mutilated on the bridge, and the unidentified man who was hit by the train approached the scene from different directions with the intention of meeting on the bridge. The killers followed Tagi Hamid. They were not interested in him, however, but in the man that he was supposed to meet. Ali Hamid, on the other hand, was killed last night, so it seems as if the information about the meeting on the bridge had been tortured out of him. He, in turn, had heard it from his cousin Tagi."

"Where does the four come in?" asked Toivakka.

"Everyone who has ever been involved in tailing a suspect knows that in order to do it successfully, you need enough people. You have to switch roles, so the target doesn't start noticing that the same guy is always at his heels. In addition, the killers intended to abduct the other man from the bridge. You can't drag a man who's struggling and afraid for his life very far without calling attention to yourself. There had to be someone there with a car. But how did the killers know that the person they were following would take the exact route he did? How did they know to have a car at the right spot? They didn't. The problem was solved by using two cars. The killers were in telephone contact with the cars and were giving them instructions the whole time. When the target approached the Linnunlaulu bridge, one of the cars was sent to Eläintarhan-tie, the other to the City Theatre. With only one car, they would have lost the guy by the railway bridge at the latest."

"Sounds like a police operation," Huovinen reflected.

"Or military," I said.

"Are you implying that a group of terrorists has set up shop here and some huge posse of foreign agents is after it?" Leivo snorted, an even more dubious expression on his face. "And why did it all happen right there on the bridge?"

"They were following Ali Hamid's cousin Tagi, because they were looking for the person he was supposed to meet. Afterwards the target was no longer of any use to them, and he was killed. The victim's face was mutilated so that he wouldn't be identified too soon."

"What do you mean, too soon?" Sillanpää wondered.

"Because they knew that, whether or not his face was mutilated, the deceased would eventually be identified. It's obvious that it's only a matter of time. So whatever they're planning on doing here will take place within a very short time frame."

My words were followed by a silence. It was broken by Deputy Chief Leivo.

"It seems to me that the theory cuts too many corners. The commander and I – and I have already discussed this matter with the commander – feel that you have much more plausible theories. I mean the one in which two men, potentially skinheads, kill a foreigner who's waiting for his friend on the bridge. The friend shows up and tries to run from them, but falls in front of a train."

"That was the best theory until we found the two new victims at the body shop," I agreed. "After that, it was clear that this wasn't a coincidence."

Leivo ignored me.

"Or drugs. Maybe they simply had a drug deal that led to an argument and the murders. That would give them a good motive for keeping quiet. Drugs would also explain Hamid's torture. He was either being punished, or they wanted information from him."

"That's possible, too… but I don't believe it."

"You don't? Well, since you're sure, why don't you tell us who the killers are?" Leivo said testily.

"If we're dealing with the kind of operation I think we're dealing with, I can only come up with two alternatives. Either a disagreement arose within a terrorist group and the more fanatic wing killed the others, or else the killers belong to the intelligence agency of some country."

Half a dozen pairs of eyes turned to look at Inspector Sillanpää. We were clearly in SUPO territory now. Sillanpää didn't even bother standing.

"We don't have any indication that a terrorist attack was being planned, and I venture to claim that we're the ones who know most about such matters. In addition, we collaborate with the intelligence agencies of numerous other countries and are immediately informed if even a single suspected terrorist approaches our little northern paradise. Agents of foreign powers aren't in the habit of coming here to carry out operations, at least on the scale that the aforementioned theory would require."

Sillanpää's delivery was convincing. And yet I still sensed that he was steering and slowing the investigation. I was good about picking up on stuff like that, or at least that's what I liked to believe.

"Simply the fact that all of the victims are Arabs shouldn't make us jump to hasty conclusions," Sillanpää continued. "Of course we shouldn't discount the possibility of terrorism either. We're looking into the backgrounds of the deceased with the help of our international contacts. I would, however, continue to urge caution in the use of the word terrorism. If it leaks into the papers, we won't have a moment's peace. And of course if we're really lucky, the story will get picked up by the international media."

"It already has," Huovinen noted. "*Aftonbladet* called a couple of hours ago and *Expressen* right after, and at that point there were only two bodies. Both of them asked if there were any terrorist links in the case. I don't get where they got that from."

Deputy Police Chief Leivo still looked peeved. He was probably wishing he could have seen his name, preferably with an accompanying photograph, in the pages of the Swedish papers.

"In any case, we need to agree on the specific communications tactics, down to turns of phrase, that we will all use. And no one slides from them."

"We won't be commenting on the case other than to state we are following the investigation, as always occurs in cases like these," Sillanpää said. "Public mention of terrorism in particular inevitably points at certain states. We can't prevent

66

the media from speculating. If police command wants to explain matters at the diplomatic level, then go right ahead, but don't get us mixed up in it."

Deputy Chief Leivo's expression grew more concerned. He clearly didn't want a diplomatic incident, even a minor one.

"If SUPO knows more about this than we do and doesn't want us fouling things up, they'd better spit out everything they have."

"I'd tell you if I knew anything," Sillanpää said. "I was just offering my opinion. I assume that's the reason I'm here."

Huovinen turned back to me.

"I propose Lieutenant Kafka decides. He's got the best sense of the case."

I eyed Sillanpää, who stared back stonily.

"I agree to some extent with Inspector Sillanpää. We're going to continue trying to figure out the identity of the unidentified victim with our own resources. If that doesn't work, then we can reconsider releasing the photograph."

Sillanpää gave a near-imperceptible nod.

On the way to my office, I remembered that my colleague who sat a few rooms away, Lieutenant Kari Takamäki, had just wrapped up an investigation of the murder of a young Arab man.

I figured I would be at least partially retracing some of the same paths as him, and I wanted all of the advice he could offer. I showed him the photos of the deceased, but he didn't recognize any of them. We chatted for a minute and Takamäki suggested that I have a word with the communications officer or imam from the Islamic Society, and gave me a name and number for both. I thanked him for the good advice.

6

Imam Omar Nader was evidently a tolerant man. At least he didn't give the slightest indication that Stenman and I were unwelcome guests, although it was unlikely that a Jew and a policewoman were everyday sights at the offices of the Islamic Society.

I had called the imam at home, and he had suggested that we meet at the society's offices. Stenman and I had agreed that I would handle most of the talking, just to be sure.

The imam was a gentle-looking man with thick-framed glasses. It was difficult to say how old he was, but I estimated around fifty. I deduced this based on the fact that the beard, which didn't really suit his round face, was going grey. In a slight contradiction to his role, he was wearing a youthful sweater.

"You said that you needed my help. How can I be of assistance?"

The imam spoke almost perfect Finnish. I had seen him on a television programme once and knew that he had already lived here some twenty-odd years.

"To start with, I'm hoping you can identify someone."

I handed the imam the photo of the body that had been found on the tracks. The photo had been retouched so that the bruising from the collision wouldn't be visible. The imam raised his glasses and stared at the picture for a long time.

"I've seen him at the mosque once, but I don't know his name. I got the impression that he was French, that's why I remember him. Is he dead?"

"Do you know whose guest he was?"

"No. Not necessarily anyone's. Perhaps he just wanted to pray and meet fellow Muslims during a trip to Finland. That happens often."

"How did you come to the conclusion that he was French?"

"I think that someone mentioned it, I don't remember who. That's the impression I was left with, however."

I gave the imam three more photos.

"What about them?"

This time a concerned and at the same time mournful expression flashed across the imam's face.

"Does this have something to do with what was on the news?"

I answered in the affirmative.

"Are they all dead?"

"Yes."

"This is a day of sorrow for me, in many ways. May Allah be merciful to them."

"Do you recognize any of these others?"

The imam hesitated for a moment, but then pointed at Ali Hamid's photo.

"He was a good Muslim, he came to the mosque often to pray. The whole family did. They're all good people, good Finns."

The imam pulled a checked handkerchief out of his pocket and wiped his brow.

"I'm afraid that this is going to bring us a lot of trouble. People have many misplaced prejudices against us Muslims. Finland has treated us well, and we don't want to repay good with evil. This is why you can be sure that the majority of Finnish Muslims condemn all forms of violence, as does the Koran. It will be sad and unfortunate if we are linked to these violent deeds. I always say that violence begets more violence."

"According to Ali Hamid's wife, her husband attended the mosque the night before last with his cousin. Did you see him?"

Once again, the imam hesitated.

"We greeted each other, but we didn't speak."

"Did you know his cousin, Tagi Hamid?"

"I've seen him a couple of times, nothing more."

"Did Ali Hamid speak with anyone other than his cousin?"

"Of course. He's doesn't go around not speaking when he's in the company of friends... But I know what you mean. I didn't notice anything like that."

For the first time, the imam sounded a little impatient.

"Could you please tell me what this is about now?"

I looked at the imam and believed he was sincere.

"We don't know yet. The murders occurred in two different places, but we know that they are related. Do you know, did these four men have anything to do with each other?"

"I don't know the other two at all, but apparently they're Arabs. There aren't very many Arabs living in Helsinki. Maybe they know each other, maybe not, I can't say."

Stenman had had enough of keeping quiet.

"Do you have any idea what might be the motivation for the killings?"

"There are some people and some parties that do not like us. I don't know what else to say. You know these parties as well as we do."

"Could it be a matter of a disagreement between two militant Arab groups?"

"There might be, and are, differences of opinion, but almost everyone is in agreement about the main issues. I don't understand why Arabs would kill each other, especially here in Finland."

I didn't know how the imam would react to the request I was about to present, but I presented it anyway.

"I was hoping you could show these photos to the members of your congregation as soon as possible. We'd be grateful for any information we can get about them."

"Do you suspect them of something?"

"We don't, but naturally we want to know why they were killed. The investigation isn't going to go anywhere until we discover the motive. We don't believe that this was a hate crime. We're particularly interested in the unidentified man you guess was French and Ali and Tagi Hamid. The fourth one is Hamid's employee. We believe he was killed simply because he was in the body shop when Hamid was killed."

The imam gazed at the images of the deceased and, without looking up, said: "I'll do what I can."

I drove Stenman home and returned to HQ to hear the latest news. I wasn't surprised to find the light still on in Simolin's room.

I had been the same way when I started in the Violent Crimes Unit. I'd sit in my office until the wee hours, sifting through the details of a case. I enjoyed being able to chat with the detectives who were on night duty and hear their experiences. I was an avid listener. We'd down cups of automat coffee and talk. Sometimes an interesting call would come in and I'd tag along. I understood Simolin better than he knew.

He was sitting at his desk, bent over a sheaf of papers. He had taken off his jacket. His shirt was blindingly white and there was a dark-blue tie at his neck.

"Aren't you tired?"

"I took a little nap. I'm still going through the last of the tip-offs."

"Anything interesting?"

"As expected, some are racist – you know, those ragheads got what they deserved, etc. There might be some important information in here too, but it's still tough to tell at this point. I've sorted them into some semblance of priority. I can read you a few."

"Go for it."

"Mrs Aune Kujala says that she saw a young, foreign-looking man lifting a bicycle into a white van in front of the City Theatre at eight-thirty in the morning. There were two men, also foreign-looking, in the car. No licence-plate number, no make. It did occur to me that to an old woman, a minivan might look like a van."

"Drop by tomorrow and find out more."

"Then there's this tip-off from a service-station owner who says three skinheads were laughing knowingly while watching the five o'clock news on the killings. We got the tapes from the petrol-station security camera and there's a pretty decent shot of all three. We're looking for them. SUPO gave us a name and address for one of them, but he wasn't at home. A patrol is going to try again later tonight."

"I don't believe they're our guys."

"Me neither," Simolin said.

"Didn't anything come in about the Citroën Hamid rented?"

"Amazingly enough, no."

Earlier that evening, Oksanen had discovered that Ali Hamid had rented a green Citroën C5 hatchback from Hertz. We didn't release the vehicle details to the media until all patrols had searched for it for a couple of hours with no results. I thought it was strange that no tip-offs from the public had come in.

"That car's got to be in someone's garage," Simolin remarked. "And it could be that it hasn't been used since it was rented. Maybe it's being saved for a specific purpose."

"Could be."

Simolin made no effort to decorate his office with anything that reflected his personality. There were no fishing or hunting pictures on the walls, no cartoons or Che Guevara posters or any other ideological material. All that was on the shelves were case folders and a slim collection of legal literature. Simolin preferred looking up information online. The sole spark of personality was the image on his computer's screen saver. It was of a Sioux Indian chief in a magnificent feathered headdress. I knew that the Indian belonged to the Sioux tribe, because I had asked Simolin.

Later I heard from one of Simolin's academy classmates that Simolin was crazy about North American Indians and had made himself a complete Indian outfit out of moose skin, plus a perfect replica of an Indian bow and arrows. I wasn't surprised; somehow I could imagine him being into stuff like that.

The information about Simolin's hobby had spread rapidly around the VCU, and for a while it was impossible for him to escape it. Whenever he was in a meeting, some wiseass would fold his arms akimbo and end whatever he was saying with: "Ugh! I have spoken!" Until the joke got old, words like forked tongue, paleface, papoose, teepee, great white chief, long knife and yellow-hair were tossed around the department in all possible contexts.

Simolin didn't get mad, he just smiled shyly. He clearly possessed that brand of quiet, stubborn resolve that shouldn't be underestimated. If Simolin had been a boxer, he would have been the kind that you could knock to the canvas time and again and he'd always just pick himself back up.

"Why weren't the images of the victims released?" Simolin asked.

I recounted the reasons that had been discussed in the meeting. Simolin didn't look convinced.

"I think the photos would have brought us some good tip-offs. Now we don't even know all their names or where they live."

Simolin was right about that. A little unexpectedly, Hamid's cousin Tagi didn't have a permanent address. He had moved a couple of months back from his place in Kannelmäki and hadn't given a new address to anyone, not even his cousin. Or then Ali Hamid hadn't told it to his wife.

He hadn't been seen at the vocational school where he was registered for weeks, and they didn't know anything about him.

The background of Ali Hamid's body-shop employee Wasin Mahmed had also been checked and everything corroborated the notion that he didn't have anything to do with the case.

"If we don't see any progress in the investigation, we can release the photos tomorrow."

"The killers might have already skipped the country by then."

Once again Simolin was right.

"Nothing we can do about it. Go home and go to bed," I said.

"Soon."

"Well, I'm going now."

My mobile rang.

"Detective Kafka."

"It's Vivica Mattsson from the City Theatre. You were here this morning."

"Hi."

I glanced at Simolin. He was already reviewing the next tip-off, and wished me an over-the-shoulder goodnight.

I stepped out into the corridor. For some reason I didn't want Simolin listening in on the conversation between Mattsson and me.

"You asked me to call if I remembered anything."

"Right... So you remembered something?"

"What someone yelled on the bridge... I just came home from rehearsal and I dropped by a convenience store on the way. There were two Arab-looking guys in there. They were arguing, and one of them barked '*Manjak!*' at the other one. I'm pretty sure I heard the word *manjak* from the bridge."

"Do you remember anything else?"

"No, I'm sorry. I'm afraid I haven't been much help."

"Every bit of new information is a help."

"Do you already know who killed those men?"

"No."

"Or you do, but you won't tell me, is that it?"

Her voice was flirtatious.

"No."

"Couldn't you interrogate me… even just a little?"

"Some other time."

"That's probably what you tell all the girls."

I wondered if she had dropped in at the pub on her way home. Nevertheless, I felt that something was sparking up between us – or else it was just wishful thinking.

"I'm sorry, when I'm tired I start saying all kinds of inappropriate things. Rehearsal lasted eleven hours. Hopefully you'll solve the case. Goodnight."

"Goodnight," I blurted out stiffly.

I looked at my phone and felt like a cardboard-dry civil servant. For someone over forty, I was still a complete amateur at verbally manipulating women.

I sat for a moment at my desk, still intoxicated by the call. Then I went online, opened up Google, and entered a search for Vivica Mattsson.

I spent ten or so minutes browsing through articles about her. I found out that she was from Tammisaari, an only child, had been left fatherless – like me – at the age of twelve, and had been a wild tomboy as a child. She had a show champion Jack Russell terrier named Ole. She spoke French fluently and was single. I exited Google and leant back in my chair. It still took a minute for me to let Vivica Mattsson go.

"*Manjak*," I said out loud.

I took my phone and pulled up the number of my old schoolmate who had lived in Israel for twenty years. He spoke both Hebrew and Arabic fluently.

My friend's wife answered and called her husband to the phone. After a brief preface, I went to the point.

"*Manjak*, nothing else, just *manjak*?"

"Right."

"It's a derogatory Arabic term, but it has at least a couple of different meanings depending on the context in which it's used. In Finland it could mean either faggot or syphilitic, for instance. Does that match what you're looking for?"

"It does indeed."

If Mattsson had heard correctly, the shouter was probably the man who fell to the roof of the train. There would have been no reason for the men standing safely on the bridge to shout. So he was probably an Arab, just as we had suspected. And the fact that he used an Arabic taunt implied that the men that he was running from were also Arabs.

I decided to get back in touch with the imam.

7

I had a one-bedroom flat in the Punavuori district, on Merimiehenkatu. I'd already lived there for thirteen years and my mortgage was practically all paid-up. If I had to describe the place in a few words, I'd call it a bare-bones bachelor pad. On the other hand, all of the furnishings, the TV and the stereo were quality stuff. A few contemporary oil paintings hung from the walls. I had got a good deal on them from my cousin, who was a moderately successful artist. He had given one of them to me on my fortieth birthday.

When my mother had died, I had brought over a couple of antiques from her apartment: a mahogany bed for the bedroom and a mirror for the entryway. The antiques were a better match for my brother's disgustingly posh place in Eira. I'm not envious by nature, but disgustingly posh was an accurate way of describing my brother's home.

Or actually the flat was his wife's, whose family was so rich that she didn't understand words like *poverty* and *deprived*, except maybe in theory.

I dumped the Chinese takeaway I had picked up on the way home on the counter and set the table. Beef in black-bean sauce and fried rice. I wasn't a big kosher freak, but I didn't go out of my way to eat pork either. I popped open a cold beer to wash down my meal.

My phone rang just as I was finishing. It was my disgustingly rich brother Eli calling.

"I saw the news. You still at work?"

"Just got home."

"I'm out front. Buzz me up and I'll come say hi."

I pressed the buzzer and waited. It wasn't like Eli to drop by without advance warning, especially this late.

Eli looked a little goofy in the gaudy tracksuit he was wearing. His shoes and outfit looked like they had just been pulled out of the packaging. I cracked a couple of beers, and my brother didn't turn up his nose. He sat down on the living-room couch. For brothers, we looked totally different. Eli was round-faced, three inches shorter and fatter than me. He played tennis, skied and played golf, but he was still always putting on weight. He looked around as if he were in the market for an apartment.

"If you're looking for a bigger place in the neighbourhood, I know about one. The heirs are selling. It'd be a good buy, even just as an investment."

"Do I look like someone who's investing in real estate?"

"I could get you a low-interest loan."

"Interest that low doesn't exist."

"Have you decided about Yom Kippur Eve yet?" Eli asked.

He had invited me to his home to celebrate the Day of Atonement. I had received a couple of other invitations as well. Evidently a Jewish man my age who lived alone was a hopelessly pitiful case. I was like a ward whose care was the joint responsibility of my whole extended family.

"Unless some miracle happens, I'll be there."

"You're not telling me that a forty-year-old Jewish cop still believes in miracles, are you?"

"Just little ones."

"Don't let a miracle come between you and your family. Silja asked me to tell you she'll be mad if you don't show up."

"I'll try."

"Uncle Dennis is going to be there, too."

"How's he doing?"

"Seems to be holding up."

I got along well with my uncle the best of all my relatives, except for maybe Eli.

"Day after tomorrow is Hanna's birthday," Eli reminded me.

I remembered. Hannah, who was known as Hanna, was my sister. She was seven years younger than me and had killed herself five years ago. She suffered from schizophrenia. The disease had flared up when she was in Israel at a kibbutz. She had been sitting at a local café one evening when a bomb-rigged car drove up and exploded. Six people died, including four of Hanna's kibbutz friends. They dug Hanna out from the under the bodies and gore. Through some miracle she only had minor injuries, but she never got over it psychologically.

"Who else have you invited?"

"Max and his wife."

Eli and my second cousin Max were partners in a law firm, Kafka & Oxbaum. Max had all the symptoms of a social-climbing arsehole times two.

"Why'd you invite Max?"

"He said it's been a while, that it'd be nice to see some relatives, like you. I had to invite him."

"You'd think that a rich fifty-year-old wouldn't have to do anything he didn't want to."

"You wouldn't believe how many things there are in life that you have to do even if you don't want to. First Mum bossed us around, then the wife, and now traditions. Sometimes I think it would have been a lot easier to have been born Lutheran."

"Especially on Yom Kippur," I added.

"Then too."

I was tired and I yawned. Eli drained his bottle and stood.

"Is it true that those guys who were killed were probably Arabs?" he asked.

I admitted it, because that information had already been reported on the news.

"Hopefully they killed each other. I mean, I hope it's not some neo-Nazi hate crime," Eli added quickly. "That's the first thing that came to mind."

"We'll get to the bottom of it."

"Does the case have anything to do with us?"

Eli's question surprised me.

"What do you mean?"

"With the Jewish congregation?"

"Why would it?"

"Everything's possible these days. Even though Finland's a little out of the way, we're not going to be left in peace for ever."

"Do you know something that I don't?"

"Of course not, it just came to mind somehow… Thanks for the beer, even though it took the punch out of the run."

"Say hi to the wife and kids."

Eli jabbed a thick forefinger at me.

"And remember: the day after tomorrow. Be there."

"I'll try. 'Night."

Eli pulled on his wool cap and bounded down the stairs. I watched from the window and saw him exit the building and turn towards the shore. Suddenly he stopped, looked around, and got into the passenger side of a Volvo hatchback parked at the edge of the street.

Eli hadn't dropped by while he was out on a run. He had dropped by on purpose.

8

When you scratch the surface of a Jewish man, his mother starts to come out, in both good and bad.

I spent my entire childhood and youth afraid that my mum would pounce just as I was kissing my neighbour Kaija Lindström in the basement, or insinuating my hand into Karmela Meyer's pants.

For her part, Mum considered men next to useless, and never glanced at a single one after Dad died. Sometimes it seemed to me as if his death came as a relief to her. Her big, black underpants billowed on the courtyard laundry line like a banner of war. It was clear to anyone who saw those panties that the front they concealed would never be surrendered again.

Maybe the worst thing was that I didn't dare to invite any friends over because Mum would subject them to a cross-examination that would conclude with her pronouncing judgment without ever giving the defence the floor.

We tried to understand Mum, because she'd been through a lot. She was born in Poland, and when Germany invaded in 1939, her mother had fled with her to Finland. She had been ten at the time. At the age of eighteen, she had married a fabric merchant twenty years older than herself. He had died in the late 1940s and the business had gone under. About a year later, relatives who were trying to marry off my father brought my mother and father together. Only a couple of months passed before Wolf Kafka was an ex-bachelor.

The union with the fabric merchant had been childless, but my mother had three children with my father: Eli, me and Hannah. When Eli was born, Mum quit her job at a hair salon.

My father, who was a hydraulic engineer, didn't have things any easier. A peace-loving man by nature, he feared my mother. Maybe that's the reason he was often away in northern Finland. He worked for a large energy company and was involved in every dam and power-plant project in Lapland.

He was also involved when the power company bought stretches of riverbank at ridiculously low prices from the locals and harnessed the rapids to churning out cash. And it was Dad's slide rule that was the source of the profit and environmental calculations for the Loka reservoir.

Northern Finland is where Dad died, too. He drowned on a fishing and hunting trip that had been organized for the energy company's upper management. The drunken CEO insisted on trying whitewater rafting, and Dad, who was the most sober of the bunch, had been forced to man the oars. The boat hit a rock and capsized. Dad's body was found the next day, a couple of miles downstream.

Jewish jokes often feature a woman who's as loud as my mother and defends her family like a tigress. I'd like to think that that's what Mum was like, but I'm afraid she looked out first and foremost for herself. In Poland she had learnt to fight for every last heel of bread. Living like that refines some people; others it turns callous and hard.

My worst nightmares started shortly after my father's death. I was a little over ten then. When Dad died, my family was left almost destitute. The energy company paid some sort of lump-sum compensation for our loss, but that money went to paying the mortgage. Mum had been working at the salon across the street from our apartment for a few years again, and soon she set up her own salon for men and women.

The way she got the money for the salon is Kafka family legend.

Mum marched into the bank where my uncle Dennis was the manager and slapped down the calculations for the amount she needed in front of him. My uncle was in the middle of some important financing negotiations and tried to escort my mother out. But Mum would not let up. She said that, if need be, she'd hang from the door by her teeth until Uncle Dennis promised to give her the money. My uncle knew my mother and understood that this was not an empty threat. When Mum grabbed the doorframe with both hands, my uncle lost his nerve and promised to loan her as much money as she could ever imagine needing. Mum thanked Uncle Dennis politely, kissed him on the forehead, and left.

The salon was a success, but for Eli and me it was a source of lifelong trauma. Mum couldn't afford to hire an assistant at the start, so Eli and I were forced to work there. We ran Mum's errands, swept up the hair from the floor, and sometimes, when it was really busy, I even had to wash the customers' hair. I hated it. I eventually started getting asthma from the hairspray and dye fumes I was inhaling, and the doctor ordered me to quit. Eli had already quit earlier under the pretence of his studies.

It was three in the morning and I was lying in bed, trying to figure out what part of my subconscious had lured Mum into my dreams. She had been dead and gone for sixteen years already.

"*Manjak!*"

Sometimes when she flew into a rage, Mum would grab my hair and let me have an earful of horrible Hebrew and Arabic insults. She'd spit them out like spells, so for a couple of weeks I'd feel like I was cursed.

I was forced to admit to myself that the Arabic curse word was what had brought Mum to mind.

Arabic?

An idea occurred to me, and I recalled the conversation I had had with my schoolmate a few hours back. What was it he had asked, when he had told me the meaning of the word *manjak*?

"Nothing else, just *manjak*?"

I decided to call my friend again first thing in the morning. If my suspicions held true, it would change everything.

9

I woke up to the sound of my phone ringing. It was five-thirty in the morning. I had slept poorly since my middle-of-the-night insight, and it took a minute before I was fully awake.

To top of it all off, I had been dreaming about playing ping-pong with a beautiful female Israeli soldier whose shirt was unbuttoned to her navel. I had been winning 7–3 when my phone rang.

"Lieutenant Toivola here from the Järvenpää police department, *morgen*."

I was not happy to hear from my commuter-town colleague, despite the impressive level of his linguistic skills.

"You folks have a search out on a green Citroën C5 hatchback. Might be that it's turned up."

"Where?"

"Kerava, a sandpit in the middle of the woods. Burnt to a crisp. I'm on the scene. The wreck's still giving off so much heat you could grill sausages on it."

"What makes you think it's the car we're looking for? The plates?"

"No, the plates were stolen in Kerava, but doesn't that say something too? This one's metallic green like yours, or at least it was. Now it's burnt black. Can still make out some of the original paint on the boot, though. Haven't been able to check the serial on the engine or the chassis yet, have to scrape off the soot first. But there haven't been any other green Citroën C5s reported stolen."

"Anything else?"

"There's a body behind the wheel."

"A body?"

"That's right, male, extra well-done. They're having a look at it as we speak."

"I'll be there in about an hour. Don't move anything."

"We won't."

The trip took an hour and seven minutes, even without me showering first; the place was hard to find. Toivola had resourcefully ordered a patrol to wait where the road turned off, and they gave me the directions I needed. The autumn sky was growing light as I drove down the forest road. It turned right at a metal shed that was leaning to one side, and then continued through a quarter-mile of dense spruce woods before coming to an abrupt end at a sandpit. The car had been driven behind a little ridge, so you couldn't see it from the road. At the bottom of the pit stood a small pool with the carcass of a shopping-cart jutting out of it. Finland was dotted by thousands of these sandpits, as if some incredibly hard-working and efficient sandpit salesman had sold the same pothole to every county in the country.

Toivola was leaning against a patrol car, sipping coffee from a paper cup. Maybe a considerate wife had packed him a Thermos and salami sandwiches that morning. We shook hands. He looked good-natured: round face, whiskers, blond. His hip-length dark-green coat was made of heavy cloth and had German-style brown-leather piping at the sleeves and pockets. His brimmed cap was also dark brown and trimmed in leather.

I wouldn't have remembered the guy's name if he hadn't mentioned it, but I remembered his face. Toivola and I had attended some class together. I didn't even remember what it was, but Toivola did.

"We were at the same self-evaluation course for officers."

86

"That's right."

I didn't want to get a reputation as an arsehole, but I wasn't in the mood for reminiscing. Toivola didn't let my reticence bother him. He was a lieutenant after all, and had been around the block a few times.

"That class sure was a waste of scarce taxpayer funds. At this age, the only way I learn is the hard way. Never make the same mistake more than three times," Toivola said, taking me by the sleeve. I let him guide me, even though I could have found the way myself. I could sense the nostril-tingling reek of burnt rubber, plastic and smoke from twenty yards away.

The car looked downright mournful. The fire had burnt it so thoroughly that you couldn't see the original colour. The tyres were nothing more than shreds dangling around the rims. The windows were broken and the metal had buckled from the heat. The water used to extinguish the flames had turned the ground around the vehicle to muck, and you could make out the white dregs of extinguishing foam inside the car. A crime-scene investigator decked out in overalls and thick-soled rubber boots was busying himself at its rear.

We stopped next to the vehicle.

"The man was most probably still alive when the car ignited or was ignited," Toivola informed me.

The charred torso of the deceased was shrivelled over the wheel as if he had fallen asleep at it. I examined the face; nothing identifiable remained. The skin, which had split from the heat, looked like a hot dog that had been roasted too long in a campfire. I could feel the heat still emanating from the car.

I frowned at the body that had spoilt my elegant scenario. This whole time I had assumed that the rental Citroën would be found near Linnunlaulu, in the place where the man who had been hit by the train left it. I couldn't come up with any reason off the top of my head for what the hell the car was doing in the middle of the forest twenty-five miles from Helsinki, and who this broiled guy behind the wheel was. In any case, it looked like he was also mixed up in the Linnunlaulu events. That meant that the total body count was now up to five, which was a lot, even for cities bigger than Helsinki.

"Can we remove the body yet?" asked the CSI. "It's interfering with the investigation of the car."

I looked at Toivola.

"As far as I'm concerned," he said.

I gave my consent.

The recalcitrant corpse was forcibly wrenched from between the wheel and the metal skeleton of the seat and lifted into a plastic body bag. The deceased lay there, arms and legs bent, as if reaching for something that he would never now obtain. The two burly ambulance drivers swung the body bag lightly up onto the stretcher and carried it off. The thought crossed my mind that some unlucky medical examiner was going to be getting an unusually messy gig.

Toivola pointed at the warped seat frame.

"An expert from the fire department examined the car. Looks like either under the seat or right next to it there was some sort of incendiary device with a smallish initial charge. The explosion wasn't very powerful, but the driver was at least knocked unconscious, and the fire took care of the rest. Died almost immediately. What do you think?"

"What about you?"

"Maybe the idea was to clean up tracks by burning the car, but the bomb exploded too early by mistake."

I could tell that my lack of a good night's sleep was still congealing my thinking. When I was tired I was grumpy and didn't bother hiding it, even from myself. But Toivola had been helpful in every way imaginable, so I tried to suppress my bad mood – despite the fact that the female soldier I had been playing ping-pong with had been extremely beautiful and ready for more than a little ball-bouncing.

I had thought about her during the drive. I was sure that she was some sort of delayed echo from my visit to Israel over ten years earlier. When I was at the Wailing Wall, a group of soldiers had showed up, machine guns dangling loosely. Two of them had been women, and one of them one of the most beautiful women I had ever seen. I was convinced she had been the inspiration for King Solomon as he feverishly dictated the Song of Songs.

It had been ten years, though, and that former Rose of Sharon had probably ballooned into a housewife in some dull Jerusalem suburb. And when her even-better-fed hubby, a hydrological and sewer engineer, walked in the door on the Sabbath, he found his surly wife and three well-fed kids in yarmulkes waiting for him.

Maybe I was just jealous. I was a Jewish heterosexual who was privately suspected of being gay or defective in some other way, like all forty-year-old bachelors.

And for Jews, the phrase "forty-year-old bachelor" was more problematic than normal, at least as far as my relatives were concerned. According to the Talmud, Torah studies are the only acceptable reason to postpone tying the knot.

Twenty years ago, I had lived with a woman for almost three years, and she and I had planned on getting married. Nothing came of it, because she felt Jewish traditions were overly oppressive. A few years later, she married a Kurd from Iraq and converted to Islam.

"Is there any information on the deceased?" I asked.

"No, or at least we don't have an identity yet."

I circled the car and stopped at the rear.

Toivola was right. The original green colour was visible on the boot. I no longer doubted that the car was the one we were looking for. I bent over to examine the inside of the boot but didn't find anything unusual. The tools that had been in the side panel had tumbled out as the plastic melted. Next to them was a mangled snarl of iron that I figured had been the stand for a warning triangle.

"Did the deceased have anything that could be used to identify him, a ring or necklace?"

Toivola dug into the side pocket of his loden coat and pulled out three plastic bags.

"A Citizen watch, a gold necklace with a Gemini medallion and the text *For Kimi, 17 June 2003*. A bunch of keys at the end of a steel chain, a large metal buckle, a couple of metal tubes blackened beyond recognition, and some unidentifiable clods." I glanced at the keys. There were three of them: two normal Abloy keys and one Abloy Disklock.

Our friend Kimi, born under the sign of Gemini, dealt another blow to my theories. My scenario didn't have room for a Finnish killer or even a Finnish accomplice. The only good thing was that now we had something concrete to grab on to.

"Judging by the necklace and the horoscope medallion, the deceased is pretty young. With that information and the name and birth date, we could try and pinpoint an identity."

Toivola nodded and showed me the buckle.

"This was in the back seat, a purse buckle, and this junk here is the contents of the purse, a tube of lipstick and the mirror from a powder case. If I'm right, there was also a woman in the car at some point. What do you think?"

I took a couple of steps back and looked around.

"About the woman?"

"About the whole thing."

"There's been a search out on the car since yesterday morning. It seems a little odd that it didn't burn until now."

"My thoughts exactly," Toivola agreed. "What do you make of that?"

"If there had been a firebomb in the car, it could have been on a delayed detonator with a long fuse so that the car wouldn't be found too fast."

Toivola kicked at a hunk of rock.

"Do you know what this place is?"

"What?"

"A spot where the local kids come to spawn. Maybe that's what the victim was up to."

"Could you find out if are there any Kimis in the area who were born on 17 June?"

Toivola promised to check and suggested: "Should we agree that you hold on to the case for the time being and we provide backup? The other alternative is to ask the NBI to help out."

I already had my hands full with the four earlier bodies, but if the fifth was part of the picture, I needed it to put the whole puzzle together.

"Sounds good."

Toivola stepped aside and made a call. In the meantime, I went over to the investigator.

"Find any footprints leaving the car?"

"The ground is too compacted and the firefighters made a mess of the rest, but let's see what we come up with. It'll still take hours for us to search the terrain… You have a pretty big case under investigation in Helsinki, don't you? And this on top of everything else."

"When do you think the fire started?"

"The call came in at four-thirty. The car was still burning hard when the firefighters arrived, so it hadn't been burning for very long."

I glanced at my watch. Twenty to eight. I knew that Huovinen would be awake by now, maybe even at work, so I called him and told him where I was and what had happened.

"We need you here, too. The deputy chief ordered the release of the victims' photographs today if the final body isn't identified. You probably haven't seen the tabloids yet?"

"Nah, what are they saying?"

"Both of them are linking the killings to terrorism and the Israeli–Palestinian situation."

"On what grounds?"

"Wasn't clear to me. When do you think you can be here?"

"I'll shoot for nine."

"I'll set up a meeting for quarter-past. Try and make it, we might be hosting some VIPs. High society, you know."

I had to hand it to Huovinen. He stood like a breakwater between me and the higher-ups and took the blows. You never would have guessed it based on his impeccably dapper appearance. Toivola walked over.

"Looks like we found him right off. Kimi Rontu, born 17 June 1979. Originally from Hyvinkää, but evidently sublets from relatives in Kerava. A narcotics violation and three car thefts under his belt. I also found out that the car wasn't here in the early evening. A couple of cars had been stolen downtown, and since we know from experience that stolen cars get abandoned here at the pit, a patrol dropped by to check it out. Time was six-fifteen p.m. That Citro didn't show up until afterwards."

I offered Toivola my praises and he accepted them, pleased.

"Could you still check one more thing? If there was a woman with Rontu, then maybe she was injured and went to the hospital for treatment."

"I should have thought of that myself," Toivola said, annoyed. "I'll have someone get on it first thing. What if we drop by the kid's place right now? We might find something there that'll shed light on all this. Maybe he brought the girl around to meet the landlords."

"I'm in a bit of a rush, but if we head out right this minute…"

"Right this minute. I know the place, just follow me."

I followed Toivola's dull grey Toyota. A car like that was meant to be driven by a modest man, so modest that it smacked of excess.

I followed him out of the woods, onto a side road, and across the main road into a neighbourhood of sparsely spaced single-family homes. The houses were the flat-roofed 1970s variety. Toivola's brake lights flashed and he made a sudden turn into the yard of a brick house. There was room for three cars in front of the garage. One of the spots was taken by a burgundy Volvo.

"Looks like there's someone home," Toivola said. He pressed the doorbell, and a tinkling that sounded like a loose-stringed harp came from inside. A small copper-trimmed overhang sheltered the doorstep.

The door opened, revealing a man of about fifty. Inexorably advancing baldness was attacking his grey, neck-length hair from the crown. Toivola introduced himself first and then me.

"According to our information, a person by the name of Kimi Rontu is subletting from you."

The man thought for a second and then asked: "What's he done?"

"Nothing. We'd like to check a few things."

"He hasn't been around since yesterday."

"You mind if we take a look around his room?"

Without saying a word, the man snatched a key from the key rack in the entryway, thrust his feet into wide-mouthed rubber boots, and stepped out. We followed him out behind the garage.

"This room has its own entrance. We've been renting it out since our son moved."

"Is Rontu a relative?" I asked.

"My wife's nephew. Kid's enough of a juvie I wouldn't have taken him in if my wife hadn't put the screws on me."

"Does he have a job?"

"Nah, lives off welfare. I don't think that boy is ever going to be much of a credit to his country."

Behind the garage there was a dented-up motorbike with a flat front tyre.

"Never fixed that either. It's been lying there all summer," he tsked.

"Was he dating?" I asked.

"Oh, I guess he had someone, this little brunette who came by the place sometimes, but I told him straight off that the apartment's only for one."

"When did you see her last?"

"A couple of weeks ago, around… It's high time I knew what you're after."

"Last night a car was burnt not too far from here," Toivola said. "A man's body was found in the car. We suspect it was your subletter."

"Kimi? What makes you think that?"

I looked at Toivola. He dug out the deceased's effects and showed them to the man.

His expression grew grave.

"Those are Kimi's… Those were on the body?"

"Yes."

The man distractedly opened the door and we stepped inside. He stood in the doorway, watching us.

The room was sparsely furnished. There was a bookcase on the end wall, and across from it a sofa bed, an armoire made of MDF and a small coffee table. A cheap stereo, a portable TV and a VCR were on the bookcase. A *Playboy* centrefold hung on the wall.

"Kimi didn't have a car… Was it an accident or a crime?" the man asked.

"We don't know," I said. "Do you know where he kept his photographs?"

Without hesitating, the man went over to the bookcase, opened the bottom compartment, and handed over a photo album with blue plastic covers. When I opened it, he pointed at a photo. It was of a young man with a buzz cut and bad skin. He was wearing jeans, a black flight jacket and combat boots. The familiar key chain hung from a belt loop. The shirt was open at the collar, revealing the gold horoscope medallion that had been found on the body.

"Flight jacket and combat boots. Was he a skinhead?"

"He didn't like Somalis or other refugees, but I wouldn't go so far as to say he was a skinhead or whatever. I'm not even really sure what that is. Someone who hates Jews?"

"Something like that. Do you know, was he involved in any violence against foreigners?"

"Never heard anything like that, I think it stayed more at the level of talk. He had a good friend who was a Gypsy, so I figure he couldn't have really hated them too much."

I browsed through the photographs. It looked like they had all been taken within the past couple of years. In one of them, a dark-haired girl was sitting in Kimi Rontu's lap. It had been taken at a party at someone's house; the table behind them was heaped with wine and beer bottles. I showed the photo to the man.

"Is this the girlfriend?

He glanced at the photo and nodded.

"You remember her name?"

"Säde. Don't know the last name. But she lived somewhere around here, because one night she walked home."

I poked around for an address book but couldn't find one. There were two almost-new car stereos in the armoire. Judging by the clipped wires, they had been removed from their cars in a hurry and without permission.

"I bet they're stolen," the landlord said. "You probably know that Kimi has some car-theft convictions, and I guess he fooled around with drugs too. There were these real pungent fumes in here sometimes... But in the end, he wasn't such a bad person, considering his background... I guess it'll always come out somehow..."

The man's voice trembled, and he turned to look out of the window.

"There's something seriously wrong with my wife's sister. When Kimi was small, she'd leave him alone for a whole day sometimes. It was thanks to my wife that nothing worse happened…"

I tried the bottom of the armoire. It was loose, and I lifted it out. In the hollow, there was a 22-calibre Bernardelli target pistol in a nylon case and a stiletto with a fake elk-horn handle.

"I don't know anything about those," stated the man.

I took the pistol and put it in my jacket pocket, along with its case. The NBI lab would have the honour of testing whether or not the gun had been fired at Linnunlaulu.

"I regret having spoken ill of him, the dead," said Kimi's uncle from the doorway.

Toivola's empathy was roused.

"That's the way we humans work, we say unkind things and then we regret it. Not too many angels among us."

We didn't find anything else of interest in the apartment. We left after Toivola asked for the key. If we needed DNA to identify the body, it would be found in Kimi Rontu's apartment in one form or another.

Outside, I thanked Toivola and shook his hand. Then I started heading towards Helsinki.

I was at HQ at five past nine. I had called Simolin on the way to brief him on the morning's events. He also had some things to report.

"The white Nissan minivan spotted in Vartiokylä was found in Herttoniemi, at the Siilitie metro station car park. The Itäkeskus patrol found it in the middle of the night. It was towed back to the police lot for examination."

I was pleased. The case was lurching forward on multiple fronts at once.

"And another thing. The bullets found at Hamid's body shop and Linnunlaulu don't match, just like we thought, but the blood on the unidentified man's hand is the same rare type as Hamid's cousin's. No traces of gunpowder gas were found on his body, and the weapon that was recovered from the roof of the train had not been fired."

Just before the meeting I had time to call my former schoolmate, and he confirmed my suspicions.

"Even though *manjak* is Arabic, it's in common use among Jews too. A lot of other Jewish obscenities are also of Arabic origin."

"What did you mean when you asked if *manjak* was the only word?"

"If a Jew really wants to offend an Arab, he says '*Muhammad manjak*', whereas an Arab says '*Moshe manjak*'."

I had been certain that the Arab who fell from the bridge had addressed the obscenity *manjak* at another Arab. The situation would be totally different if the target of the slur had been a Jew.

There was indeed high-level participation at our morning meeting, just as Huovinen had anticipated. Police Commander Tuulia was sitting at the head of the table, and Deputy Police Chief Leivo sat on his right. The last time I had seen Tuulia in an investigation meeting had been in connection with the police killing in Punavuori, and that had been several years ago. Inspector Sillanpää was sitting next to the wall, rocking back in his chair – without falling, no matter how hard I wished he would.

After Huovinen's briefing, I reported on the latest developments in the investigation. They must have been more favourable than Tuulia had expected, because his stony expression softened. He had probably included a wish in his bedtime prayers that the perpetrator would turn out to be a normal criminal, your basic Finnish murderer. He wasn't any more interested in exoticism than Leivo, although he was a lot thicker skinned. The dead Rontu took the case in a normal direction.

"Do you have any theories about what the car was doing in Kerava if it was being used by the man who was killed at

Linnunlaulu, and what the young man who was found in the car had to do with it?" Tuulia asked.

I replied that my theories still had gaps in them.

"Let's hear them anyway."

"Maybe someone was waiting in the car while two others met on the bridge. He saw what happened to them and fled the scene. He figured that there would be a search for the car and drove it far enough away to hide it. Rontu happened to be at the sandpit and so the perpetrator was forced to kill him. Afterwards he ignited the car. Or maybe the man who died at Linnunlaulu simply lived out there and came to Helsinki by train."

Tuulia looked a little disappointed.

"Couldn't the sandpit guy – Rontu, was that the name? – be one of the killers?"

I said I didn't believe he was.

"You don't? This Rontu has a criminal record. I think it's a bit too much of a coincidence that he would just happen to be in the wrong place at the wrong time."

I hesitated for a second, but then I decided to play my Israeli card.

"*Manjak!*" Tuulia repeated. "Based on one curse word we're supposed to believe that the perpetrators were Israeli? So if the word 'fuck' had been used on the bridge, we'd assume that one of the crooks was American? We can't afford to be labelled anti-Semites on such flimsy grounds."

"It's pretty hard to accuse me of being an anti-Semite," I said. Huovinen laughed.

"It's not a matter of one police officer, but of the entire organization," Tuulia snapped.

"I'm just repeating what a witness heard."

"One witness."

"Another witness is also certain that there were foreigners speaking a language that sounded like Arabic on the bridge. It'd be nice to hear what SUPO thinks."

Sillanpää sat up a little straighter.

"About what?"

"Do you believe that the killers could have been Israeli?"

"The killers could just as easily be African Bantus or Indian fakirs as Israeli. The citizens of every country kill each other. We haven't got to the point where the lamb and the lion go frolicking around in peace and harmony."

Leivo frowned.

"Let's stay on track, shall we?"

Leivo indicated the tabloids in front of him. I had taken a glance at the articles. Both of them referred to an anonymous source according to whom the method used to execute the three dead men was similar to the one used by the Israeli intelligence agency Mossad. All of them had been shot multiple times in the upper body and once or twice in the head. In addition, there was a direct quote from the paper's "Arab source", who considered the killings part of Israel's policy of assassination, designed to sabotage the emergence of an independent Palestine and fan conflict within the Arab community.

"Does anyone know anything about this?"

Everyone glanced around, but no one said a word. I eventually asked Sillanpää: "What sort of cooperation does SUPO have with the Israeli security police?"

"The same kind as with the intelligence services of other friendly nations. We exchange information when necessary."

"Have you exchanged information in this instance?"

"I'm not authorized to give out information regarding intelligence cooperation."

"That's too bad. If the killers are Israeli, we have to suspect that the perpetrators are Israeli intelligence agency personnel. It's pretty hard to imagine Israeli civilians getting up to something like this on their own here. And Mossad has operated abroad before, even in the Nordic countries."

Sillanpää snorted dismissively.

I ignored him and continued: "And if it is Mossad, that

means that the victims were terrorists. They're not interested in normal criminals."

During my officer's training, I had read all the literature on Mossad that I could get my hands on, and I was sure I knew more about the topic that anyone else present, with the possible exception of Sillanpää.

"What do you think, Inspector Sillanpää?" asked Chief Tuulia, mustering all the authority he could. But Sillanpää was not to be shaken.

"It's hard for me to imagine a reason why Mossad would come to Finland to kill Arabs whom they suspect of being terrorists. They have enough problems of their own. All they would have needed to do is give us the information, and we would have taken care of it."

I was starting to get annoyed with Sillanpää.

"Everyone knows that Mossad executes pre-emptive and retaliatory strikes on foreign territory. Maybe they got their hands on some information that gave them a reason to strike."

Everyone turned back to look at Sillanpää.

"There are all kinds of legends and fairy tales going around about Mossad," he said. "The majority probably started by Mossad itself. They make mistakes just like everyone else. In Lillehammer, Norway, they killed an innocent Moroccan-born waiter because they thought he was a terrorist. Five Mossad workers and aides who had participated in the assassination operation were convicted. In reality, Mossad is the same kind of intelligence and security service as all the rest, and conforms to the same laws. The bosses are equally stupid everywhere; all they think about is their careers and all they care about is getting a pat on the back from their superiors."

He glanced instinctively at Commander Tuulia. It was like someone had pressed a Stop button, the silence was so sudden. Sillanpää continued, as if he hadn't noticed anything: "Generally speaking, of course. Besides, Finland and Israel are friends. Operating here illegally would be such a big risk for relations that it would require approval at a ministerial level."

Tuulia and Leivo clearly took Sillanpää's remark about the stupidity of bosses personally.

Tuulia spoke: "There's no point wasting time debating; we don't have enough facts for that yet. I'd like to hear some constructive suggestions, if anyone has any. I've decided that the photos of the deceased will be released to the media, if his identity is not ascertained this afternoon."

No one had any suggestions, and the commander ended the meeting. I was about to leave when Tuulia gestured me aside.

He still looked grim.

"I've had several people contact me about you."

"What about?"

Tuulia cleared his throat.

"Regarding, shall we say, a conflict of interest."

"A conflict of interest?"

"A Jew investigating the murders of Arabs. I'll tell you frankly that doubts have been presented that suggest that, due to your Jewish background, you might not have the motivation to find the perpetrators."

Even though I had suspected something like this, I was still offended.

"I'm first and foremost a police officer, second a Finn, and only third a Jew."

The commander eyed me for a moment but then gave a strained smile.

"Well said. I'm sure you'll do your best."

Tuulia nodded and left, escorted by Leivo. Huovinen, who had been waiting in the sidelines, came over to me.

"What was that all about?"

I told him.

"Such bullshit," Huovinen sighed.

I went to Simolin's office. I was just stepping in when my phone rang. It was my brother.

"It's kind of a bad moment..."

That wasn't going to stop Eli.

"We need to meet you, Silberstein and I."

"I'm busy, in case you didn't notice."

I was annoyed by the fact that my big brother Eli took it for granted that I would be at his beck and call.

"So are we. We can come there if you just tell us when."

"What's this about?"

"You'll find out. I think you'll find it interesting, too."

I gave in. "At one at the Hotel Pasila, but fifteen minutes, tops."

"Thanks, we'll see you there."

I stepped into Simolin's room, where I also found Stenman. Simolin was busy doing something at his computer.

"Anything in the latest tip-offs?"

Simolin spun around in his chair.

"Nothing special, but the medical examiner confirmed that the body that the nose and ears had been cut from wasn't shot until after being stabbed in the chest with a knife, and only after he was lying on the ground. Pretty bizarre, at least when you think about the time, the place and the conditions under which it all happened."

I thought about the time, the place and the conditions. A meeting on the bridge, which was packed with joggers and commuters every morning. Someone follows one of the people coming to the meeting, the person coming to the meeting is surprised, one of them is killed, and there's an attempt to kidnap the other one. He manages to get away, pulls out a gun, but falls to the roof of the train and dies. Those who attempted the kidnapping try to escape in a white minivan that had been spotted the previous night in Vartiokylä, where an Iraqi body-shop owner and his employee had been killed. Bizarre was the wrong word, though. That impression just resulted from the fact that our information was incomplete. When we got more information, the logic of events would be revealed.

"What about the security cameras?" I asked Stenman.

"Nothing on them either. I'll get the cassette from the Siili-tie metro station soon, but the camera doesn't cover the car park, and I don't think the men who dumped the car left by metro. Everyone knows that there are surveillance cameras in the metro."

"But they still left the area somehow. Try to pinpoint the time the car was abandoned and figure out what public transportation serves the area."

"I'll try, but I'm sure they were picked up in a car."

Oksanen stormed in in his coat. He was wearing a copy-company scarf and a sweatshirt from a German car manu-facturer.

"What's next?" Oksanen asked. He was two hours late, but I didn't ask where he had been. He always had a slate of good excuses and I was tired of listening to them.

I remembered Lieutenant Toivola and called him on the spot.

"I was just about to call you. You guessed right, the girl was injured in the fire. She went to the health centre in Korso to get her burn wounds treated. We have a name and an address. We're going to pay her a visit. You want to join?"

"Definitely."

Then I remembered that I had promised to meet my brother and Silberstein.

"I have to be back by one."

"We won't even be cutting it close," Toivola said optimisti-cally. "And one other thing. The serial on the car's chassis has been checked. It's the car you're looking for."

He gave me the girl's address. We agreed to meet in front of the house.

I filled in Stenman, Oksanen and Simolin on the latest from Toivola.

"It'd be good if you came along," I said to Stenman. "The girl might be in a state of shock; she might be more willing to speak to a woman."

I told Oksanen to go through the tapes from the metro station camera that Stenman had been promised. Oksanen glanced at his watch with a frown. He had probably set up a negotiation with one of the sponsors of the police-guild rally club. I trusted Simolin so much that I gave him free rein to decide what to do.

The house was almost new and looked expensive. It clearly wasn't a prefab; it had been designed by an architect. From the road you saw a high, white plastered wall and narrow vertical windows. There was a glossy metallic black BMW hatchback in the drive and a "Beware of the Dog" sign on the gate.

The door was opened by a woman of about forty. She smelt trouble and had her defences up from the start. A short-legged beagle that didn't look the tiniest bit aggressive scampered at her feet. I allowed Toivola, as the senior officer, to handle the introductions.

"I'm sorry, but I'm in a hurry. Could you come back some other day?"

"Unfortunately we're in a hurry too," Toivola said.

"I was just leaving."

Toivola didn't let up.

"I'm afraid that's too bad," he said.

The woman didn't make the slightest indication of inviting us in. She stepped out and pulled the door closed behind her.

"The matter concerns your daughter. Her burn wounds were treated at the Korso health centre. We'd like a word with her."

"She's sleeping."

"We're going to have to ask you to wake her up."

The woman crossed her arms across her chest. She was clearly defending her nest.

"Don't you understand? She's sick and she's sleeping. She's taken a powerful sedative."

But Toivola was relentless in his persistence. The woman realized she wouldn't be able to get rid of us and gave up.

"Well, come on in then. But I'd like to ask you to leave as soon as possible."

The interior of the home matched the exterior. All of the furniture was designer goods: carefully selected and expensive.

The woman hurried upstairs. She returned a couple of minutes later.

"My daughter will be right down. Before that, I'd like to hear what this is about. My daughter is a minor, so as her guardian, I assume I have that right."

I asked her how old her daughter was.

"Seventeen."

The girl was the same age as my nephew and godson Leo. In my godfatherly eyes, he was still a child.

"We're investigating a car fire. We believe your daughter was present when the car was burnt."

"Was it an accident?"

"It might have been, but someone died."

"Who?"

"We suspect it was your daughter's boyfriend."

"Kimi?"

"Yes."

"That's impossible! Don't you think Säde would have told me?"

The daughter came downstairs, a bathrobe wrapped around her nightshirt. One half of her face was bandaged. She looked as though she'd been crying. The mother stood and placed a protective arm around her daughter.

The girl sat down on the sofa. Stenman went over next to her.

"You can probably guess why we want to talk to you."

"Tell them everything," her mother encouraged her.

"Where did you get the car?" Stenman asked right off the bat, as if she already knew the whole story. I would have used the same tactic myself.

"Kimi and his friend found it."

"Stole it, you mean?"

"Yeah… or I mean the keys were inside."

"What happened at the sandpit?" Stenman continued.

"Kimi and I went there last night. We slept in the car… I told Mum I was at my friend's place… In the morning I went to pee and when I came back, the car caught fire or exploded. The door was open and the flames hit my face… Then the whole car burnt up… I ran away… Once I got to the main road I called a taxi and took it to Korso. I waited for the health centre to open and then I came home."

"If you slept in the car, why was your boyfriend in the front seat?"

"We were just getting ready to leave."

Now I asked a question: "Did the car explode or did it catch fire?"

"It exploded… At least it burst into flames… they were coming out of the window… I could hear Kimi yelling… then the whole car was on fire…"

The girl collapsed into sobs, and we let her mother soothe her for a moment.

I glanced at Stenman, and she continued the interrogation.

"Where did Kimi and his friend get the car?"

"I don't know, I wasn't with them then. From somewhere pretty close by, I guess."

"Did Kimi tell you that the keys were in the car?"

"Yeah, and I saw them too."

"What's Kimi's friend's name, the one who was with him when they found the car?"

"Tomi, Tomi Siltala."

"Can you tell me where we can find this Tomi?"

"In Kerava, in prison."

"In the Kerava prison?"

"Yeah, he was on leave… He went back yesterday."

* * *

I had been to the Kerava prison before. Back in the day, it had housed mostly young or first-time offenders. Nowadays lots of other kinds of criminals were jailed there too. The prison's buildings sprawled across a broad expanse in the middle of some fields. The old prison building was as stately as a manor house; the new juvenile department built in the Sixties stood farther back. The prison also had a greenhouse that produced some of the prison's food, a car workshop, a barn and wood and metal workshops.

Siltala was working in the metal workshop, which was located between the old building and the new one, in the former stable. When we arrived, he was finishing a solid-looking sauna stove with a corner sander.

Toivola watched him work with interest. "The sauna stove for my nephew's cabin in Mäntyharju was made here. Gives a nice steam."

The guard interrupted Siltala's handiwork and brought him over to a break room that stood near the doorway. The kid's overalls were full of holes from soldering sparks. He could tell we were police, and his demeanour turned aloof.

"Sit," I ordered. He sat on the bench. His narrow face framed lethargic eyes and a moustache of peach fuzz. He was only about twenty.

I asked the guard to leave us alone and said to the kid: "This is an unofficial interrogation. We couldn't give a crap about the fact that you and your friend ripped off a car, but we're interested in everything else. Tell us how it went down, and the theft will stay our little secret. Help us and we'll remember you."

"Did Kimi rat on me?"

"Kimi's dead."

"Don't yank my chain, I just saw him yesterday."

"Your buddy died today, early this morning. The car you stole caught fire. He burnt along with the car. I could take you to go have a look at him; on the other hand, a grilled body isn't pleasant to look at."

The kid thought for a moment.

"Fuck me!"

"That's not all you have to say, is it?" Stenman prodded gently.

"I just went along for the ride. Half an hour at most."

"Where did you find the car?"

"A little ways outside town. It had been left on one of the forest roads. The key was in the ignition and all the doors were unlocked."

"What were you guys doing there?"

Despite his young age, Siltala had the body language of a professional crook. He eyed us and thought for a second before continuing.

"Kimi had bought an unregistered .22 target pistol from somewhere and we were just going to go into the woods and try it out, shoot up a few beer cans."

He stopped mid-story. I encouraged him to continue.

"We were on the forest road when we noticed the car – Kimi took a look in the window and saw that the keys were inside. He tried the door, and amazingly enough it was unlocked. Kimi jumped behind the wheel and I got in the passenger side. We forgot all about going shooting."

"Then what?"

"The car hadn't been there for long, because Kimi said the engine was still warm. I was pretty surprised that someone could be dumb enough to leave the keys in the car and the doors unlocked. Just to be sure we waited for a second, but no one came."

"Was there anything else in the car?"

"Like what?"

"Anything personal that doesn't belong to a car's standard equipment. The car was a rental."

"Nothing that I can think of, at least."

"How much petrol was there?"

"Almost half a tank."

"Then what did you do?"

"We drove around Kerava for a while, but then my leave was about to end so I went home and Pops gave me a ride here. Kimi took off in the car. He said that now that he had a decent ride for once, he was going to pick up his girlfriend and sweet-talk her into going off somewhere to screw. Is that who told you about me, Säde?"

"Did you see anyone else when you left the forest road, or anything else, for instance cars?"

This time, he didn't have to think twice.

"There's a bus stop right where it hits the main road. There was a car waiting there and some guy was just getting into it."

"What kind of car?"

"Ford Focus, that colour that looks like an old lady's underwear, real light green. Normal four-door. Stockmann Auto tag in the back window."

"Do you remember anything about the plate number?"

The kid frowned in thought.

"Was it Finnish?" I helped.

"I guess, because I definitely would have remembered if it was foreign."

"Try to remember more."

"The number was short; foreign plates are normally long. This one had four characters at most, could be that there were only three."

"Like EO-1, or what?"

"Exactly."

"And the man?"

"Pretty old, at least forty."

"That's pretty old, all right," Toivola grunted.

"What did he look like?"

"His hair was kinda grey and he had glasses. Clothes must have been pretty normal cause I don't remember them."

"Did he look like a foreigner?"

"Maybe, I'm not sure. He was at least fifty feet away and Kimi was hitting the gas as hard as he could."

"What then?"

"Kimi freaked out when the dude looked at us a little too long. At first we were afraid that the car was his and that they'd follow us, but luckily they didn't."

"What about the driver, did you see him?" Stenman asked.

"Nothing except that it was a woman."

"Brunette, blonde, young, old?"

"More like young and I think dark hair, but there was glare off the window and I couldn't really see."

"What did you guys do after that?"

"Drove around the back roads and ripped off... Kimi ripped off new licence plates from this one car. We went to the sandpit to put them on. Then I had to come here."

"How well did you know Kimi?"

"Pretty much as long as he's lived in Kerava. We were at the same summer job."

"What did he think about foreigners, like Arabs, for instance?"

"Not much anything. Sometimes when he was drunk he'd say that someone needed to draw a line so they don't steal all the apartments and jobs. The only Arab we know is this guy Hasid, he's got a pizza place off the square. Kimi thought he was cool."

We talked with the kid until he convinced us that he had nothing more to tell us. I gestured the guard over. I asked the kid to contact us if he remembered anything.

"You promised that the car thing is gonna stay between us..."

"It will."

"Can you hook me up with something a little extra?"

"Like what?"

110

"Like a short leave... Just tell them that you need me for some important IDing. They're not gonna check up."

"What do I look like, Santa Claus?"

The kid hadn't expected too much. He gave up right away and stood, looking preoccupied.

"How did the car catch fire?"

"We're investigating that right now."

"Man, talk about lucky. I could have fried in there too."

"That's right. Take this as a lesson and mend your ways, or next time you won't be so fortunate," Toivola advised.

The kid left, reflecting on his good luck.

"I'm guessing that good advice is going to go to waste," Toivola said, watching him walk off.

Before we began our journey home, we agreed that Toivola would go with Siltala to take a look at the spot where the car was found and have the terrain searched.

On the way back into Helsinki, I distinctly felt the extraordinary burden of responsibility carried by a lead investigator from the Violent Crimes Unit. If a theft, break-in or incident of tax fraud didn't get solved, it didn't arouse any particular passions. But if a homicide remained unsolved, it left a blood-red mark on the forehead of the investigative lead. Plus, a killer on the loose was a real risk factor. It was the nightmare of every violent-crime investigator that an unsolved crime would lead to another.

At the top of the unofficial ranking of violent-crime investigators were those who didn't have a single unsolved homicide to their name. This was the case despite the fact that everyone knew that solving a crime was as much a matter of luck as skill. It just seemed like some people ended up with all of the particularly difficult violent crimes.

Stenman guessed what I was thinking and said: "This is clearly crossing municipal boundaries. We could ask the NBI for help."

"No cause for that yet. The investigation is moving forward the whole time."

"This isn't a normal case. It wouldn't hurt."

For some reason, Stenman's proposal bothered me, even though I knew it wasn't a demonstration of lack of confidence. She noticed this and added: "I'm just betting that we haven't seen the end of this, and we already have five bodies."

"That last body doesn't belong to the same group as the others. It has to be a coincidence."

"I agree, but the firebomb wasn't a coincidence. Normal criminals don't use firebombs."

"I never said anything about normal criminals."

"Who, then?"

I didn't answer, and Stenman didn't expect me to, either. For the rest of the drive, we barely said a word. Both of us were probably trying to come up with an answer to the question that had been left hanging in the air.

10

My big brother and Silberstein were sitting at one of the side tables at Hotel Pasila, cups of coffee in front of them and looking sulky, even though I'd informed them I'd be at least fifteen minutes late. I was twenty minutes late.

I ordered myself a coffee, too.

Raoul Silberstein was the chair of the Helsinki Jewish congregation and usually the one to make media statements on any issue related to Jewishness, whether it was the situation in Israel and Palestine, circumcision or the ritual slaughter of animals, *shechita*. Silberstein was intelligent but a little narrow. I, for one, found it hard to imagine anything that would make him laugh.

Eli glanced at his watch and gave me a disapproving look.

"If you're in a hurry, let's get back to this at a better time," I said. "I've got my hands full, too."

Silberstein waved his hand dismissively. He was a thin, hook-nosed man with thick, dark hair. Rumour had it that he dyed it. He was dressed in a grey suit and a dark-blue tie, and a dark-blue poplin coat hung from his chair. Leaning forward as he sat, Silberstein looked somehow predatory.

"If the matter is important, the time must be found."

A cup of coffee appeared in front of me. I looked questioningly at Eli. He in turn looked at Silberstein, who instantly appeared to assume the lead.

"You're investigating a case in which four foreigners have been killed, evidently Arabs, correct? Can you tell us what it's all about?"

"If you read the papers and watch the news, you'll know."

"You know what I mean. We're not interested in what they say on the news."

"Anything that isn't told on the news isn't meant to be told."

"You're not taking us seriously," Silberstein said, staring coldly at me.

I stared back and did a pretty good job of it. I noted that as a police officer, I was bound to confidentiality.

"You know we're not simply asking out of curiosity."

Silberstein's tone goaded me into taking a tough stance.

"I don't really care what your reasons are for asking. I cannot give information about a criminal investigation to outsiders. If you don't believe me, ask the lawyer who's sitting next to you. He knows what being under an oath of confidentiality means."

Eli's face darkened. He was afraid his little brother would shame him in front of the congregation bigwig.

"Ari, don't make this too hard for us."

It was my turn to glance at my watch.

"If you've got something on your mind, spit it out. I'm investigating a murder case and I've got a lot on my plate."

Silberstein fiddled with his wristwatch. It was gold and looked like the kind that a faithful employee got for working at the same company for thirty years or turning sixty.

"We're not outsiders. We come to you as Jews who want to protect our long-suffering people and the members of our congregation, including your relatives, friends and acquaintances, from violence."

"I want to protect everyone from violence."

"But you're also a Jew, you can't avoid that fact. By helping us, you also help your people."

"True, I'm a Jew, which is why I'm not going to buy a pig in a poke."

Silberstein glanced at Eli. The red of Eli's face deepened. The expression I had used had been mildly inappropriate.

"I never would have believed that your brother would joke about such a serious matter," Silberstein said. "I knew your father, your mother. Your uncle is my good friend, and I attended your bar mitzvah. Why are you doing this to me?"

Eli took me by the elbow and squeezed hard. "Ari, this is really serious."

"You mean you think I should commit an act of criminal misconduct without knowing what this is all about? That sounds like a bad deal to me."

Silberstein pointed at me. His forefinger bore a ring with a black stone in it.

"Am I to believe my ears? You don't trust the chair of your congregation and your older brother, a counsellor at law?"

"I'll ask you the same question. Don't you trust me?"

Silberstein's hand clenched into a fist. If I had been a boy, he would have grabbed me by the scruff of my neck and shaken me or twisted my ear.

"If you have information that I, as an officer of the law and the lead investigator on the case, should know, then tell me," I said. "Otherwise..."

Eli glanced at Silberstein. I gulped down my coffee and stood.

"It was nice seeing you two."

I managed to take two steps before a cry from Eli stopped me.

"Ari, don't go!"

I turned around and sat back down.

I could tell from Silberstein's expression that he was no longer my friend, bar mitzvah or no.

"What I'm about to tell you is confidential. Your brother and I are responsible for security matters at the congregation.

That's why we want to know if anything has come up during the investigation to indicate violence against the congregation or the synagogue."

I looked at Eli, both slightly surprised and at the same time amused. Eli was the last person I would have pictured as the sword and shield of the congregation. He was exceptionally timid and terrified of all forms of physical violence. I was also surprised because Silberstein had just revealed that some sort of security organization existed within the congregation. There had been rumours for years, but no one had ever confirmed them. The official line was that the police and SUPO answered for all security matters related to the congregation.

"I'd like to know what answering for the security matters means in practice," I said.

"That's not relevant now," Silberstein replied, his lips pursed.

For Eli's sake, I made a conciliatory gesture.

"Neither the congregation nor the synagogue have been mentioned in any way."

"There are all kinds of rumours going around," Eli insisted.

"I'd love to hear them."

"According to the rumours, two of the dead Arabs were al-Qaeda terrorists and our synagogue was their target."

"It's news to me."

Silberstein looked at me dubiously. Doing so was clearly inherent to his nature.

"We have reliable sources," he noted, stressing the word *reliable*.

"Then your reliable sources know more than the police do. What else do they know?"

I looked at my brother expectantly.

"There's talk of weapons and explosives that have been smuggled to Finland for the terrorist strike."

"If that's the case, that's Security Police territory."

My mobile rang. I glanced at it. It was Huovinen.

"I'll be there in a few minutes," I answered.

"Come straight to my room."

I placed my phone on the table.

"Is there anything else I can do for you gentlemen?"

"But the timing," Silberstein insisted. "I don't believe in coincidences in matters like this, and even if I did, I always assume the worst."

"What timing?" I wondered.

"The New Year and Yom Kippur."

"They happen every year."

"But the Israeli foreign minister doesn't visit our synagogue every year."

"It's true," Huovinen said. It was drizzling and it had been since I returned to police headquarters from Hotel Pasila. I had just told him what I had heard from Silberstein.

I tried making my voice sound sarcastic. "Considering the capabilities of modern technology, communication has been pretty slow, don't you think?"

"I know. But I haven't been withholding information. I just heard about it myself half an hour ago, that's why I called."

"What's going on?"

"The information about the visit has been kept in an extremely tight circle for security reasons. The only people who have known about it are the highest political leadership, the police command, the Security Police, a few key people from the Helsinki Jewish congregation and the Israeli embassy. The visit is completely unofficial and is taking place at the congregation's invitation. Evidently Szybilski, the Israeli foreign minister, feels particular sympathy for the Jewish congregation here, because during the war it helped his grandfather and his family emigrate from Austria to the US through Finland."

"So why's the information being released after all, then?"

117

"Because it leaked somehow. SUPO has been getting enquiries from the press. They haven't commented, but it's definitely going to go public via that route. And it would come out anyway."

"What else important has been kept from me?"

"Don't take it personally. The same things that were kept from me. The man who was found on the bridge has now been positively ID'd as Tagi Hamid. In addition, we've received information that he has terrorist connections. He's believed to have been in contact with a terrorist named Ismel Saijed, who's being hunted as a suspect in half a dozen bombings. He was last spotted over a year ago in Syria. Then some intelligence came in that he's in Denmark. The unidentified man who was hit by the train may be Saijed; it's difficult to get confirmation because there are no good photos of him, or fingerprints either. There would have to be some reason for his presence here. Szybilski's visit would fit the bill best."

"I'm guessing the information on Tagi and Saijed didn't come from Interpol?"

"No, from the Israeli embassy. First to SUPO, from there to the ministry, and from there to us."

"Where did the Israeli embassy get the photos of Tagi Hamid and the other man?"

"Probably from SUPO. Routine exchange of information between security agencies, like Sillanpää said."

"Who did you hear about Saijed from?"

"Through my own sources... OK, from Superintendent Kekkonen."

"What else did Kekkonen tell you? Did he mention guns?"

Huovinen smiled.

"Looks like you two have the same sources. Tagi Hamid's cousin is suspected of helping Saijed smuggle weapons and explosives into the country from Russia."

"I'm presuming you mean the Israelis suspect him."

118

"It could be that SUPO has some intelligence of their own that they're holding back for the time being, intelligence acquired, for instance, from Russia."

The new information roused new questions. If Ali Hamid's cousin Tagi was a terrorist, what reason did Saijed have for killing him? I posed this question to Huovinen, too.

"I couldn't come up with any other reason except that Saijed suspected Tagi of being a traitor and getting confirmation for his suspicions through torturing Ali Hamid."

I couldn't help playing the "if" game a little longer.

"If Tagi was a double-crosser, then who was footing the bill? SUPO?"

"That's a pretty surprising wager," Huovinen conceded. "But possible. I've heard that SUPO's been trying to recruit Muslim immigrants. But the Israelis suspect that Saijed killed Tagi Hamid because Hamid and his cousin wanted to jump ship in the middle of the operation."

"So it's possible that the attack is still being planned?"

"So it would seem. To top it all off, the Israelis believe a big-time terrorist named Bakr is involved. He's worked with Saijed before."

Stenman stuck her head in the door.

"Toivola's been trying to call you." I had turned off my phone because I wanted to talk with Huovinen in peace. "He asked you to call him right away."

I turned on my phone and called.

"I told that pretty constable not to take this as telephone harassment," Toivola said. "It's pure business. We went with the Siltala kid to the place where they jacked the Citro. I brought in a few patrols and a dog to scour the terrain. Didn't go to waste. We found another body. Foreign. Beaten and shot in the head. Been dead twenty-four hours at most; in other words it looks like he was brought in the car that was burnt last night."

"Where was the body found?"

119

"Only ten yards from the spot where those boys snatched the car, or as it says in the law books, seized it without authorization. A little less than a mile from the sandpit where you were this morning."

"Did the body have any identifying papers on him?"

"An Israeli passport. According to it, the deceased is Ben Weiss, from Jerusalem."

"I'll be right there. I'll call for directions from the car."

Huovinen was looking at me expectantly. When I told him what I had just found out, he snapped:

"Someone owes us a damn good explanation."

11

Driving to Kerava three times in one day was starting to exceed the limits of my patience. This time, Simolin came along. He was enthusiastic, filling in the gaps in the "chronological chain of events" in his notebook during the drive.

Huovinen had sent me off with some parting words: "We're up a huge goddamn creek here. The Helsinki police department doesn't have the resources to deal with an imported Middle-East crisis. If the Israeli embassy is in touch, tell them immediately to call me. Don't even give them your shoe size."

I had met the Israeli ambassador and knew that he could be effective at pressuring you and throwing you off balance. I also knew the embassy's head of security and was sure that he wouldn't have the tiniest qualm about squeezing what he could out of our slight acquaintance. In matters like these, delicacy was unheard of.

It was equally clear that Ben Weiss, who had been found shot in the head, had not been out in the woods picking mushrooms, no matter what the embassy claimed.

Toivola had given me precise directions. The place where Weiss and his life had parted ways was easy to find.

The forest had been thinned, and there were stacks of cordwood at the side of the road. Toivola's Toyota was parked next to one. A police car and an ambulance were also at the scene. A forest tractor had cleared a small opening around the stack; behind it stood a stand of thinned spruce and a sheer rock face. A reporter from the local paper was lurking behind the police tape with a camera and took a photo of me.

Toivola's face was showing clear signs of exhaustion. He was probably in the middle of the biggest brouhaha he'd ever see.

"The good thing about this is that the day can't get any worse," Toivola said.

"Let's hope not."

We followed Toivola into the forest. Several uniformed police officers were scouring the terrain. The body was at the foot of a small spruce. There was a contusion from a blow on his forehead, a deep cut, which looked like it had been made with a knife, in his cheek, and a bullet hole at his temple. The face also showed other signs of violence.

The deceased was at most thirty-five years old. His hair was blond and his cheeks were heavily stubbled. He was wearing a dark-blue tracksuit.

"The medical examiner estimated that he was killed yesterday, sometime during the day," Toivola remarked. "And roughed up before, probably tried to get to talk. Wasn't there some of the same business in those cases of yours?"

I told him that the killed body-shop owner Ali Hamid had been tortured.

"Something about this Weiss interested the killer," Toivola reflected.

I remembered something and glanced at the soles of the deceased's shoes. There was gravel in the treads, the same kind as on one of the Linnunlaulu bodies. Toivola looked at me, baffled.

"According to the CSI, the deceased was dragged here, in other words the killer was alone. The terrain is so hard that no other tracks were left behind."

Simolin bent over next to the body and touched his hair.

"Dyed. It's dark at the roots."

"What did you find on him?"

"Aside from the passport, a wallet with a little money in it, a multi-tool, a Seiko watch, no other effects… and this…"

Toivola showed me a small plastic bag containing a pistol shell.

"We found the shell on the forest road. He was shot on the side of the road, but we haven't found the bullet yet, even though we've searched with a metal detector."

"Has anyone been asking about him?"

"Besides me and the people who are here now, only my superior and you know about this."

"And at this point, no one else needs to."

"What about SUPO?" Simolin asked.

"Them least of all. Where's the passport?"

Toivola handed over the plastic bag containing the passport.

I took the passport and examined it. Ben Weiss, born in Jerusalem on 26 April 1969. In the photo, Weiss was jutting his jaw defiantly towards the photographer. He also had dark hair. What sense did it make to dye his hair blond? I said to Toivola: "I'll take the passport in for examination. It might be forged."

I heard the low rumble of a powerful diesel engine. A dark-green Land Rover pulled up next to my car, and two men stepped out. I immediately recognized both of them. One was Inspector Sillanpää from SUPO; the other was Simon Klein, the head of security from the Israeli embassy.

Toivola glanced at me.

"Judging by the way they carry themselves, servants of the state. You know them?"

"SUPO and the Israeli embassy."

"Speak of the devil."

When I saw Sillanpää striding towards us with Klein in tow, my first reaction was extreme annoyance. I had decided to twist SUPO by the nose, and some traitor had immediately leaked. My annoyance was increased by the fact that Sillanpää was schlepping along the representative of foreign country.

I ordered Simolin to take a face shot of the deceased with a digital camera and walked up to the newcomers.

"This crime scene is closed to outsiders."

"Do you mean him?" Sillanpää asked, nodding in Klein's direction.

"As far as I'm aware he's not a police officer."

Klein understood the delicacy of the moment and maintained his composure. "I was just offering my help. If the deceased is an Israeli citizen, I may know him."

Klein, who was married to a Finn, had come to Finland over two years ago and spoke the language almost perfectly. At the Israeli embassy, the head of security rotated every three years. Maybe the embassy was afraid that a longer post would lead to Finlandization.

"There are over five million Israelis. Isn't the probability pretty small? And if we need help with identification, we'll be sure to get a photo to you."

Klein shrugged. Sillanpää's eyes bored into mine.

"These kinds of cases work best if there's some give and take and everyone shows a little goodwill. Nitpicking isn't in anyone's interest."

"I'm the lead investigator and I'll decide how good-willed or nitpicky I feel and how much I want to give. Could you please wait in the car, Mr Klein?"

I had met Klein on several occasions. I had even been to the sauna with him before at the police-guild cabin in Lauttasaari, but now I addressed him with deliberate formality. It helped maintain distance.

Klein smiled, but then he gave me an "I'll remember this" look, turned, and walked away.

"Pretty full of yourself," Sillanpää muttered. "Klein only had good things to say about you on the drive up. He won't any more."

"What if the deceased had been working for the state of Israel? Wouldn't it be pretty stupid to show your hand too early?"

"That's a pretty ballsy conclusion. And even if he was, don't you trust us to take that into consideration?"

"I'm playing it safe."

Sillanpää shook Toivola's hand and circled the body, looking at it from all angles.

"Doesn't look Jewish."

"Hair's been dyed," Simolin pointed out. He was standing stiffly behind the corpse and didn't like the situation any more than I did.

Sillanpää held out his hand and asked for the passport.

"What passport?" I tested.

"There was a passport on him when he was found."

Sillanpää's source was good.

I showed the passport and said, "Don't mess it up."

Sillanpää pulled on his gloves. "Looks authentic. It wouldn't take Klein more than a few seconds to confirm authenticity. He has a laptop in the car and a direct connection to the Israeli population registry and passport office. But if his help is no good…"

Sillanpää knew how to be a pain in the ass, but I didn't take the bait. I snatched the passport back from him.

"Did he have anything besides the passport?"

"Normal stuff, a watch and a wallet, but there was only money in it, euros. The clothes are international brands."

"Do you think this guy was at Linnunlaulu?"

"I do. Probably one of the two from the bridge."

Sillanpää glanced at Klein, who was talking into a mobile phone next to the Land Rover, and then asked: "Am I right in interpreting that this guy and the two bodies from Linnunlaulu were in different camps?"

"That's what I believe, at least."

"How could he have ended up here?"

"First tell me something."

"What?"

"Did Klein contact you or did you contact him?"

Sillanpää considered for a moment.

"I contacted him. I thought he would be of assistance in the investigation. Your turn."

I had been thinking about the situation the whole drive up and could only come up with one good explanation.

"We have an eyewitness who says two men in tracksuits ran in the direction of the City Theatre soon after the altercation. Apparently there was a man sitting in a green Citroën in the vicinity. He had driven the man who later got hit by the train to the scene. The driver somehow or another forced one of the two runners, in other words Weiss, into the car. Maybe the runners split up on Eläintarhantie, one of them noticed the car and tried to apprehend the driver, but things ended up going the opposite way. I'm ninety-nine per cent sure that the deceased was brought here in the Citroën that was burnt nearby early this morning."

"I heard about that. What does it have to do with the case?"

I told him.

"Bad luck for the kid."

Sillanpää nodded in Klein's direction.

"Wouldn't it be wisest to use Klein's help to check Weiss's passport?"

Sillanpää was right, but I decided to string him along a little longer.

"Soon."

Toivola slapped a hand down on my shoulder.

"Think I'm gonna take my lunch break. That OK?"

"Of course."

Toivola's departure gave me a natural reason to walk towards the cars.

"Keep me up to date, won't you?" Toivola asked, poking his head out of his rolled-down window.

I promised I would. I went over to him and said: "Remind them to do a gunpowder-gas test on the body, and that shell needs to be compared to the bullets that were

126

found at the body shop right away. At least the calibre is the same."

Toivola nodded and sped off. I watched his car recede. I had to admit, Toivola and his Toyota both had a certain everyday charisma.

I authorized the ambulance drivers to take the corpse away. They were tired of waiting and got right down to business.

Klein was leaning against the side of his SUV. I handed him some disposable plastic gloves and the passport.

First he examined the passport with his naked eyes, then he pulled out a loupe and stepped into the car and tapped the passport number into the computer. It only took a few seconds to establish the connection.

Klein compared the information in the passport with the information he got from the computer and handed the passport back to me.

"Genuine. Ben Weiss, trades in furs. Lives and works in Jerusalem."

"Doesn't really fit the picture."

"I think it does. He reported he would be taking three hundred thousand dollars out of the country to buy furs. Maybe he got mixed up in the wrong company and was kidnapped or murdered."

Klein's theory came too quickly and too ready-digested. He had had time to think about what story would be the best one to offer.

"Horribly wrong, if those two dead men are terrorists, as you suspect."

He lifted the computer up in front of my face.

"See for yourself. Weiss can't have had anything to do with those men."

The information Klein had given was on the screen, but I didn't buy it. If Ben Weiss was the kind of guy I thought he was, he could have arranged himself an ID with Adolf Hitler's name if necessary.

Klein eyed me appraisingly.

"I really shouldn't tell you this," he said. "According to the currency export claim, his business partner is a company called Arctic Furs. Out of Helsinki. I'm sure you can get more information about Weiss and his affairs there."

Klein's helpfulness was suspect. It was even more suspect because I knew that Arctic Furs was owned by a Jewish businessman named Josef Meyer. He was a member of the board of the Helsinki Jewish congregation and the treasurer of the congregation's primary fund. Meyer's daughter, my former girlfriend Karmela, lived in Israel and was married to a captain of the Israeli air force.

I didn't really get along with old man Meyer, and he had been hoping to make me his successor in the fur business. Aside from the fact that the field held no great fascination for me in the first place, I was allergic to animal dander. And so I took off for the army right after my university exams, and when I got back Karmela was dating the son of the carpet-shop owner. He was a Tatar. The Tatar vanished from the scene within six months, and Karmela travelled to Israel to lick her wounds, which is where she met her future husband.

"Thanks. We'll be in touch with Meyer." I gestured for Simolin, who was standing off to the side, to come over.

"I think we'll be heading back to Helsinki."

Klein panicked.

"I'd like to discuss the deceased."

"Yeah?"

"Do you already know how he… how the death occurred?"

"For investigative reasons I can't reveal any details."

"I helped you verify the name of the deceased. I even told you something I shouldn't have," Klein reminded me.

"And I already thanked you. Was there anything else?"

"The killers, is there any new information on them?"

I shook my head.

"Investigative reasons. Anything else?"

Klein got the point.

"No."

After we had driven to the main road in silence, Simolin said: "Someone's leaking everything to SUPO."

"Yup."

"But you can't leak what you don't know."

I glanced at Simolin. He was holding a white slip of paper in his fingers.

"Parking stub. In the pocket of the deceased."

My mood improved noticeably. With some good luck we might be able to squeeze a surprising amount of information out of a parking stub.

As we approached Helsinki, Simolin called the parking-services office. We found out that the stub was from a machine in the Töölö district, on Aurorankatu.

"Let's check on that soon," I said. "But first let's go take care of this one other thing."

12

Seeing Josef Meyer was never a pleasant experience for me. He considered me the primary culprit in the calling off of his daughter's wedding to me and her subsequent move to Israel. For some reason, Meyer had treated me coolly from the time Karmela and I started dating. Maybe it was my fault. I clearly wasn't his ideal son-in-law. According to my uncle, the coolness was due to the fact that he had been forced to refuse Meyer a loan when he wanted to expand his business.

Meyer had once been one of Helsinki's most successful fur merchants, but time had passed him by years ago. The shop was as gloomy as a mortuary and just as old-fashioned. Its decline had begun with the death of Meyer's wife and his daughter's move to Israel. Nor was the profitability of Meyer's business improved by the fact that both animal activists and neo-Nazis had used his display window for target practice.

Meyer's furs were just as outdated as the mannequins in the window, and all of his remaining customers were elderly. Meyer had experienced the same fate as my mother. When my mother closed her barber shop-slash-salon in the Seventies, hairstyles that had been in vogue in the Fifties were still being advertised in the windows. One greasy-haired model looked exactly like James Dean, and another like Marilyn Monroe.

There wasn't a single customer in the shop. Everywhere you turned you could sense that the company was dying and

Meyer had already given up. For him the shop was some sort of escape to a happier time. That's why he didn't want and couldn't bear to change anything. He preferred to cling to his memories and go down with the ship.

On the way into Helsinki, I had told Simolin about the history Meyer and I shared. He had listened with interest and posed a few cautious questions about my relationship with Karmela Meyer. I suppose he imagined that the dating relationships of Jews were a lot more exotic than those of other young people.

I only managed to take a couple of steps before sneezing. I had forgotten about my allergies. I knew that spending even a few minutes among the furs would be pure hell.

Meyer emerged from the back room in his black suit so quietly that he took us by surprise. He recognized me immediately.

"Mr Kafka. So you're still in the neighbourhood."

After I broke up with his daughter, Meyer had begun to address me formally. It was actually a relief; forced intimacy was much more awkward.

I sneezed again and could feel my nose starting to run. Luckily I had a few tissues.

I immediately explained our business. I wanted to get out of there as fast as possible.

"It's true. Ben Weiss was here a couple of days ago discussing potential cooperation."

"What sort of cooperation did you discuss?"

"He proposed that I act as his buyer in the next fur auction. It's early next year."

"Why?"

"Because I'm familiar with the markets and sellers here and because Finland is one of the world's leading fur exporters. He didn't know anyone here; he used to go through German brokers."

"Did he indicate why he picked you specifically as a partner?"

"I got the impression that someone had referred me to him."

"How did your negotiations end?" Simolin asked.

Meyer glanced at him, but turned to address me.

"I promised to look into the possibility, but I also told him that I'm gradually getting out of the business, because I don't have a successor."

As he spoke the words, he looked at me accusingly.

"Why are you interested in Weiss?"

"He's dead."

I looked at Meyer as I said this. He didn't look surprised, despite the fact that next he asked three questions all at once.

"Dead? Weiss is dead? How?"

"He was killed."

"When?"

"Yesterday. Do you have any idea who might have done it and what their motivation might have been?"

"No, it must be an accident, unless…"

"Unless what?"

"He led me to understand that he had a lot of money with him. He said that he would open an account here if we came to an agreement."

Meyer was not a good actor, not even amateur-dramatics calibre. He repeated everything as if he were reciting memorized lines.

"Were you in touch with each other after his visit?"

My nose was running like a tap and my eyes were itching. I was having a hard time concentrating. This gave Meyer the advantage.

"No. He promised to get back to me before he left."

I noticed that there was a security camera above the register. I pointed at it.

"We'd like the tape from the security camera."

"It's broken," Meyer said, and started straightening out some fox furs hanging from a rack.

"How did he first get in touch with you, by phone or letter?"

Meyer's demeanour sharpened, and he thought for a second.

"He called from Jerusalem before he came."

"Where did he get your contact information?"

"My impression was that he got it from one of my acquaintances in Israel. I didn't ask who."

"Of course not," I muttered. "Does anything else come to mind?"

"No, I'm sure it must have had to do with the money. What other reason would anyone have for killing him?"

"Do you know where he was staying and if he knew anyone in Helsinki?"

"No, we only discussed business."

"In what language?" Simolin asked from behind my back.

"How so?"

"I'm assuming he didn't speak Finnish. Did you speak Hebrew or English?"

The question surprised Meyer, and he was forced to think again for a minute.

"German and English."

I blew my nose and made for the exit.

"Kafka."

"What?"

Meyer waved his hand in a broad arch, looking at me with bottomless melancholy.

"This would all have been yours now, if you had married Karmela. She would have made you a good wife."

Apparently he sincerely believed I was bitter about losing those heaps of hair.

"Is it really better being a bachelor at the age of forty?" he asked.

"It has its advantages."

I sneezed three times in the entryway.

"I don't think you would have made much of a fur sales-man," Simolin remarked. "What do we do now?"

I blew my nose.

"Let's go take a look at that parking meter."

The parking meter was behind the curved annexe to the Parliament House. A small bakery-café stood opposite. We went over and showed the photograph of the deceased Weiss. The person at the counter didn't recognize him, even though she had been at work on the right day.

I stood next to the meter and looked around. As I turned towards the Parliament House, I practically jumped for joy. Between the original building and the annexe, a set of granite stairs rose up to the former, and a silvery security camera gleamed above them. We walked around to the main entrance of the Parliament House and asked the guard sitting in the lobby's glass cubicle to call the head of security and ask him to come down. Fifteen minutes later, we had the videotape containing the footage that had been recorded by the security camera on the Aurorankatu side of the building two days earlier. I had shamelessly lied that we were investigating an assault that had taken place on Aurorankatu, and the head of security had looked suspicious. Maybe he recognized me from the newspaper photos and knew what I was investigating. For some reason, my name stuck in people's heads. But he still didn't have any reason to not give me the tape.

As we returned to the car through the fine drizzle, I re-membered the thing that had been bothering me.

"Where was that white minivan that was found at the Siilitie metro station stolen from again?"

Simolin pulled out his notebook. His handwriting was meticulous, each line was exactly the same length. My notes were always a huge mess. A word here, another there. No one could make anything out of them except me, and not even me all the time.

"It was registered to some antique shop, on Freda or Eerikinkatu I think."

"Oxbaum Antiques?"

"That's the one."

I stopped for a moment. I felt dizzy. Josef Meyer was Jewish; Levin Oxbaum, the owner of the antique shop, was Jewish; and his son Max was a partner in my brother's law firm, which was located on Aurorankatu, only fifty yards from the parking meter.

It was almost six p.m. and the drizzle hardened into a real rain. I shivered.

"Let's go straight to HQ after all."

Huovinen was still at work. He seemed anxious, and it took a lot to make Huovinen anxious.

"The Israeli ambassador called me to express his displeasure that we had not given enough information to Klein, even though the victim was an Israeli citizen. He threatened to call the Minister of the Interior, said they're golf buddies."

"That's exactly why."

"They want the body. You know how stubborn your people are about funerary rites."

Of course I knew. Jewish tradition mandated that the deceased be buried within twenty-four hours. Every Jewish congregation had a burial-preparation office, a *chevra kadisha*, a holy society that took care of burying the dead.

When my dad died in Lapland, two men from the *chevra kadisha* were sent there to wait for the coroner to finish his work and then brought the body back to Helsinki for burial on the double. The practice was so established that a Jewish body took priority over others in autopsy lines.

Even though I honoured Jewish traditions, I had my limits. In the case of a crime, the *chevra kadisha* could wait.

"We won't turn over the body until all tests and exams have been conducted and identification is certain."

"That's what I told him, and for some reason he didn't like it. According to the ambassador, Ben Weiss was a respectable businessman who was the victim of a crime and doesn't have the slightest thing to do with the events at Linnunlaulu."

"What about the photographs?"

"They've been released through the Finnish News Agency, and we're also asking for information about both Tagi Hamid's and Weiss's movements. Oksanen and Stenman are accepting tip-offs all evening. Some have already rolled in."

I remembered Toivola and called him. He was still at work.

"Did you get the gunpowder-gas results yet?"

"Not yet. I lit a fire under them, though, and they promised to get them to me today."

"What about the shell?"

"Tomorrow at the earliest."

"Call me as soon as the results come in… even if it's late."

"Will do."

"What gunpowder-gas test results?" Huovinen asked.

"If traces of gunpowder are found on Ben Weiss's hands, then he was most definitely one of the shooters at Linnunlaulu."

"Let's hope to God they are, then. That'll shut the ambassador up," Huovinen said hopefully. "Your brother called, too." Eli was acquainted with Huovinen, but not well enough to call him without good cause.

"Why?"

"Tried to wheedle information about the investigation. He had heard a rumour that the killings had something to do with the Jewish congregation. And before that, I got a call from the chair of the Jewish congregation."

"Silberstein?"

"Yup. Asked the same thing. Has every Jew in Finland been recruited to snoop on us?"

"So it would seem."

I told him that Meyer, who had confirmed Ben Weiss's fur-dealing alibi, was a Jew, and so was the antiques dealer whose stolen vehicle had been used at Vartiokylä and probably at Linnunlaulu too. I also told him that my brother and the chair of the Jewish congregation had already paid me a visit.

Huovinen looked at me gravely.

"The way you talk about it, it sounds like you don't believe in coincidences."

"At least I believe that Meyer lied to me. And that if he lied, he was protecting Weiss. I can't think of any other reason for protecting him except that Weiss isn't who he was pretending to be. The cooperation between him and Meyer sounds fishy anyway. Meyer had dropped out of the race ages ago, so why would an eager young fur dealer want to work with him? There are better partners to be found in Finland, Jewish ones too."

"Do you believe that your brother and Silberstein could have got information we don't have yet through their own channels?"

"I believe that they are in some way involved without knowing it, as are Meyer and Oxbaum. Their Jewishness alone doesn't explain everything."

Simolin knocked on the open door and said: "You want to come watch the tape?"

"What tape?" Huovinen asked.

When I told him about the parking stub found on Weiss's body and the footage shot by the Parliament security camera, Huovinen got excited.

"Are you serious? I want to see it too."

We went into the conference room, pulled up chairs, and sat down in front of the TV.

Simolin turned on the VCR. The clock was running at the bottom of the screen. It was still five minutes to the time that the parking stub was dispensed. Simolin fast-forwarded, and a white minivan flashed across the image.

"Stop!" I ordered.

The white vehicle was at the right edge of the camera's field of view. The camera was about ten yards from the meter. It was impossible to make out the licence-plate number, but Simolin tossed out a guess.

"Probably the stolen minivan."

The minivan approached and stopped. Simolin went up right in front of the TV.

"That's it, I can already make out the plate."

The vehicle backed up next to the meter. The passenger door opened, and a blond man stepped out.

"Definitely, that's him," Simolin repeated.

"That Weiss?" Huovinen asked.

"Yup."

Weiss dug into his pockets and walked towards the meter, stopped, studied the coins he had pulled out, fished out a couple, and dropped them into the meter. While waiting for his stub, he glanced around and noticed the camera.

"He noticed the camera," remarked Huovinen.

Weiss turned his back to the camera. After getting his stub, he started heading for the vehicle. At the same moment, the driver's door opened and a dark-haired man twisted himself out.

"Got 'em both," Simolin said excitedly.

The dark-haired man pointed a remote key at the van to lock the doors. The van's lights flashed, indicating they were locked. He took a few steps in Weiss's direction, and his face was clearly visible. Weiss gesticulated an order to him. The man appeared confused, glanced directly at the camera out of instinct, turned, and stroked his jaw with his left hand. It was as if someone had pressed my internal pause button. My stomach wrenched.

"Go back to the dark-haired guy," I said.

Simolin rewound and stopped at the point where the man

stepped out of the van. He went around to the pavement and turned towards the camera.

I saw a hard, muscular face and close-cropped hair. The man was tall and lean.

Huovinen looked at me.

"What now?"

"I want close-ups of both men."

"Can I fast-forward now?" Simolin asked.

"Go ahead."

The men walked in the direction of Mannerheimintie and stepped off-screen.

I pondered what I had seen. The security camera was blurry and it had been hard to distinguish the men's faces. Still, I was sure. I knew the dark-haired man, even though he had changed and aged twenty years. I was sure of it.

His name was Dan Kaplan. He had moved to Israel in 1985 to do his military service there and never came back. Before that, he had been my best friend since first grade. He had picked up the thoughtful chin-stroking from a Clint Eastwood Western that we had seen together.

You couldn't fool Huovinen. He asked: "Do you know him?"

I nodded.

"I think he's my childhood friend. His name is Dan Kaplan. I saw him last ten years ago when I was in Israel. At that time he was a major in the army's special forces."

"What the hell is he doing here?" Huovinen wondered out loud.

"That's what I'd like to know."

"Not trading furs, I bet," Simolin said.

My phone rang. It was Toivola.

"Those boys went all out, the gunpowder results came back in record time. They're positive."

"Thanks. Now go home and get some rest."

"I think I will. I already called the old lady and asked her to heat up the sauna."

"You've earned it ten times over."

Toivola laughed in satisfaction. People were given far too little praise these days.

I said to Huovinen and Simolin: "Traces of gunpowder were found on Weiss. In other words, he was at Linnunlaulu and fired the gun."

Huovinen rose so suddenly that he almost knocked his chair over.

"Make sure it's Kaplan and put out an APB on him… what do you think, is he dangerous?"

"If he wants to be."

"Do you think he wants to be?"

"It looks like it."

"Mention in the APB that he's dangerous and possibly armed."

"Are there any better pictures of him?" Simolin asked.

"I took some photos of him on my trip to Israel, but they're already ten years old."

"His family must have more recent ones," Huovinen suggested.

"I'll try to get my hands on them."

13

It was the seventh day of the month of Tishri, and the ten days of repentance were already leaning towards Yom Kippur. Jews believe that there is a book in heaven in which a person's every deed, word and thought is recorded. The book opens on the second day of the New Year holiday and God reads what each person has done. Based on this, he decides our fates: who must suffer death, who may live, who will be made poor and who rich, who may live in peace, and who will be cast into ruin.

However, this judgment is not final. Everyone has ten days to reflect on their deeds and pray to God for forgiveness. During the ten days of repentance, one must settle one's quarrels, pay one's debts, and ask for forgiveness from those one has trespassed against. Only after that may one hope for mercy and forgiveness from God.

During the ten days of repentance, attendance at the synagogue was much higher than normal. Now it was almost packed.

Looking from the podium, the *bimah*, the Kafkas sat at the front right. In addition to me, there were only two Kafkas present, my brother Eli and his son Leo. Eli was sitting hunched over so far that he looked almost like a dwarf among the tall chairs. His yarmulke grazed the back of the bench in front of him. Knowing my brother, the position was excessively pious. He glanced at me out of the corner of his eye but didn't say anything.

The seats to our right were reserved for the Oxbaums, and the Weintraubs were at our left. The Kaplans sat, from our perspective, behind the Weintraubs. Their family was represented solely by Salomon Kaplan, Dan's father.

After the service ended, I loitered in the foyer. My brother Eli came over to me, looking put out.

"What now? Don't try and tell me you're here to pray."

"Of course I am. I have plenty of things to repent for."

My brother greeted people walking past on both the right and the left. He was clearly an important and well-known person in the congregation, which was no surprise to me. The surprise was how rapidly it had all happened. Just a few years back, he had, at least when he was drunk, laughed at the silliness of the activities of the congregation's "old guard". Now he appeared to be one of its mainstays.

"I want a word with you a little later," I said.

Eli frowned. My tone was clearly too bossy when you took into account that he was, after all, the older brother. He didn't answer, he just kept on walking.

The next person to stop and talk to me was my now-retired English teacher, and before long my former religion teacher joined us. When they left, I was approached by the leader of the Maccabi table-tennis club, who reminded me that I would be welcome in the club veterans' series.

Veterans' series sounded so bad that I immediately drove it from my mind. In my high-school years, I had been the greatest talent in the history of the club, and I would have been accepted for grooming for the national team. But when Karmela Meyer and her D cups entered the picture, my adolescent hands found better things to do.

It wasn't until the police academy that I took up ping-pong again and immediately rose to the top ranks of the police-guild table-tennis club. At least there was one thing I was better at than my brother.

I forgot all about ping-pong when I saw a grey-haired, bearded man with a black, silver-tipped cane exit the sanctuary. I positioned myself in such a way that he was almost forced to bump into me.

I turned and faked surprise.

"Mr Kaplan! It's been a while."

Kaplan couldn't see well without his glasses, but as he came closer he recognized me.

"Ari! Is that you?"

"It's me, Mr Kaplan."

"You've become a real celebrity. I'm very proud of you."

I'd always liked Salomon Kaplan. I had spent a lot of time in their home, and they had always treated me like a son. If it was mealtime, they would set a place for me; if it was teatime, a cup would be poured for me, too. I was a shy child, but Salomon Kaplan and his wife Ethel had broken through my defences.

Salomon Kaplan was a master tailor by profession and Ethel was a housewife. She had died a couple of years back. It had been a tough time for Salomon, because his and Ethel's marriage had been a real, genuine love story. I never once heard them fight.

I was envious of Dan for many reasons, but most of all of his parents and the love they showed their children.

"Being on TV a few times doesn't make you a celebrity," I said modestly.

"I've read about you in the papers, too."

"It's just the job."

Kaplan appeared a tad reproachful, but only a tad.

"Ari, we don't see you here at the congregation very often."

"I'll try to mend my ways."

Salomon smiled. "There are probably a few too many of us old codgers standing in the way."

143

I decided that it was the right moment to get to the point.

"Have you been to Israel to see Dan lately?"

"I don't have the energy any more, I can't stand those long flights. They've even been pestering me to move, but there's far too much commotion and hubbub there. Everybody talks too much."

I chuckled. Salomon sounded like my Uncle Dennis.

"Has Dan become talkative too?"

"Well, not Dan of course, but his wife is a real motor-mouth."

"How's Dan doing, is he still with the army? I haven't heard from him in years."

"That's a shame, and you were such good friends... The army? Not any more, I guess. I don't really know what he does these days, but they're doing well. Nice house and a new car. My son doesn't talk much about his doings."

"Has he brought his family over to Finland yet?"

Salomon Kaplan's friendly eyes were strangely bright for someone his age.

He squinted a little. "Oh, I've asked them, but they haven't deigned to grace me with a visit."

"I heard somewhere that Dan was in Finland."

"I'm pretty sure I'd know if he were. Who told you that?"

"Someone mentioned it in passing. It would have been nice to see him again after such a long time."

Kaplan gazed off into the distance. For a moment it looked as if he were about to say something important. Then he said, a little wistfully: "Sometimes when I look out the kitchen window, it's almost as if I can see you two playing there in the yard while Ethel prepares the Sabbath meal... Ethel was so fond of you..."

I knew it. And that Ethel adored her son. Dan was the son every mother wished for, and every mother-in-law's dream son-in-law. Fun, bright, athletic and handsome.

We had known each other since the first grade. The Kaplans had moved to Helsinki from Turku, and Dan started at the Jewish school in the middle of the school year. I remember when Ethel brought him there. It was raining, and we were floating boats made from wine-bottle corks in the schoolyard gutters. Dan had come over to watch us play and introduced himself precociously. It turned out that he lived in the building next to ours. We walked home from school together, and from that day on we were best friends until he moved to Israel.

Salomon Kaplan raised his cane and headed towards the door, dragging his right leg slightly.

I watched him go and felt like a real jerk. Here I was playing my best friend's elderly father – and in the synagogue, too. For once I'd really have something to repent for on Yom Kippur.

Eli was talking with Silberstein in the foyer. I hung back a couple of yards.

"Have you considered what we discussed yet?" Silberstein asked, like a teacher who imagined his punishment had proved effective on a lackadaisical student.

"Haven't had time."

Eli glanced at the stone-faced Silberstein.

"You go ahead, Ari, I'll be out in a couple of minutes."

It was cold outside. A sliver of moon and a couple of the brightest stars could be seen among the clouds.

I had to wait for Eli for almost ten minutes. We walked over to his Audi, which was parked on Freda.

I sat down in the leather passenger seat. The car smelt new. Eli started up the engine, and the car purred softly to life.

"You have a new car," I remarked.

"Buy my old one. I would have got so little in exchange that I didn't have the heart to give it up."

Eli's former car was a five-year-old BMW hatchback.

"It's too hard finding parking downtown."

"Get a spot in your garage."

145

"You're overestimating a cop's salary."

"Fair enough."

"What are you mixed up in?"

"What do you mean?"

"Where did you get your information?"

"There are rumours going around."

"When you know more than you should about things you shouldn't know about, you might end up being suspected of complicity. Six people are dead."

"That's why Silberstein and I came to meet you. We don't want anyone else to die."

"Who is Ben Weiss?" I asked sharply.

"A fur dealer from Israel."

"No, he's not."

"Then I don't know. I met him when he came to the office to see Max. Max advised him on some contractual matters."

"Have you heard that a car was stolen from Max's father?"

"No. How so?"

"It was found at the Siilitie metro station in Herttoniemi. Ben Weiss used it. He was found a day later in Kerava, dead."

I could see from Eli's expression that he didn't know about Weiss's death. His alarm was genuine.

"Believe me, he's no fur dealer," I said. "And everyone who tells you so is lying."

I almost felt sorry for my brother. He started desperately trying to figure out what he was mixed up in.

I asked him: "Who told you that Weiss is a fur dealer?"

"Silberstein."

"Why, where did he hear that?"

"He said that Weiss came to the synagogue. He had asked if Silberstein knew some Jewish lawyer who could advise him in local banking matters. Silberstein directed him to us."

"To your office, or did he mention Max specifically?"

"Silberstein said he gave him our firm's name. Max happened to be there when Weiss contacted us and got the job."

Eli was beginning to see that he had got mixed up in something that he could most easily extract himself from with my help.

He stopped at the traffic lights at the old opera house. The restaurant Bulevardia was being remodelled. When Dad was still alive, he'd take us to Bulevardia for Sunday lunch now and again. We'd always sit upstairs at the window table. Maybe the choice of restaurant came from the fact that Dad had been born at the corner of Hietalahdentori Square and Lönnrotinkatu. The building had been damaged in the first bombings of the Winter War. A disco that Dan and I used to go to all the time was near the same place.

The lights changed. Before he started off, Eli glanced over at Bulevardia.

"Bulevardia's being turned into some trendy joint too. You remember Dad's Sunday lunches? One time he admitted to me that the manager was some army buddy of his. That's why we always went there. He got a discount."

Eli's revelation amused me.

"Is that why?"

"That's why. Our clan's known for its stinginess."

"Speak for yourself."

We arrived in my neck of the woods. Eli pulled up in front of my building.

"At whose instigation did you come to ask me for information about the investigation?"

"Silberstein's. He was certain that the deaths were related to the foreign minister's visit. He doesn't believe in coincidences."

"I suppose he had some theory to support his suspicions?"

"We've received several threats in Arabic. They say the synagogue is going to be blown sky-high."

"Letters?"

"And a videotape. We turned it over to the Security Police."

"What was in it?"

"An armed man with a scarf around his face holding a sign that read 'Free Palestine' in English. He spoke Arabic and said that Jews are not safe anywhere in the world and that we had been selected as the target of a strike by al-Qaeda and the Martyrs' Brigade unless we publicly denounced Israel's policy of occupation."

"Al-Qaeda and the Martyrs' Brigade. Almost sounds like we're part of the big bad world that's out there. Little Finland has finally had the honour of making it onto the terrorists' hit list."

"Are you making fun of this?"

"No, I'm surprised."

"When we heard about the killings at Linnunlaulu, Silberstein said that al-Qaeda and the Martyrs' Brigade had planned a joint attack during the foreign minister's visit, but then the organizations had had a falling out over something and started killing each other."

I had no doubt that Silberstein had a taste for fabricating conspiracy theories, but his theory tasted too ready-digested, just like Meyer's explanation of his and Weiss's cooperation in the fur trade.

"Pretty bold conclusion from so little information," I said. "What's it based on?"

"I don't know, but Silberstein and Meyer have good contacts in Israel."

"What does that mean?"

"I'm not sure. But I know that Silberstein went and visited Meyer a few days ago, even though they're not on speaking terms. Meyer's son-in-law is in the Israeli army."

"Meyer's son-in-law is a pilot. How the hell would he know what al-Qaeda and the Martyrs' Brigade are up to here?"

"Maybe he has connections in Mossad."

"And Mossad would tell Meyer's son-in-law, 'Now be sure and warn your father-in-law that al-Qaeda and the Martyrs' Brigade might attack in Finland'?"

"I'm just telling you what I know."

"How does Weiss fit into the picture?"

Eli shook his head.

"And what about SUPO, what did they do when you told them about the threats?"

"They promised to organize security for the synagogue for the duration of the visit and protect the foreign minister."

"Was Sillanpää the one you talked to?"

"Yeah, Inspector Sillanpää."

"Have you guys been in touch with the Israeli embassy or has anyone from there been in touch with you?"

Eli gave me an irritated look.

"Are you interrogating me? Even though you're a cop, you're still my little brother."

"I want to know what you're mixed up in and how deep. Have you been in touch with them?"

"Silberstein and I met the ambassador and the embassy's head of security once."

"Why?"

"We were discussing the foreign minister's visit and the related arrangements."

"Did the ambassador mention anything about risks related to the visit?"

Eli thought for a minute. He was by nature timid and satisfied with his lot; he didn't want to put what he had achieved at risk. And now we were talking about matters more significant than screwing a female client on his desk or on the oriental rug in his office.

He had told that story once when he was with me and my subordinates in the sauna at the police-guild cabin. He didn't do it because he was drunk; he did it to spike his status among the coarse, crude police officers. He had later regretted his revelation so much that he had gone to synagogue every night for two weeks to ask God for forgiveness – not for what he had done, but for the fact that he had blabbed.

"Silberstein told me that Mossad had provided intelligence – or I mean he didn't talk about Mossad, he said the Security Police – indicating that there were several Arabs living in Helsinki who had connections to terrorist organizations, two of whom were suspected of participating in multiple bombings against Jewish targets. So you can understand why we were worried. The foreign minister of Israel was coming here on a visit, and at the same time hard-line terrorists with false identities who were known to have procured explosives and weapons from Russia were hiding out here."

"If Mossad knew that there were terrorists here, why didn't they just go ahead and tell us who they were?"

"Maybe they did, but only to SUPO."

Eli looked at his handsome watch. He had received it as a birthday gift from his wife. It cost twice as much as Lieutenant Toivola's Toyota.

"I promised I'd be home before ten."

I knew I'd been a little rough on Eli. I still wanted to know one more thing, though.

"When were you tapped for the congregation's security gig?"

"It's been a couple of months already."

"The decision about the Israeli foreign minister's visit had already been made then, hadn't it?"

"Yeah. It takes months to organize a visit like that, because…"

Eli wasn't an idiot. He turned to me.

"Why are you asking me that? Are you saying that the whole thing was planned so…"

"Goodnight, Eli."

I got out of the car and shut the door.

I had only slept a few hours the previous night, and those few poorly. I was bushed.

I made myself an egg sandwich, listened to Billie Holiday for a minute, and then fell asleep. That night I didn't play table tennis with a beautiful Israeli soldier, but with Karmela Meyer. She was naked and played a lousy game. I hit a sharp backhand and the ball got caught between her melon-sized breasts. Right when I was dislodging the firmly trapped ball, my phone rang. I had just got my hands full of Karmela and I didn't want to wake up. But the caller was sadistically persistent.

I glanced at the clock as I answered. It was already ten past seven. I felt like I hadn't slept a wink. It was Simolin.

"Got a good tip-off about Hamid's cousin. According to the caller, Tagi was renting a studio apartment in Kallio. The caller was Tagi's landlord. He read this morning's paper and ID'd him from it. I promised I'd come by right away."

"What's right away?"

"I could pick you up. I'm at HQ."

"Thanks. In half an hour in front of my building."

"See you then… and sorry I woke you up."

14

Tagi Hamid's apartment was in an old building on Toinen
Linja, across from the Kallio municipal centre. The landlord – a skinny guy, about seventy – was waiting in his car
out front. The car was a brand-new, silver-grey Volvo. He
eyed us but didn't get out until we parked. He was wearing
a tracksuit that rustled as he walked; it was in stark contrast
to the status projected by the car. He was carrying a plastic
folder under one arm.

"Harjumaa?" I asked, just to be sure.

"That's right, and I assume you're from Criminal Investigations… I trust you, but I'd still like to see that badge if
you don't mind."

I showed him my police ID, and so did Simolin.

"There's so much at stake here you can't afford to take
any of it lightly."

He clenched the folder under his arm as if it were full of
top-secret information.

I conceded that he was right; there was no call for light-
heartedness.

Harjumaa began flipping through his folder, intermittently
wetting his finger in his mouth. He evidently had psoriasis,
because the nail was as hooked as an eagle's talon. He showed
the rental agreement, holding the contract at a safe distance.
I did manage to note that Hamid's rental agreement wasn't
the only one. He was clearly a wealthy man who raked in
sizable sums through his property rentals.

"Here it is," he said, his hand and voice trembling. He took a step backwards when I reached for the folder.

"Could I get a better look at it?"

Harjumaa hesitantly stepped closer.

I examined the contract. It had been signed a little over two months ago, and the rental period had been noted as "month-to-month, with a two-month notice period". Harjumaa had demanded three months' rent in advance – 1,350 euros.

The apartment was not even two hundred square feet.

"This is what you get for being a nice guy and trying to help someone out. That's the last time I ever let to a foreigner. I'm losing out on a month's rent here."

He looked at me as if seeking sympathy for his tragic fate.

"Don't you get to keep the deposit?"

"That won't go far if I have to clean up after him and fix the place up. If I could start over, I'd become a plumber. They really bleed you dry."

"How many apartments are you renting out?"

Harjumaa considered for a moment whether this information was classifiable as a trade secret.

Wiping his brow, he confessed: "A few... but the taxman makes sure that you can't get rich off of being a landlord. First headaches and worries keep you up all night and then you barely break even. And the renters... they're real trouble-makers these days, they complain about everything. It's never warm enough, or it's too hot, or then the soundproofing's bad, or the toilet's broken. Nothing's good enough. And of course they ought to get hardwood floors and triple-glazed windows for free."

Harjumaa's dramatic gestures and the greed emanating from his voice made him seem like the prototypical blood-sucker.

I wouldn't have been surprised to see him throw himself to the ground and shower himself in ashes in the throes of rent-loss agony.

"Isn't 450 euros a pretty decent return on 190 square feet?"

"You have to take into consideration all the trouble I go through. Plus the expenses. And the money invested in the apartment. I could get more out of it elsewhere, and with less effort, too. But someone needs to put a roof over people's heads."

"I'm taking this, it'll be returned to you in due time," I said, showing him the rental agreement.

The apartment was on the second floor. The window looked out onto the dumpsters in the courtyard.

"Nice view," Simolin remarked.

The furnishings were sparser than sparse: a small table and two flea-market chairs.

The bed also looked like a flea-market acquisition. A grey blanket had been tossed across it.

On the floor there was a stack of books, a cassette-player boom box and a portable TV, but the apartment still didn't look like a student shack.

I held out my hand to Harjumaa.

"I'd like the key please. I'll get it back to you as soon as the apartment has been searched."

"It's the only key and I need it. There's someone coming to look at the place this evening who wants to move in right away… every day it's empty ends up costing me."

I snatched the key.

"How did Hamid hear about the place?" Simolin asked.

"I had an ad in the paper."

"Did he speak Finnish well enough?"

"No, he had someone with him, some relation, an older man who spoke Finnish. When I wondered whether or not I dared to rent to a foreigner, he said he lived in Finland and had his own company. Promised to back his relative."

"Was his name Ali Hamid?"

"Ali something."

"Is this where you met them?" I asked.

"Right here. I was getting the place ready."

In the kitchen there was a newish refrigerator and a mustard-yellow stove with a frying pan and a small steel pot on top. The tap was dripping. Harjumaa noticed and rushed over to turn it off.

"Always leaving the tap running… as if water didn't cost anything."

The dripping didn't stop in spite of Harjumaa's efforts. It was the seal that leaked.

"Just had this fixed a year ago. Plumber just about robbed me blind, too."

"Did you see whether they came in their own car?"

"No, there was someone else coming to see the place and I stayed here to wait."

"And it was just the two of them?"

"I guess, at least no one else came upstairs."

Simolin measured the apartment with his eyes.

"Does the place come with basement or attic storage?"

"There's a walk-in and a potato cellar in the basement. The attic is for drying clothes."

"Thanks for your help," I said. "I'll let you know as soon as you're allowed to enter the apartment again."

"What about tonight?" Harjumaa nagged.

"Not a chance. I'll be sure to let you know."

Harjumaa was an obstinate soul. He still wouldn't leave.

"It wouldn't take more than ten minutes. I'd just give them a quick tour. Remember, I was the one who was prepared to help out the police here…"

Simolin took Harjumaa by the shoulder and escorted him brusquely into the entryway.

"We'll let you know."

"If I had known —"

Harjumaa's words were cut off as Simolin pulled the door shut behind him and snapped: "I would have whipped out the tear gas next."

Our preliminary investigation of the apartment was soon completed. In the wardrobe there were a few shirts and pairs of underwear, a couple of pairs of trousers, a grey jacket, a hooded nylon parka and an empty plastic suitcase. There was nothing in the pockets, not even a bus ticket. In the entryway there were dark-brown shoes and a ski cap, in the kitchen just the bare necessities.

Simolin looked around in wonder.

"How can anyone live without collecting the tiniest slip or scrap of paper? Trouser and shirt pockets totally empty. Even the garbage was empty."

"Maybe he was anticipating that the place would be searched."

"He didn't have anything on him when he was found, either, not even keys or a mobile. Where are they?"

"Let's take a closer look," I said.

Twenty minutes later, we had examined the bottoms and backs of the wardrobes, gone through the clothes once more, the air circulation vents, the food supplies and the insides and backs of the fridge and the oven. Simolin also cracked open the backs of the television and the boom box and peered inside. It wasn't until we got to the combined toilet-shower space that we scored. When I lifted up the drain cover, I spotted a plastic bag. I pulled it out into the light. Inside there was a small wad wrapped in plastic, a roll of cash as fat as my forefinger, and a Yale key.

The cash was hundred-dollar bills.

I carried our find into the kitchenette and poured the contents out onto the counter. I took the wad and made a small incision in it. White powder drifted out.

Simolin glanced at me: "Maybe this is a drug thing after all."

I considered this for a moment and then rejected it. The packet weighed ten grams at most. The substance might have been for Hamid's own use, or for a little income on the side. Business of that scale doesn't involve murders.

Simolin counted the cash.

"A thousand dollars."

"Should we call in a dog?"

"Let's go down to the basement first."

The basement smelt of mouldy clothes and mothballs. We found the right walk-in, but it was empty and there wasn't a lock on the door.

We went back out into the corridor. I noticed a grey door on the opposite wall. Behind it, a hallway stretched back. It was about ten yards long and lined with rows of numbered doors on either side.

I looked for number five, which was the number of Hamid's apartment.

I fitted the key into the lock and turned it.

On the floor there was a long nylon gym bag. I yanked down the zipper and saw half a dozen bricks, slightly larger than a cigarette carton, wrapped in brown resin paper. It took a second before I realized what they were.

On the other hand, the dark-green metal tube was a cinch to recognize. It was a disposable grenade launcher. The bricks wrapped in paper were plastic explosives. Next to them lay a gleaming black machine gun, a dozen electric blasting caps and a device that looked like a delayed detonator.

"If you want peace, prepare for war," Simolin muttered. "Looks like this guy was planning a little military campaign."

The bag also contained an English-language pocket calendar. I took it and locked the door. We went back up to Hamid's apartment, where I called the police bomb squad. I didn't believe that the explosives were dangerous, but I didn't want to transport a loaded launcher and dozens of kilos of bombs to HQ in our car.

As I waited, I studied the calendar. Simolin was curious and squeezed in behind me.

The calendar had been primarily used to make notes on meetings, phone calls and other everyday things. I searched for the day when Hamid and Harjumaa had signed the rental agreement. The meeting place and time had been marked in block letters. The calendar also contained Arabic notations.

As I browsed through it, a piece of paper that had been folded into quarters fell out. Simolin picked it up, studied it for a minute, whistled softly, and handed it to me.

A rough map had been sketched on it in ballpoint pen. The place was easy enough to identify. Lapinrinne, Malminrinne and Malminkatu.

The location of the synagogue had been circled.

I opened the calendar again and looked up 3 October.

A small Star of David had been scrawled there.

On 3 October, the foreign minister of Israel would be visiting the synagogue.

15

From the masses of clutter in the window of the pawnshop, you would have imagined that it was the owner's life mission to collect stuff, not sell it. We stepped in, and I introduced Stenman and myself.

"You called in a tip-off about the Kerava homicide," Stenman said.

"Kafka, was that the name?"

I knew what was coming. "No, I'm not related to the Kafka who owned the pawnshop on Pursimiehenkatu."

"No?"

The sparse-whiskered, middle-aged man was organizing the heap of stuff that filled the counter. He must have had an amazing visual memory or excellent notes. There was more junk than a couple of small factories could produce in a week. Stenman slapped Ben Weiss's photo down in front of him.

"Is this the man you saw the day before yesterday around two p.m.?"

"Beautiful autumn sunshine out there," commented the man, gazing out at the street through the dusty window. Then he took the photo and peered at it myopically from under his glasses.

"Sure looks a lot the same. They wanted to break a bill for parking, but I told them that I'm not a change machine. If I got a euro for every time someone asked me to change money, I wouldn't have to do anything else."

"What do you mean, they?" I asked.

"There were two of them. The other one spoke and this guy was silent."

Two thirty-year-old men barged in, preceded by wafts of booze breath.

"Howdy. Isn't this the place where you can buy and sell, trade and steal?"

"Please state your business, gentlemen," said the shop owner.

"You got rolling papers?"

"All right if I take care of this?" the owner asked me.

I nodded.

"How many?"

"Make it five."

The owner searched the shelf for the box of cigarette papers and placed five packs on the counter.

"Anything else?"

The man fished into a large sack at his feet and pulled out a bright-red accordion.

"Kid's accordion. Quality goods."

He whipped up a fast-tempoed trill on his button-box.

"No thanks, I already have two."

"But do you have a kids' model? Made in spaghetti land."

"No thanks. Anything else?"

"So what is it you buy around here, if a top-of-the-line Italian accordion isn't good enough?"

"Nothing at the moment, I have to get rid of the old ones first. Two euros and fifty cents."

The man who had remained silent dug some coins out of his pocket and handed over exact change.

"Bye now," the owner said.

The quiet man stepped out; the other one squeezed the accordion, emitting a hippopotamus-fart burst of noise pollution, before exiting with the instrument dangling from his hand. It was like a creature that had fallen from outer space and been killed by having its neck wrung.

"How can you remember the man?" Stenman asked as soon as the croaking of the accordion had faded.

"What a couple of kooks," the owner said, watching in fascination as the man walked off. "From the hair. It was blond, but it looked dyed and he looked foreign."

"What about the other guy?"

"Finnish, at least spoke darn good Finnish. No accent, or at most a teeny one."

"What did he look like?"

"That was the other reason why I remember them. The guy talked like a Finn but looked like a foreigner. I thought he must be a Tatar or a Jew. There's a carpet shop right nearby that's owned by a Tatar, there was something similar about them. But this one looked like he meant business."

"How old was he?" Stenman asked.

"Maybe forty, something around there."

"How was he dressed?"

"Neatly, I think he was wearing jeans, some kind of sweater and a smart jacket."

"And the other one?"

"I don't remember, I think the same. Normal."

"Did the men talk to each other?" I asked.

"No. The blond one didn't say a peep."

"So you didn't change their money, then?"

"Nope. A matter of principle."

"So what happened then?"

"There's all kinds of odds and ends over by the window. He picked up a small screwdriver and asked how much it cost. It cost a euro. He paid with a ten. That's how they got the change."

"Did you see what kind of car they had?"

"A white minivan. It was parked on the hill there on Albertinkatu."

* * *

The autumn sun was shining outside, making even the bleak apartment buildings look pleasant and giving off a nice warmth. I opened the buttons of my coat.

"We need to figure out what they could have been up to here," Stenman said, looking around.

"Guys like that don't drive around sightseeing."

"I think I know. Oxbaum's antique shop, which is where the minivan that the pawnshop owner also saw is registered, is only a hundred yards away... and Meyer's fur shop is almost as close."

"Which one are you thinking?"

"Oxbaum. Let's go over and have a chat with him while we're here."

Our little jaunt was a bust. A sign hung from the door that said ON HOLIDAY.

"How convenient," Stenman said.

I thought for a moment and then said: "Oksanen is looking for the Ford Focus, you head over to Toinen Linja to help Simolin. Tagi Hamid's neighbours need to be questioned, the super too. There's someone I need to talk to."

My uncle Dennis Kafka was by far the closest person to me of my entire extended family, if you didn't count my brother. My uncle had been a father substitute for me after Dad had died. He had supported our family in plenty of ways besides granting Mum the loan to set up her hair salon. He had regularly given her money for Hanna's, Eli's and my studies. Uncle Dennis had even bought skates for Hanna and me when Mum couldn't afford it.

In addition, he donated substantial sums to the congregation's assistance and loan fund, which helped needy Jewish families. This gave him the status of a well-respected man in the congregation's eyes, even though he wasn't a very active congregant.

More than the financial support, I appreciated the way he

always treated us, his brother's children. Like Salomon Kaplan, he noticed my shyness but didn't throw his hands up in the air. It was only in retrospect that I learnt to appreciate sufficiently how much of his time he gave to me, despite the fact that he was a busy man with a family of his own. He'd chat with me until he got a response. He was always interested and never arrogant. You could talk to him about just about anything.

One of his children died of an overdose at a little over the age of twenty; another moved to Israel and is now a citizen of that country; a third lives in Stockholm. His wife died about ten years ago.

We met at Sibelius Park. My uncle was a dapper gentleman, grey-haired and fine-featured. He wore a pale-grey felt hat and carried a silver-handled cane, even though he didn't need it. There was a bit of the dandy in him, or more than a bit, actually.

"I heard you're coming to Eli's on Thursday," I said.

"It's nice that at least someone remembers."

My uncle smiled to show he was kidding. He knew he was popular with his relatives; more invitations were showered on him than he could ever accept.

"You're in the middle of the biggest case of your career. Why are you wasting time going for a walk in the park with your old uncle?"

"That's exactly why."

My uncle stopped and clasped his hands behind his back. It was one of his usual poses.

"I don't follow."

I told him about Silberstein, Meyer, Oxbaum and Ben Weiss.

"I want to know what they're mixed up in."

"Do you think I know?"

"If anyone does, it's you."

"Most likely the matter is simpler than you think," my uncle said. "Some party has asked for help and appealed to their Jewishness."

"Mossad?"

"That's quite a hypothesis, but it's not impossible. The visit of the foreign minister is an extremely volatile matter."

"Have you heard about Mossad's Jewish collaborators who live abroad?"

My uncle laughed. "We've read the same book. Do you believe it?"

"What about you? Do you believe that locals could be involved?"

"I suppose that's possible too, but it's pretty hard to imagine Meyer or Oxbaum as Mossad's errand boys, they're so cautious and timid. I could almost see Silberstein doing it, or what?"

"The request for assistance could have been fed to them in a form they could digest. Oxbaum was asked to arrange a car and report it stolen, Meyer was asked to provide a suitable alibi for Weiss. Not such a big deal. Plus, both of them have kids living in Israel. That could have been used."

"By Weiss's death at the latest, they'd start to suspect."

"Maybe that's exactly the reason Oxbaum took off on holiday. Meyer might be packing his bags as we speak."

"Pretty amusing, or what?" my uncle said. "Two Jews suspecting a Jewish conspiracy."

"I'm not amused. Someone's trying to suggest that I'm not qualified to take the case because of my heritage, and if this keeps up, it won't be long before I will be."

"Do you believe that a strike is still being planned against our synagogue or the Israeli foreign minister?"

"That's what it looks like, at least. Today we found guns and explosives on a person who's tied up in the Linnunlaulu case and who has terrorist contacts."

I knew I was revealing confidential information to my uncle, but he was the only relative I trusted. He was also the only one who would definitely be able to help me out, one way or another.

"Then it might all be exactly what it looks like: Israel found out about preparations for a terrorist attack and sent people over to ensure that nothing happens. The Israelis got on the terrorists' trail. There was a confrontation at Linnunlaulu that resulted in bodies on both sides."

My uncle stopped and sat down on a bench. He inhaled deeply. The trees in the park had already yellowed, because the summer had been extraordinarily dry. Between the rowing stadium and the marina, the sea glistened in the sun.

"Autumn is certainly beautiful in Finland. When I was younger, I also considered moving to the Promised Land. I spent over six months there in the Fifties, building roads, but I had enough of it. I visited there three years ago, and everything was even worse. And that atmosphere of hatred on top of everything else. But most of all I was bothered by the heat, I never would have got used to it. I would have missed the Finnish autumn and spring, and maybe the winter a little too. After sweating for six months, I couldn't get enough of the cold. If it's cold you can put on more clothes, but if it's hot the most you can do is strip naked. I honestly believe that God could have chosen a better spot for the Promised Land."

My uncle picked up a maple leaf that had drifted to the bench.

"God's miraculous handiwork. This little leaf is more beautiful than some synagogue. I've always felt that even just sitting here on this park bench under the falling leaves, I'm closer to God than in any synagogue, no matter how encrusted with gold."

"Will you help me?" I asked.

"Have you considered how far you're prepared to take this investigation, if you start running into friends and relatives or people fighting for a good cause?"

"I never forget that I'm a Jew, but first and foremost I'm a Finnish police officer."

"Then I'm on your side."

I looked at my uncle's deeply lined face and didn't doubt him. He was on my side.

I told him that we were looking for Dan Kaplan in connection with the Linnunlaulu killings.

My uncle had already reached that point of age and experience where you no longer clap your hands in surprise or cry out in amazement. He satisfied himself with a nod.

"Is that who you meant when you said I might run into people?"

"No, I was talking generally. This Dan Kaplan, he was your best friend, wasn't he?"

"He was."

"And then he moved to Israel. Went into the army and did well. Salomon Kaplan's son, war hero in Lebanon. What has he done?"

I told him everything I knew about what Dan Kaplan had been up to in Helsinki and the fact that a warrant was out for his arrest.

"Did you know he was here?"

"No, no, I didn't. It looks bad... for Kaplan's son."

"Sure does."

"What are you planning on doing?" my uncle asked.

"Bringing him in."

My uncle's gaze focused on a woman who was walking her dog about twenty yards away.

"Have you considered something? If this is what you think it is, then you're the most important person in the whole investigation and your doings are of interest to a lot of people. Her, for instance."

The woman was thirtyish and dark-complexioned. She was wearing a fur-trimmed jacket and low-heeled walking shoes. There was nothing odd about her complexion in and of itself, because a lot of embassy people lived in the area. After the small, wiry terrier finished its business and covered it with a few kicks of sand, the woman started heading towards us. We sat silently and waited. The dog stopped at the end of the bench, and she glanced at us. She had beautiful features, but wasn't in the same class as the Israeli soldier of my dreams. My uncle raised his hat, and the woman smiled.

Once she had made it twenty yards past us, my uncle said: "I've been coming to this park almost every day for five years and I know every single dog in the area by sight. I've never seen this one before. And that woman clearly didn't know the dog or its habits. I'm sure it isn't hers."

If someone was following me, they were doing a good job, because I hadn't seen anyone on my tail. I parked my car in about the same spot on Aurorankatu where the white minivan had stood three days earlier.

Eli's firm Kafka & Oxbaum was located in a set of elegant old offices. A *mezuzah*, a small brass case containing excerpts from the Torah, hung from the doorframe. No other signs of Jewishness could be seen, unless you counted a photograph where Eli and Max posed with a fat man in a yarmulke. Judging by the background, the photo had been taken in Jerusalem.

Eli dealt mostly in corporate law; his speciality was international contract law. Now and again he'd descend among the hoi polloi. According to him, he only took criminal cases to maintain a feel for the field. His partner Max Oxbaum, on the other hand, specialized in copyright law.

Eli wasn't around, but Max was. He was reading a thick folder in his office and looked a little surprised to see me.

Max was in his shirtsleeves, but he was wearing a tie. The shirt was light blue with white pinstripes. A black leather belt vanished somewhere in his fifty pounds of excess mass. As a young man, he had been like a fat version of John Steed. He had started going bald before the age of forty; only a few wisps of hair remained above his ears. Like my brother, he had an exorbitantly expensive watch.

Max held out his hand and said: "I would have called if you hadn't showed up."

"Why?"

"Why... Because of Ben Weiss, of course. You're the one investigating his death."

"Who told you?"

"Meyer... he was shocked. Who would have ever believed that something like this could happen in Finland?"

"I would. It happens everywhere, except Disneyland. Why did Ben Weiss need your help?"

"He wanted to know about Finnish copyright practices. He was planning on manufacturing some Finnish fur models in Israel."

"What did he tell you about himself and his business?"

"Not much. He was feeling out the possibility of partnering with Meyer and asked what kind of man he was. I told him everything I knew. He was supposed to go back to Israel on Monday. That was about it."

"Where was he staying?"

"Some hotel, I guess. I don't know."

I already knew that Weiss hadn't been staying in a hotel. That had been checked out.

"Did he know anyone here?"

"I'm sorry, I don't know. The meeting only lasted about half an hour."

I looked around silently for a minute. Then I looked at Max again while continuing to remain silent.

Max began to fidget anxiously.

"Did you have any other questions?"

"Where's your father?"

"My father?"

"There's an 'on holiday' sign in the window."

"In France. He and Mum have a small place near Nice."

"When did he leave?"

"Day before yesterday."

"Of course they did."

I stood to leave. I stopped in the doorway and asked:

"Who's the fat guy in the picture?"

"In what… oh, that one, Benjamin Hararin. He's one of Israel's richest businessmen. Construction business, speciality chemicals, financing. Eli and I met him when we were in Jerusalem."

"Are you guys in business together?"

Max's expression became simultaneously cagey and insinuating.

"Perhaps. But it's better if I don't say anything more at this point."

On the way to HQ, I thought about Dan Kaplan. The childhood bonds of friendship had loosened years ago. When I had met him on my previous trip to Israel about ten years ago, we had spent a couple of evenings together.

Even though we had had a good time, things had been a little strained between us. He had become aggressive and cynical.

Still, it was difficult for me to think of him as a common criminal, the kind who it was my job to pursue.

Nor was catching Dan Kaplan going to be easy. He was in the country under an assumed name; that had already been checked. The fact that he hadn't seen his relatives, even his father, indicated that he wanted to keep his presence in Finland secret. And if Dan was currently a Mossad agent, like I believed, he had the support of the entire organization behind him. Everything he did had been planned in advance, and the moments when things could go awry had been taken into account.

Yet I was certain that Dan was still in Finland. If he had been sent here to prevent a terrorist attack, then his job was still unfinished, and Dan Kaplan wasn't the kind of man to leave a task undone.

I found Simolin in Stenman's room. Both of them glanced at me.

I asked if there was any news on the Focus yet.

"Oksanen's still looking into it," Simolin answered. "He likes car stuff."

"Come take a look at this," Stenman said.

There was a photograph on her computer display. I took a closer look at it.

"Tagi Hamid," Stenman prompted.

"Where'd the photo come from?"

Stenman scrolled downwards, revealing text in English.

"We got a more detailed response from the Danish security police to the enquiry we sent out through Interpol, or actually it came to us through SUPO. Hamid lived there a couple of years ago, and he has contacts with several Palestinians who knew a terrorist named Ismel Saijed."

I asked Simolin what we had got from Tagi Hamid's neighbours.

"The next-door neighbour saw a foreign-looking man and woman enter the apartment the other day. That's all. Hamid was a quiet guy, didn't come or go much. Most of them had never even met him."

I asked Stenman to continue.

"Saijed lived in Copenhagen from 1999 to 2001, and he has a forged Danish passport that he uses to go by the name of Issa Shamahdi."

Stenman clicked the front page of the passport up onto the screen. The photo was of a middle-aged, curly-haired man with a heavy beard and thick-rimmed glasses. Even just shaving the beard would change his appearance completely.

"The Danes presume that he has several other Danish passports. If he's in Finland, as the Danes and Israelis suspect, then he's probably using the passports here. Quite a coincidence that Hamid comes to Finland from Denmark at the same time as Saijed is suspected of entering the country."

"The suspicion is based solely on tip-offs, I assume?"

"At least for now," Stenman admitted. "According to the information from the Danish police, Saijed travelled to Athens in June 2001 and participated in the attack on the El Al passenger plane. The plane was shot at simultaneously with two bazookas, but one of the grenades missed and the other one didn't explode, it just passed through the plane. Members of several terrorist groups participated in the attack. The Israelis picked up his trail, but then he disappeared. Saijed has a long career as a terrorist. He began in his twenties and took part in a bombing in Paris in 1980. The bomb blew up in front of a synagogue; three people died and about twenty were injured."

"Hopefully he'll never kill again," Simolin reflected out loud.

"The end is the most interesting part, to me at least," Stenman remarked. "The Danish police claim to have wiretap information according to which terrorists are planning an attack in Finland. The architects of the attack are presumed to be Saijed and Hassan Bakr, who has done gigs for Abu Nidal's terrorists and others. Bakr has arranged dozens of bombings. In 1986, two of Abu Nidal's terrorists attacked a synagogue in Istanbul with grenades and sub-machine guns. Twenty-one Jews died, three of them rabbis. Bakr is believed to have planned the attack. His favourite targets are companies owned by Jews, Jewish restaurants, synagogues and the like."

Stenman took a small pause.

I was certain that Denmark had got most of their information from Israel, and that SUPO knew it too. If SUPO wanted more information, it had to play with Mossad's cards. I still didn't understand what point there was keeping information from us.

171

"Do the Danes also have a passport photo for Bakr?" I asked.

"No. And no fingerprints for either."

"That would have been too easy. And we haven't got anything on the deceased that got hit by the train?"

"The fingerprints have been sent out through Interpol, but we haven't heard anything. I can try and hurry them up," Simolin said.

"Do it."

I digested Stenman's newsflash for a moment longer.

"So the man who was waiting for Saijed in the Citroën might have been Bakr."

"It crossed our minds too," Simolin conceded. "And he had accomplices too, or at least one accomplice, the woman."

"I believe that the woman is Finnish," Stenman said. "In the first place, not many Arab women have driving licences, and in the second place, it's difficult to imagine an Arab woman getting up to something like this. Besides, Arab women usually come to Finland with their families. We need to start looking for an Arab who's shacked up in his girlfriend's apartment."

"Have you requested the phone records?" I asked Simolin. "We might be able to pinpoint the apartment based on calls Hamid received at the body shop and at home."

"If he called from there," Simolin added.

The sounds of hurried footsteps came from the corridor. Oksanen charged in chomping on a slice of pizza, a can of diet soda in his other hand.

"I think I found the car."

For once, Oksanen appeared to be as interested in his work as he was in his rally club.

"It was a lot of work, but I finally got it. I figured out what that guy meant by the colour of an old lady's underwear. It's a pretty rare colour, but still, over four hundred of them were imported to Finland. I didn't get anything that way, or from Stockmann Auto either. Besides, the car might have changed owners after they sold it. The short plate number is what saved the day. Only six Ford Focuses in Uusimaa County had one. One was a foreigner, a Moroccan guy by the name of Murak Laya. Just to be sure, I checked out the others too. One was a vocational-school teacher, the second a prison guard, the third a computer operator, the fourth a physiotherapist and the fifth a daycare-centre director. The Moroccan is the only one where everything fits. It's owned by an auto lot in Vantaa, but Laya holds the lease. He lives in Koivukylä. I put out a search on the vehicle, and fifteen minutes ago we got a call from Vantaa. A patrol found the car near Laya's place. I told the patrol to sit on both."

After finishing, Oksanen rewarded himself by biting off a hunk of pizza and washing it down with a swig of soda.

I asked: "Did you have time to find out what Laya does?"

"According to his application for a residence permit, he works at a paint plant in Vantaa. He has one suspended sentence for narcotics."

"Get his information to Karvonen right away and tell him about the weapons we found at Hamid's place. Let's let the SWAT team bring this guy in."

"You mean SWAT chief Karvonen?" Oksanen asked.

"Yeah. This guy might be dangerous. He must know Bakr, Saijed, or Hamid, or maybe all three…"

"I'm kinda busy… I thought…"

Oksanen's phone rang. He shoved the slice of pizza into his mouth and dug his phone out from the pocket of his tyre-company coat. Next he placed the can of soda on the table and grabbed the pizza slice with his left hand. After completing this complex set of manoeuvres, he was finally able to answer.

He listened for a minute and swore: "Fuck, you're not screwing with me, are you… don't move a muscle, I'll get some people over there right away."

Everyone turned towards Oksanen, who looked like he had been struck by lightning.

"Some woman just entered Laya's apartment and the place blew totally to shit."

16

Oksanen's description was more accurate than he could have imagined. By the time we arrived, fire and rescue were already gathering up their hoses. There were also two ambulances on the scene, and the Vantaa police had cordoned off the area.

I slipped under the tape and appraised the aftermath of the explosion. The building was a four-storey Seventies prefab. There was a car park, a sandpit and a swing, and a shed for dumpsters; a smattering of pine trees represented nature. A dozen windows were blown out, and glass shards and furniture were strewn across the yard. From the remains, it was easy to determine which apartment the explosion had occurred in. A scrap of fabric that looked like a bedspread hung from the pine tree standing in front of it, and a tongue of soot a few yards long licked upwards from the window. I went over to the fire marshal and introduced myself.

"Can't go in there yet. Might be more explosives; the bomb squad is checking the apartment and the car first."

"Any victims?"

"One. The woman who entered the apartment. The pressure from the shock wave slammed into the upstairs and downstairs apartments with the most force, but luckily they were both empty. Neighbour's an elderly woman, she was taken to hospital for tests."

"How'd the apartment look?"

"Bad. All the contents were destroyed, but the walls and ceiling are intact, there's about an eight-inch hole in the floor. Victim's in unidentifiable condition."

"How big an amount of explosives are we talking about?"

"Hard to tell; there was more than one explosion. A big explosion was heard first, followed by several smaller ones. We found signs indicating grenades. There were also guns in the apartment, or at least one sub-machine gun plus ammo. That's why I ordered that the apartment be checked before we let anyone else in there."

Stenman came over to me.

"The officers who saw the explosion are waiting in the car, if you have a second..."

I thanked the fire marshal and followed Stenman.

The men were sitting in the back of the van, looking grim. I shook hands with both of them.

The older, bald officer gave a brief report of what had happened.

"Did the bomb go off as soon as the woman stepped into the apartment?" I asked.

"No, a light came on in the apartment, then it took five, at most ten seconds before it blew... and a few seconds later there were at least two more explosions, not as powerful. All the debris flew out into the yard during the first explosion."

"You knew which apartment it was?"

"Sure. We received instructions to watch the car and the apartment and if necessary apprehend anyone... that is, if they tried to leave with the car."

"Where did the woman approach from?"

"From over there."

The younger officer pointed at the end of the building. We had just come from that direction ourselves. Behind the building, only fifty yards away, ran a busy arterial road served by a local bus route.

"So she came on foot, not by car?"

"If she came by car, then it had to be farther off."

"Did she have anything with her? Carrying anything, a bag or something like that?"

"A purse. White leather."

"And you didn't see anyone else in the yard?"

"When it exploded, you mean?" asked the bald police officer.

"Yeah."

"No, almost definitely not. Before that, there were two little girls on the swing, but someone yelled for them to come home."

Yelled. It sounded so old-fashioned. Nowadays a mum was more likely to call her kids on their mobile phones than bother to step out onto the balcony and yell for them to come home.

The car door opened. Simolin peered inside.

"There's someone here who wants to join you."

Sillanpää climbed into the van and sat down next to me.

"Evening. Inspector Sillanpää from the Security Police. I'd like to hear everything once more from the start."

The police officers told him everything they had told me. I didn't feel like sticking around for the rerun, so I hopped out.

Sillanpää evidently couldn't come up with any more questions than I had. A couple of minutes later, he emerged from the van.

"Looks like it's time for us to clear the air," he said, attempting a smile. "Your boss already let me have it, so go a little easier on me, huh? Try to keep in mind this isn't a simple matter."

"What matter are you talking about?"

Sillanpää steered me aside.

"You already know that we received a tip-off just a little over a week ago that a couple of big-time terrorists were holed up in Helsinki – we're talking international elite. We got names, but they weren't of much use, because both of them had false identities and evidently Danish passports as well. All the other distinguishing characteristics were old too; we didn't even have fingerprints for them. Both had lived in Denmark for a long time, one was apparently married there. Someone was right when they said that something's rotten in the state of Denmark."

I started to suspect that Sillanpää was trying to butter me up by telling me everything I already knew.

"Tell me something new."

"The information came at a fucked-up time, frankly speaking, because a couple of weeks earlier the foreign ministry of Israel had contacted us and informed us that Foreign Minister Szybilski was intending on visiting the Jewish congregation in Helsinki during their Yom Kippur. The foreign minister didn't want any official visit or protocol; he just wanted to pay his respects to the congregation. The only meetings Szybilski would have would be informal discussions on the situation in the Middle East with the prime minister and the minister of foreign affairs. We were told the duration of the visit would be two days. When we were informed about the visit, we were also presented with a request to take a group from the Israeli security police around to the stops on the itinerary in advance, let them familiarize themselves. This is normal protocol in such situations, and we didn't have any reason to say no. Five men from the security police arrived a week ago. Everything went as usual. They were here for four days."

"They're the ones who told you about Saijed and Bakr?"

"We already knew about them, but we got some updated intelligence. We were told that in addition to Bakr and Saijed, a UK citizen named Tagi Hamid who had previously procured weapons and explosives from Russia for terrorists was hanging out in Helsinki. Surprisingly, we found Hamid easily. It turns out that Hamid's cousin who had been granted Finnish citizenship also lived here."

"Ali Hamid," I said.

"Right. Israel didn't have any information on this cousin, so in other words Ali was innocent and only died because his cousin had got mixed up in some bad stuff, the same with his employee at the body shop… I heard that you found some of the weapons and plastic explosives that Hamid had procured."

"Some?"

"According to our intelligence, there were many times more explosives and three launchers. It could be that some of it detonated in Laya's apartment. Laya's still missing, though, and so is Bakr. And that means that we still have a problem."

"We're not sure yet that the man who got hit by the train was either Saijed or Bakr. As a matter of fact, we still don't have a clue as to his identity."

"The Israelis believe he's Saijed."

"On what grounds?"

"They won't say. They just talk about their sources."

It seemed strange that Sillanpää was still willing to believe the Israelis, even though he had been screwed over like us. It was clear that the Israelis were doling out information bit by bit, and only as much as they considered necessary. If they wanted to play, I'd play too, and I didn't want Sillanpää to reveal my cards to them.

"As I recall, the day before last you still believed that the events at Linnunlaulu and Vartiokylä didn't have anything to do with terrorism," I reminded him.

Sillanpää grunted.

"The commander and the rest of upper police command knew the whole time what was going on. The tactic had been agreed on with them. We had to maintain a low profile. Keep in mind, the foreign minister is arriving next week."

"You said that all the guys from Mossad left Finland."

"You better believe it. I escorted them to the airport and put them on the plane myself."

"Why?"

"Because my bosses and I wanted to be sure that they left."

"What about now?"

"We want to know who's behind the Linnunlaulu killings, and we also want to get the rest of the explosives out of here before the visit… and of course apprehend Bakr, Laya and the accomplice."

"What information do you have on Laya?"

"We knew that he and Tagi Hamid were meeting. He didn't have a record, and we evidently didn't take him seriously enough. We staked out his apartment a few times, but then we concentrated on locating Bakr. We had our hands full with that."

"Did Laya have a girlfriend?"

Sillanpää nodded.

"I'd say she's an ex now."

"She may have been the woman seen in Laya's Focus in Kerava. In which case it's more likely that the man who got into the car was Laya and not Bakr."

Sillanpää still wanted to hear how we had picked up Laya's trail and what we knew about him.

When I had told him, Sillanpää held out a hand.

"So, a clean slate?"

I shook the hand, even though I was sure that Sillanpää hadn't changed his ways. Either that, or he had a different conception of a clean slate than I did.

I left for home around nine p.m. By then I had learnt that sixty grams of hash and twenty-five grams of amphetamines had been found in Murak Laya's apartment. On the way, I ordered a pizza. There were a few cold beers in the fridge, and I had already mentally cracked one. Life was more pleasant if you rewarded yourself now and again.

I had just hopped off the tram at Viiskulma when my mobile rang. After a moment of silence, I heard a voice say: "Hey Ari, nice to hear your voice. It's been a while."

I recognized the voice as easily as the figure from the Parliament House security camera. The caller was Dan Kaplan, my friend who had a warrant out for his arrest.

"Hi Dan. You still in Finland?"

"I'm afraid so."

"In Helsinki?"

"Maybe. Is it true that you're looking for me?"

"Maybe."

"Ask me what you want to know."

"Where are you?"

Dan chuckled.

"Let's not get down to the nitty-gritty just yet."

"Then tell me what happened at Linnunlaulu. You were there, weren't you?"

"I must admit I was."

"Why were you there?"

"I was travelling with Weiss as a bodyguard of sorts. Maybe you haven't heard, but I quit the army and set up my own company in the security field. I also work as a bodyguard."

"Why did Weiss need a bodyguard?"

"Weiss came to Finland, at least in his words, to buy some furs, and he was carrying a lot of cash. He and I bowl in the same league, that's why he extended me an unofficial invitation. According to Weiss, I wasn't actually working, more on holiday and as a travel companion. He paid for my trip and expenses and promised me a thousand dollars on top."

"Doesn't sound like much of a holiday."

"No indeed."

"What happened to Weiss?"

"Usually the first thing you ask a friend who you haven't seen in ten years is how he's doing."

"How are you doing?"

"Not so great. My boss didn't like me and made my life such hell I had to quit. I'm on the verge of getting a divorce. Other than that, everything's great. Hopefully for you, too."

"Can't complain."

"I heard you're still a bachelor. What happened to that foxy redhead that you came to Israel with? Heli, wasn't that her name?"

"We parted as enemies."

"You happen to have her number? How are things going with the ladies otherwise?"

I told him that for the past couple of years I had stuck to one-night stands.

"Ari, I've always said that you're full of surprises. When I last —"

I interrupted him: "What happened to Weiss?"

"All right, down to business. Weiss was an exercise freak and always went running at seven a.m. I had to go with him, of course. We ran along Töölönlahti Bay, and when we were about maybe fifty yards from the Linnunlaulu bridge, we saw two men were fighting on it, or at least that's what we believed. One was lying on the ground and the other one was having a go at him. Then the guy got up and kicked the guy on the ground so hard that he rolled down the embankment. When he took off in the other direction, we ran after him. From the bridge I could see that the guy who took a tumble down the slope was lying there all bloody."

"Was he still alive?"

"I didn't have time to check, because Weiss followed the other guy and caught up to him on the bridge. I had to go help Weiss. By the time I ran up, the other guy was reaching for his gun. I pulled mine out faster and aimed. He was dark-skinned, looked Arab. He went nuts and scrambled over the railing onto the edge of the bridge. At the same time, a train came from the north and he lost his balance and fell…"

I had a few seconds to consider what Dan told me. His story seemed solid.

"Then we noticed this other Arab-looking guy standing at the far side of the bridge. Weiss wasn't the type to stand around thinking; he attacked him. The other guy took off and Weiss went after him. I followed, of course, because I was afraid that Weiss would get into more trouble... I have to admit, I've let myself get a little out of shape. By the time I got to the park, Weiss was right on the guy's heels. There was a car at the side of the road with someone sitting behind the wheel. The guy who was running from Weiss suddenly stopped and pulled out a gun. He aimed at Weiss and forced him into the back seat of the car. Right when I made it there, the car sped off... End of story. It's fucked up, huh? Weiss had a wife and three kids. I know the wife pretty well... imagine what it's going to feel like telling her about all this when I was there."

"Have you heard anything from Weiss since then?"

"Why would I have?"

"If he was kidnapped, there must have been a reason. Ransom or something."

"I'm pretty sure the reason was real simple. He screwed someone over and paid a big price for it."

"What do you mean, a big price? Do you know what happened to him?"

"Well I doubt they'd kidnap him and then pat him on the head and then tell him, 'Skedaddle on home now.'"

"Tell me about the car."

"Green Citroën hatchback. Finnish plates. Now of course you're going to ask me why I didn't contact the police..."

"Why didn't you contact the police?"

"I didn't have my phone with me, and I had a minute to think about what had really just occurred. I was most surprised by the fact that we happened to arrive on the scene right as that guy was getting killed. Weiss picked the route. He studied the map in the phone book for a long time before we left and called someone. Of course I also wondered why the men kidnapped Weiss."

"What conclusion did you come to?"

"That he had got mixed up in something criminal, money laundering or something similar, maybe even drug trafficking, and that he was supposed to meet the guy who got killed. Weiss was a mysterious guy. One of my police buddies warned me about him. I should have listened. Weiss had a lot of dough and lived large, too large considering the scale of his business."

"Meyer claimed that he was negotiating some fur deals with Weiss."

"Meyer's practically senile. It would have been easy for a guy like Weiss to lure him in as a front for his operations. He was amused by how enthusiastic Meyer was. Believe me, Meyer was just part of the scenery."

"So why didn't you ask Weiss to his face what he was up to?"

"I did. He laughed and said that he was making deals, fur deals, and he intended on getting rich off them."

"Did he meet anyone besides Meyer?"

"He went to your brother's office to consult Max Oxbaum."

"What about?"

"No idea. I waited outside."

I thought for a minute. Dan's lengthy explanation sounded just as believable as a story patched together from half-truths might sound when told by a good liar. Dan predicted what I was about to ask and said: "After I thought about it, I thought it would be smartest not to call the cops. I called the Israeli embassy and told them everything or almost everything. They promised to contact the police."

"Who did you talk to?"

"Head of security, I think the name was Klein. Of course you don't understand why I had to give a crap about Weiss's doings unless I was involved too. I told you I have a security company in Israel. It's a pretty tightly regulated business down there... all it takes is one little mess and I lose my permit. Weiss's death looks like more than a little mess. And

184

another minor detail... I'm in Finland on a fake passport and my weapon isn't legal here either."

"On a fake passport? Why?"

"Because I suspected that Weiss might get me mixed up in something. I have friends in Mossad and it was easy to get my hands on one. I did consider not coming at first, but Weiss promised me a good fee. Money doesn't grow on trees, and to be honest, business sucks. I needed that grand bad."

"You said that you were here on a business trip, but you're not staying at a hotel. We checked all of them."

"Weiss arranged an apartment with the help of a friend. But don't bother asking where it is."

"So why call me then?"

"You're investigating the case. Now you know how it really went down. As a policeman, you know that the most probable story is usually the right one. Weiss got mixed up in some shady deals and did something that someone didn't like."

"There's still a warrant out for your arrest. I'll give an old friend the best advice that I can. Come meet me."

Dan was silent for a moment.

"I don't think I will. No offence, Ari."

"Then I'm going to have to bring you in, and that's going to get a little nastier."

Dan's voice took on a taunting tone.

"Do you remember how we used to play cops and robbers when we were kids? You never caught me. And when we made up secret codes, I always cracked your messages, but you were never able to crack mine."

"I'm a big boy now."

"So am I."

An ambulance came from the direction of Iso Roobertinkatu, sirens blasting. When it arrived at Ratakatu, it sounded like it was echoing. It took a moment for me to get what the deal was, and I started running towards the ambulance.

When I got to the square, I stopped. At the corner of Iso Roobertinkatu, a man stood watching me. There was about forty yards between us. He waved at me and disappeared around the corner.

I ran as fast as I could, but it wasn't fast enough. When I got to the corner, I saw a silhouette disappear down Fredrikinkatu. By the time I got there, I couldn't see anyone any more, and I had to rest. As I heaved there, doubled-over, I decided to start exercising again.

I took off jogging towards Bulevardi, even though I knew I had lost the game. At the corner of Bulevardi, my phone rang. I answered it, still panting.

"Nice how you picked up on that," Dan said. "You've improved, but luckily for me you're in pretty lousy shape. Not that you've ever been a very good runner."

"*Moshe manjak!*" I swore into the phone.

Dan laughed.

"Next time I'll have to be more careful. I just wanted to see you. Goodnight."

17

Dan Kaplan, who are you and what are you doing? I kept asking myself these two questions over and over without getting anywhere.

I was sitting by the shore at Kaivopuisto Park, letting myself be buffeted by the sharp wind coming from the direction of Tallinn. The most powerful waves broke over the sea wall and threatened to plunge onto the path. The light from the lighthouse at Suomenlinna swept across the sea-sky.

When I was a few years old, Dad used to drive Eli and me to the Kaivopuisto shore often. The car was a pale-green Ford Taunus and Dad was proud of it, even though it belonged to his employer. We'd walk from the Restaurant Klippan to the Hernesaari shore, and Dad would buy us all ice creams. I also remember how we'd feed the crumbs of the waffle cones to the ducks, and how I once fell into the water while I was following a fluffy little duckling.

And yet sometimes I suspected that I had imagined all this, or heard about the walks from Eli.

I asked him about it once, and he claimed that he didn't remember anything about Sunday strolls. I was sure he was lying, although I couldn't come up with any reason for why he would.

A fire-engine-red American hot rod drove past me, stereo blaring. The noise annoyed me, because it momentarily blocked out the sound of the wind and the waves and threw my thoughts into turmoil...

Dan's call had been precisely the sort of bravado that he used to love – but that he'd still be acting that way at the age of forty? I didn't know what to make of it. I got up and went and stood right at the edge of the sea wall. The sea surged over the stones. Watching it mesmerized me the same way as staring at a fire.

Dan's story filled in most of the remaining gaps about the events at Linnunlaulu and was otherwise believable. Furthermore, it fitted with the narcotics conviction info we had on Tagi Hamid and Laya. But it still didn't explain why there were weapons and explosives in Hamid's apartment. It was hard to believe that a drug dealer would work as the weapons connection for terrorists.

A car pulled up next to me and flashed its lights. I would have preferred to sit staring at the waves for a minute longer and then headed home to bed, but duty called. I climbed in next to Simolin.

Hussein, the brother of Wasin Mahmed, who had been killed in Ali Hamid's body shop, had called the duty desk and said that he wanted to speak with the investigator. The desk sergeant had contacted Simolin, who had called me and then the brother and set up a meeting. The brother had a pizzeria in Herttoniemenranta.

Mahmed had been sidelined in the investigation as a matter of procedure, because from the start it had seemed clear that Hamid was the target. I had ordered Oksanen to go by his place and contact his relatives, but I didn't know if he had done it yet.

It took a second before we found the pizzeria in the labyrinthine new residential neighbourhood. The area had previously been an oil terminal with gigantic oil tanks.

It was about twenty minutes to closing and there were only two customers. Mahmed's brother was maybe around thirty-five. The skin on his downcast face was pitted.

He led us over to a side table and asked if we wanted anything, on the house. We thanked him and declined.

Hussein Mahmed sat down across from us. He was wearing a T-shirt with the pizzeria logo on it.

"I'm sure it was a drug thing. My little brother mentioned it a few times."

"A drug thing?" Simolin wondered.

"Hamid, the guy who Wasin was working for, sold a lot of drugs. Big business."

"How did your brother know?"

"He saw two French guys come by, they looked like real bad criminals. Hamid was afraid because he didn't quite have all of the money, and the men were angry. They spoke Arabic and Wasin heard that they were talking about money. The men said that Hamid would be really sorry if the money didn't turn up."

"When did this happen?"

"Two weeks before they killed him."

"You believe that the men killed him?"

"Who else?"

"Try to remember what else your brother told you," Simolin asked.

The last of the customers left. Hussein waved at them.

"After the men left, Ali called his cousin. He said that he had to get money from somewhere… Then he said that the Israelis wouldn't agree to give them any more money."

"Did Ali use the word Israelis?" I asked.

"My brother said Israelis. Ali spoke Arabic."

I considered what I was hearing. Had Dan told me the truth after all? Was Ben Weiss involved in financing the drug trade? But why the hell would drug traffickers be planning a strike against a synagogue?

"What happened then?"

"My brother wanted to quit working for Ali, but he couldn't find a job anywhere else. He wanted to save money and set up his own body shop and then go and bring back a good wife from Iraq. My brother was a good man, a hard worker."

A shade of sorrow cast the man's face into an even deeper gloom.

"How did he get the job at Hamid's?"

"Through me. Hamid told me that he needed a good mechanic. My brother was working as a cleaner then. He had gone to car-mechanic school. Hamid gave him a job. Now I regret getting it for him."

"How long had he worked for Hamid?"

"Over six months."

"How well did you know Hamid?"

"Not well. I just talked with him at the mosque sometimes."

"What about his cousin Tagi?"

"I didn't know him at all. My brother said that he also sold drugs. He was not a good man."

"How did he know that Tagi Hamid sold drugs?"

"I don't know, but that's what he said."

"Where did Wasin live?"

"He had a room behind the body shop. Sometimes he stayed with me, but he was looking for his own place the whole time."

I remembered the pigeonhole of a backroom at the body shop. There had been a suitcase full of clothes and few personal belongings there. They had been searched.

"Did your brother have a girlfriend or any friends?"

"No, he was always studying at home or else he was at the mosque. He didn't like going to the discos or bars."

"Why didn't Wasin contact the police?" Simolin asked.

"He didn't dare. Hamid is a Finnish citizen and his employer. He was afraid they wouldn't believe him and that he would be killed. Hamid was a dangerous man."

"Did your brother see the French men again?"

"No. He came by here two days before he died. He told me that he had been in the backroom when he heard Tagi tell Ali that he had set up a meeting on some bridge. My brother didn't understand what bridge they were talking about. Tagi had said that their friends would come there and take care of the whole thing and after that they wouldn't have anything to be afraid of any more."

"Friends? Did your brother understand what Tagi meant by that?"

Hussein didn't answer. Suddenly he remembered something and yelled into the kitchen: "Eija! Come here!"

A thirty-year-old woman in a chef's uniform stepped out of the kitchen.

"Eija is my wife… tell the police what you saw."

The woman hesitated for a moment, but then she walked over to us.

"I saw Ali Hamid meet a man from the Security Police near Itäkeskus. The man got out of Hamid's car right when I was riding past on my bicycle."

"How do you know the man was from the Security Police?"

"I used to work with his wife. I saw her with her husband when I was selling stuff at the Hietalahti flea market last summer. I had no problem remembering him."

"What's the wife's name?"

"Irma Sillanpää."

18

Sometimes disordered thoughts sort themselves out overnight. This time it felt like they had got even more muddled. When I woke up at seven, the first thing I thought about was Vivica Mattsson, as if she had settled into my head during my sleep and waited for me to stir.

"Vivica Mattsson," I muttered to myself as I shaved.

I had to admit, she had made an impression on me. I had thought about her on numerous occasions and even considered different ways of approaching her. It would have been easiest to go meet her under the pretence of wanting to confirm whether what she heard shouted from the bridge could have been either "*Moshe manjak*" or "*Muhammad manjak*".

A former colleague of mine had bumped into his current wife while questioning her in an assault case. He kept coming up with excuses for questioning her until the opportunity arose to invite her for coffee.

Another policeman I knew married the girlfriend of a criminal he was hunting, and a third couple was formed when a colleague from Violent Crime was trying to find the apartment that had the best view of a shooter holed up in the building opposite. Now he sees the spot they cornered the guy from his own window every day.

I opened the ventilation window to check the weather. Chilly and a light fog. From the window, I could see the building across the way and folks going about their morning business. At one window, a guy in his undershirt was taking the last puffs of his cigarette. Then he stubbed it out on the window sill and flicked it into the street.

Outside, I breathed in the damp air and buttoned up my coat. An opening car door flashed at the left edge of my field of vision. I instinctively turned to look.

"Kafka!"

The person yelling was Klein, the head of security from the Israeli embassy. I walked up to his car.

"You have time for a coffee?"

We headed over to the Primula Café at Viiskulma. Klein ordered us a couple of coffees and sat down across from me.

He didn't look nearly as competent as his position demanded. His eyes were bloodshot and he had a cold.

"I want to apologize for stepping on your toes. I was trying to help. I was the one who called Sillanpää; he was just being friendly. Don't blame him."

I sipped my coffee and let Klein talk.

"After you and I met, I started thinking about things. I was in touch with Jerusalem yesterday and asked the police there to look into Ben Weiss's background. It looks like I painted an overly rosy picture of him."

I raised my eyebrows a little.

"Weiss really does have a fur company, and he reported business as the reason for his trip. However… the police in Jerusalem informed me that the tax authority has been looking into Weiss's affairs, and he's suspected of tax fraud and money laundering. And according to tip-offs the police have received, he also has connections to certain major-league drug traffickers, who in turn have a lot of contacts in the Russian mafia. You're aware that a lot of Jews have moved from Russia to Israel. There are criminals among them, and unfortunately they often continue their illicit activities in their new homeland."

"So Weiss wasn't here to buy furs?"

"That's what it looks like. I'll be honest, someone in Israel screwed up. We should have been informed about Weiss so we would have known to look out for him... we believe he was supposed to pay for a drug shipment on behalf of some criminals who live in Israel. The tax authority conducted an investigation of Weiss's corporate accounts, and it revealed that payments made to them lead back to certain shady enterprises. They're linked by a complex web of sham companies."

"What do Weiss's drug deals and terrorists like Saijed and Bakr have to do with each other?"

"We're not sure. We have two theories. We know for certain that Tagi Hamid used and probably also dealt drugs. Maybe that's how he and Weiss ended up working together. Tagi Hamid used at least amphetamines and heroin. It's not easy being a terrorist; it's tough on the nerves."

I encouraged Klein to continue.

"Could be that Saijed or Bakr or both found out about things somehow, flew off the handle, and killed the two of them. The simple fact that Hamid was in contact with a Jew could have been enough to make men like Saijed and Bakr suspicious, especially since they were planning a terrorist attack at the time. In their minds, Hamid had made an unforgiveable mistake that put the whole strike at risk."

"Are you sure they were planning a strike, or is that a guess?"

"The Israeli security service received certain information about the weapons and explosives. We also know with one hundred per cent certainty that Tagi Hamid has procured weapons from Russia – the kinds of weapons that are only suitable for terrorist use."

Klein took a handkerchief from his pocket and wiped his running nose.

"I'm sorry. I was out on the Baltic fishing with friends and caught a cold... Another possibility is that Weiss was kidnapped because the kidnappers discovered he was a rich Jewish businessman. Weiss had a lot of money on him, hundreds of thousands of dollars. The money's missing. He was killed because he was Jewish. For guys like that, it would be three birds with one stone: take a Jew's money, kill him, and then use the stolen money to buy weapons to kill more Jews."

"There's only one but," I noted. "We're not even sure that the guy who got hit by the train was Saijed and that Weiss's killer was Bakr. Neither one has been identified yet."

My phone rang. It was Huovinen.

I stood up and stepped a few yards away. Klein tried to look hurt.

"Where are you?" Huovinen asked.

I told him.

"That Murak Laya who's being sought for the explosion in Vantaa just turned himself in at HQ. He's in custody."

"I'll be right there."

I went back to the table and tried to remember what I was saying before Huovinen's call. Klein was faster.

"According to the information we have, they are Saijed and Bakr. The source is extremely reliable. Saijed and Bakr have worked together before, and both of them left Denmark at the same time. According to our source they came here. We'll be happy to offer you expert assistance in identifying the deceased, if that's acceptable to you."

"I was under the impression that you don't have any fresh photos of them, not even fingerprints."

"We have our methods."

"One more thing about the latter theory. If Weiss's murder was political, how come no one has exploited it?"

"Because things went awry and one of the kidnappers died."

"And the man who was with Weiss?"

"You mean Dan Kaplan, or Josef Kayly, the name he was going by here?"

"What do you know about him?"

"Please understand that this is extremely embarrassing for us. In principle, Israel protects her citizens tooth and nail. We believe that Kaplan is involved in Weiss's death. If the first theory holds true, he was here protecting the interests of the Israeli criminals. If the latter theory is true, he was in on the kidnapping and helped Israel's worst enemies... You Finns have a fitting saying for this. The one about the goat and the cabbage patch."

"The goat guarding the cabbage patch."

"That's the one. Kaplan was like the goat guarding the cabbage patch."

"Isn't he in the service of the Israeli army?"

"Was. A few years back, the army discovered some cases of weapons theft. Kaplan was implicated, but they couldn't gather sufficient evidence of criminal activity against him. Nevertheless, he was forced to leave the army. After that, he set up a security company with a dodgy reputation."

"Do you have an idea of why Tagi Hamid's cousin Ali was killed then?"

"Maybe he had got mixed up in the drug dealing or the kidnapping and once Tagi botched things they didn't trust him any more. Wasn't the burnt car his or rented by him? Another possibility is that Bakr, Saijed or Kaplan didn't want to split Weiss's money with anyone else."

"Do you know where Kaplan is?"

Klein sneezed again.

"No. We'll do anything we can to help the Finnish police apprehend him, but he's a tricky bastard... and he has a lot of contacts from his army days. The Jerusalem police have been tailing him for years, but they've never caught him red-handed."

"We've checked every hotel in the Helsinki area. Neither Kaplan nor Weiss stayed at any of them. Do you know where they were staying?"

"I'm afraid not."

I considered how much I could reveal to Klein. Then I decided I didn't have anything to lose by rattling his peace of mind a little.

"Weiss had business dealings with a Jewish fur trader, he consulted a Jewish lawyer, and Weiss and Kaplan used a car that was stolen from a Jewish antiques dealer."

"Blood is thicker than water. You know that Jews prefer dealing with Jews."

"Why did they have to steal the car?"

"Because they were involved in criminal activity. Maybe they heard about Oxbaum's van and trip by accident."

"I never said that the stolen van was Oxbaum's."

Klein looked at me almost sympathetically. It annoyed me, because it reminded me of my brother Eli when he was a move away from checkmate. It made me want to get my butt kicked by him the old-fashioned way rather than lose the game.

"It's part of my job to be on top of things like that."

"You know everything else, but not the things that would help us."

"We'll get Kaplan as soon as he returns to Israel."

I reminded Klein that that wouldn't do us much good, because Israel doesn't extradite its citizens.

"We can still question him, and maybe even allow the Finnish police to interrogate him. If he was mixed up in Weiss's death, he will definitely be prosecuted. Israel is a democratic state and operates under rule of law, the only one in the Middle East," Klein added.

"I want a recent photo of Kaplan."

"I'll try to get you one."

Observing my reaction, Klein asked: "Is it true that Kaplan was your childhood friend?"

I answered in the affirmative.

"What about nowadays?"

"He's a criminal suspect I'm looking for."

Klein glanced at his watch.

"Unfortunately I have to get going, I have a meeting with the ambassador… we sincerely hope that Bakr is found and apprehended prior to the visit of our foreign minister. I hope you're taking this seriously enough; he's a dangerous man."

Klein rose, and so did I.

In the doorway, I asked him casually if any Mossad agents were still in Finland.

"No… Why would they be?"

I don't know if the question surprised Klein, but nonetheless, he hesitated for a second.

"I didn't do anything wrong. I lent my car for a couple of hours. Is that a crime?"

Laya was on the verge of crying. He hugged his arms around his chest and tried to pull himself together.

"I loved Taina. If I had known, I would have gone myself…"

A stream of tears rolled down from the corner of one eye. I didn't doubt that his grief was genuine.

Murak Laya was a small man a little over thirty. His hair was short and curly. He was sitting on a concrete bed in the lock-up at headquarters. Stenman and I had been interrogating him for almost an hour. Simolin and Oksanen were on the other side of the wall, listening to the interrogation through a speaker and immediately verifying anything they could.

According to Laya, this is how it had all happened:

Laya knew Tagi Hamid. They had met at an establishment frequented by Arabs and hung out there together on a few evenings. Hamid had a lot of money, so he treated. When Hamid had moved to the apartment on Toinen Linja, Laya had helped out with his car. A week ago, Hamid had explained that an important friend of his might need a car for a few hours and asked if Laya would agree to rent his in exchange for good compensation. Initially Laya had been hesitant, because he suspected the car would be used for criminal activity. Hamid had laughed and promised that there was no danger of that. Laya had eventually given in, and Hamid had told him that someone would be in touch if his friend ended up needing the car.

The day before yesterday, Laya had received a phone call. The caller was a man and spoke French. He had asked Laya to drive the car to a certain spot in Kallio and tape the keys to the bumper. The caller promised to return the car to the same place and leave the fee in the glove compartment. And that's exactly what had happened.

The caller hadn't given his name, and the number had been blocked. After seeing Hamid's photo in the paper and hearing what had happened at Linnunlaulu, Laya had panicked and tried to think what he should do. He had told his girlfriend about lending the car, and she had demanded that he contact the police.

"What was your girlfriend doing at your apartment?"

"I asked her to pick up the car and then come get me. The keys were inside the apartment."

"Why didn't you pick it up yourself?"

"I was at work."

"Where?"

"The paint plant… in Vantaa."

"Let's forget the car. Hash and amphetamines were found in your apartment."

Laya grew grim. Perhaps he thought that the drugs had been destroyed in the explosion and subsequent fire.

"They were only for my personal use."

"And a sub-machine gun and grenade shards. The investigators believe that one of the grenades exploded or that there was a home-made bomb inside the apartment that exploded and detonated the grenades. The question is whether the bomb exploded by accident or on purpose."

Laya looked genuinely surprised. For a moment, his mouth actually hung open.

"I don't have a sub-machine gun or any bombs or grenades. I hate weapons. The people who planted the bomb also planted the gun. Maybe they want you to believe I am some kind of terrorist or big-shot criminal."

"Who are they? Who are you talking about?"

Laya almost lost his temper. "Don't you understand – the same men who killed Hamid, or else then it was the man who borrowed my car."

"What do you know about them?"

"Nothing. I read about it in the paper. I'm not stupid, I don't believe it's a coincidence."

"You also dealt drugs to Hamid. You'd think you'd know at least something about his business partners."

"No, I didn't. I lent some to him a couple of times, but I'm not a terrorist. I left my own country to get away from violence. I hate it. I've lived here seven years, and Finland is my second homeland…"

"You lent him drugs?"

"He didn't have any money and he said he was going to be getting some and a big load of amphetamines and hash. He promised to give it all back to me… he had once before…"

"Was it because of drugs that someone killed Hamid and tried to kill you?"

Laya thought for a second.

"I'm positive that it all has to do with Tagi. He was always afraid that something would happen to him. He said that if he held on to a few good cards, he might live. He never said who he was talking about."

"What did he mean by good cards?"

"Some kind of important information."

"And he didn't say what?"

"No, but once he met someone and he asked me to photograph the meeting. I took a picture when they met at Kaisaniemi."

"When?"

"About two months ago."

"Where's the picture?"

Laya wiped a tear from his cheek.

"At Taina's place."

"That still doesn't explain why someone tried to kill you. How would anyone have known about the photo?"

Laya's voice rose to a shout: "I don't know, I've been racking my brains, but I don't understand! I'm not some mafioso, I'm a normal man who has only done some small-time stuff."

"What if Tagi told someone about the photograph, and about you too?"

"Why would he? He was afraid."

"Did he tell you who he was afraid of?"

"One time when we had done some hash, he said something, but at the time I thought he was just babbling. He told me how someone thought he was so smart, but that he would scam all those Jewish bastards. He said that if the bait is good enough, you can use it to hook however big a fish you want."

"Jewish bastards?"

"Or he actually used a nastier word."

"*Moshe manjak?*" I suggested.

Laya was surprised. "You understand Arabic? That's exactly what he said."

"You suspect that he was involved in the drug trade with some Jews?"

"Yeah, but I'm not totally sure. He was always so careful, so careful."

"What about his cousin Ali, the one who owned the body shop? Was he in on it?"

Laya nodded.

"I think Ali funded the business. I was along once when Tagi got half a kilo of hash from the body shop… I don't know where it came from."

"Many kilograms of plastic explosives and heavy weapons were found at Tagi's place. Could Tagi or Ali have been planning a terrorist attack?"

Laya wiped his eyes as if he were drying tears, but he let out a laughing sound.

"Tagi? He always said that he couldn't give a shit about religious stuff, live and let live, as long as he can live the way he wants. For him, the good life was a beautiful woman, a new Mercedes, and a nice house on the beach. He wanted to live comfortably and party. Ali was the same way, went to the mosque to pray, but money was always the most important thing. Men like that can't be terrorists."

Laya's girlfriend's apartment was in Tikkurila. We entered with the keys Laya had given us. The photo was there where it was supposed to be, in an envelope taped to the bottom of the breadbox.

The photo had been taken at Kaisaniemi Park. It was summer, and the greenhouse at the botanical gardens could be made out in the background. The men were standing next to each other, talking. One of the men was Hamid. The other was even easier to identify: Dan Kaplan. It had been ten years since I had seen him last, and now I was running into him everywhere.

"Why did Hamid want the meeting with Kaplan to be photographed?" Stenman wondered.

"I don't know."

"Maybe Kaplan was in the narcotics business with Hamid and figured he could blackmail him with the photo if necessary."

I looked at the picture thoughtfully.

"Laya said that the photo was taken two months ago. We don't have any information indicating that he was in the country then. He must have been travelling on false documents," Stenman continued.

I was starting to believe that Dan was no longer the man he was when he left Finland. Still, it was hard for me to imagine him dealing in drugs. I could only think of two reasons why he would have met with a drug trafficker like Tagi Hamid in Finland without contacting his friends or relatives.

Klein had said that Dan had been forced to resign from the army for stealing weapons. Dan had said basically the same thing in slightly different words. I didn't believe either of them.

The surroundings of Ali Hamid's body shop hadn't changed since our previous visit. Autumn was a few days further along, and the trees had shed more leaves onto the roof of the RV. Soon it would be covered in snow, and Jäppinen would be shovelling himself out like a vole.

I knocked on the door. Stenman was standing behind me, as chic as ever. A half-length sheared fur had replaced the English oilskin. It looked warm and expensive, like Stenman herself. She was a little too aristocratic for my taste, but there was still something about her.

I liked her.

I said: "Take a look in the window."

There was a curtain blocking it, but Stenman peeked through the crack.

"There's someone in there, all right."

I banged on the door with my fist. The tone of my banging wasn't apologetic, it was authoritative.

"Who the hell… at this hour…"

For Jäppinen, at this hour meant nine-thirty. He clearly wasn't a morning person.

He opened the door in his boxer shorts. His hair was sticking out all over the place, and we were assaulted by a gust of fermenting interior air.

Jäppinen noticed Stenman and blushed.

"Can't a man even get dressed?…"

He yanked the door shut. Stenman looked at me, amused.

"Aah, the bachelor life, so glamorous and carefree."

"Ain't that the truth," I agreed.

Suddenly Stenman looked thoughtful.

"That was quite a stench that wafted out. Did you smell?…"

I gave her a questioning look. Then I understood. I stepped aside and made a call.

I was hanging up just as the door opened. Jäppinen came out, fully dressed and his wet hair slicked back. Even though it was almost foggy, the light blinded him, and he squinted his night-owl eyes. Feeling his way, he cautiously lowered himself to the RV steps. His tremulous hands moved to his lap.

"You said that Ali Hamid used to work for you and then he bought the body shop?"

"That's right."

"How much did it cost?"

"He got a package deal: all the equipment, three lifts and the other big-ticket machines, plus all the tools, screwdrivers and everything, and a loyal customer base on top. I got three hundred and fifty thousand marks… I gave him a good-guy discount, but I respect a hard-working man, and that's what Ali was."

"So about sixty thousand euros."

"Around there."

"And he paid all at once?"

"Course. Got the papers and receipts to prove it."

"Where did he get the money?" Stenman asked.

"The bank, I guess… or wherever people get money from… He didn't have that kind of dough himself, they were renting, and raising a big brood like that costs a mint."

"We believe that Hamid was dealing drugs. Did you ever see anything like that?"

Jäppinen glanced around furtively. He cleared his throat and fished a half-smoked cigarette out from his pack.

"No… no… I never did."

"Did he give you the money in cash or was it transferred to your account?"

"My account, the whole shebang."

"I'd like to see the receipt," I said.

"Now?"

"Yes."

"I don't remember where it is right now… You mind if I look for it and give you a call… I could use a lift down to the Teboil for my morning cereal."

I looked into Jäppinen's beady eyes and changed tack.

"I just made a call and asked a few questions about you. You've been convicted three times for narcotics violations. Use and smuggling."

Jäppinen's expression froze, then he swallowed and said: "That stuff's ancient history. Back when I was a young…"

"I can call in a drug dog to come sniff out your RV."

Jäppinen grew pale and his upper body swayed as if he were about to faint.

"Don't bother. Is it really that big a deal if I take a few puffs for my own pleasure sometimes, an old man like me? Who's getting hurt?"

"We're interested in Hamid, not you."

Jäppinen lit his cigarette and took his first drags of the morning.

"He was dealing hash and amphetamines. I don't know how much, but I'd buy small amounts from him sometimes. He said he'd quit as soon as he got his finances in order. He used to send money back to just about his entire extended family in Iraq or wherever it is Kurds live these days."

"What about his cousin Tagi?"

"Yeah, he was in on it too."

"Anyone else? The killings might have something to do with the drugs."

"He said the drugs came from Spain and Morocco. I don't know who he bought them from, not a Finn at least. Could we —"

"Just one more question. Did you see anything that evening when Ali and Wasin were killed? Think carefully; you don't want to make the biggest mistake of your life."

"Two cars… and a few guys… a white van and a Passat."

I had a photo of Oxbaum's stolen Nissan in my pocket. I showed it to Jäppinen.

"That's what it looked like at least. I remember the plate number, it was JFK-37. JFK are the initials of that Yankee president and thirty-seven happens to be the year I was born."

"What about the Passat?"

"Dark and a diesel. Didn't see the plates."

"But you saw the men?" Stenman suggested.

"The white van came first, but I didn't see when it came. I only saw when the guys were leaving. The yard lights are pretty bad and I couldn't see very well, but I heard them talking in some foreign language, I don't know which one. I thought they were Ali's or Wasi's Arab buddies."

"Do you remember any words?"

"I'd been drinking a little that day and I had just woken up. My head's like a Swiss cheese when that happens. The guys got out of the car and drove away, and I didn't give the whole thing any more thought. I went to Teboil, and when I got back, I had a couple of beers to take the edge off and then I cracked open the vodka. The Passat showed up almost right after. There were two men in it. I saw them go into the shop. While they were in there, I headed around back to take a leak, and when they came out I heard one of them saying fuck and shit over and over and call someone. He was looking around, but luckily there weren't any lights on in my RV, and he didn't see me."

"What did he say?"

"He said that Ali was dead and asked what they should do. Whoever was at the other end must have said something, I guess, because he answered that there are only two options. Then he said they needed to meet that night and rethink the whole thing. That was it. The guys got in the car and drove off."

"What did you do?" Stenman asked.

"Got tanked and didn't wake up until you came knocking on my door."

"I don't know anything about my husband's money. He worked hard and was frugal; he saved every mark."

Hamid's wife had already got over the worst of her shock. She had been forced to. Even though her husband was dead, she still had four children who required her attention. The children were at school and the apartment was quiet. Hamid's photograph was on the living-room table; a candle burnt in front of it.

"The body shop cost sixty-thousand euros," Stenman pointed out.

"Maybe he borrowed the money from one of his friends… He didn't get it from the bank… I would have known about that."

"Did you have a joint bank account?"

"No. I have my own account, and my husband gave me money when I needed it."

"Do you know how much money is in your husband's account?"

"Yes. The bank sends the statements here."

"Could we have them?"

Hamid's widow walked over to the living-room bookcase and pulled out a black plastic folder from the bottom drawer.

"All of the statements and company papers are here. You can take it with you."

"What will you do with the company?"

"I will try to sell it."

"Who handles the company's books?"

"I don't remember her name, but it's in the papers."

The woman suddenly looked anguished and tired.

"How have you been managing? Is there anything we could help you with?" Stenman asked.

"No thank you. I will be fine. I have to be strong for the children."

"Has anything new come to mind that might be of interest to us?"

"No…"

Then she appeared to remember something.

"There is one thing. Two days before Ali's death, a Finnish man called here asking for him. He didn't tell me his name. I asked him to call Ali's mobile phone or the shop, but the man said that no one was answering at either. The man left a message for Ali and asked me to tell him that it was about the rental car."

"Did he leave his number?"

"He just asked Ali to call."

"Could the caller have been one of the customers from the body shop?"

"No, Ali didn't give out our home number to them. It was unlisted."

"What did he say when you mentioned it to him?"

"Nothing, but he went immediately into the other room and called from there with his mobile."

"Did you hear what he was talking about?"

"I heard him say that he didn't want to get mixed up in it any deeper. That he just wanted to warn him, but that he couldn't help out any more. Then he hung up."

"Why didn't you tell us about the call earlier?" I asked.

The woman looked frightened.

"Did I make a mistake? I'm sorry… the caller was Finnish, and you just asked about his friends and a man who spoke English and Arabic."

"Did you know that your husband's cousin Tagi used drugs?"

"Yes, my husband told me, he was afraid... he was afraid that Tagi would get caught and he would drag his relatives into it."

"Did your husband know where he got the drugs from?"

"No, he said that he didn't want to have anything to do with it. He believed that using drugs was against the Koran."

Stenman drove and I studied Hamid's papers. According to the last statement, there had been slightly over fourteen thousand euros in Hamid's account. The withdrawals and deposits appeared normal.

I looked through the company papers, but I couldn't detect anything out of the ordinary in them either. I couldn't find any loan papers, nor was there anything else that would have explained where the money necessary to buy the body shop would have come from. Among the papers was a copy of the power of attorney granted to the bookkeeping company. I called information and asked for the bookkeeper's number and called her. She was suspicious and called back through the police switchboard. The firm had one fifty-thousand-euro loan that had been taken out from an Estonian finance company.

"The name of the company?"

"Baltic Invest."

"Are there any names on the loan papers?"

"The usual ones. The CFO of the company and so on, in other words the party granting the loan... and here are the names of the Finnish intermediary company and contact person."

"You mind giving them to me?"

"Kafka & Oxbaum, Attorneys at Law. Evidently Eli Kafka, Esq., has acted as the contact person."

* * *

"As far as I'm concerned it doesn't disqualify you, but let's let Simolin look into any matters related to the company," Huovinen said from the window. Whenever faced with a difficult decision, he would stand up, conduct a visual inventory of the room's furnishings, and go stare out the window.

"The bureau's white-collar-crime unit has good contacts in Estonia, the police and the tax authorities. If there's anything fishy about the company, it'll come out."

"How could Hamid have known about Baltic Invest?" I asked, mostly rhetorically.

"Word probably gets passed around the immigrant community. Maybe he couldn't get a loan here and decided to get one from Estonia."

"The wife didn't know anything about the loan. And Hamid didn't have any collateral."

"I think that's normal in that culture. And maybe the company and its inventory covered the collateral. The loan's not very big. Or else some friend of Hamid backed it."

My conception of the Hamid cousins, especially Ali, had already gone through the wringer several times. At first he was an upstanding family man, Muslim, and a hard-working entrepreneur, then he turned into a drug peddler and a SUPO snitch. I remembered what Hussein Mahmed had said about him: Hamid was a dangerous man.

If Klein, as head of security at the Israeli embassy, hadn't so conveniently joined in the chorus, I would have been sure this was just an everyday case of drug-related crime.

19

My uncle's apartment occupied a third of his building's top floor. The living room gave onto the sea, and through the trees you could make out the rowing stadium and the marina, which was buzzing with autumnal activity. In 1992, it had got down to seventeen degrees below freezing on the night of 15 October, and the shoreline had frozen. Boaters were a long-memoried lot; they hadn't forgotten. They wanted to get their boats onto dry land and up for the winter in plenty of time.

There was a fireplace in the living room, in front of it a cigarette table and two well-worn club chairs, the kind inhabited by gentlemen in smoking jackets and silk scarves in old-fashioned advertisements. The chairs smelt of cigars, even though my uncle had stopped smoking years ago, when his asthma started getting bad. Maybe he allowed his guests to smoke so he could catch just a tiny whiff of the pleasure he had lost.

I was sitting in one of the chairs, waiting for my uncle to get ready.

"Which one would you choose?"

My uncle showed me two ties. One was burgundy, the other one dark grey.

"The red one."

My uncle put on the burgundy tie and flashed himself a smile so broad that his gold-bound ivories winked in the mirror.

"Ready."

When I rose from the chair, it made a hissing noise as the leather, freed from the pressure, sucked in air.

I helped my uncle on with his overcoat.

"I've been thinking a lot about this case of yours, but all I can say is that it's about something major. What you told me about your brother came as no surprise. I had heard about his affairs. Yet the fact that one of the men who was killed was a client of his is still a shock."

"To me too. And an exceptionally unpleasant one."

"You can rest assured that your brother doesn't have anything to do with the murder. He wouldn't dare to be involved in anything like that."

"I believe that, but he might not have any idea of what he's involved in."

"It'll provide a nice topic of conversation for this evening, anyway," my uncle grunted. "Sorry to joke about such a serious matter, but Eli and murder don't really add up."

I agreed. But I still wasn't amused.

By the time we arrived at Eli's, the other guests were already there. Eli's wife Silja received us, hugging my uncle first and then me.

"It's wonderful you could make it, even though you're so busy at work."

If I had a line-up of middle-aged women in front of me that included one millionaire, Silja wouldn't have been the first one I would have pegged. She was a big-boned brunette who at first glance called to mind a farmer's wife. But if you looked closely, you could find small, subtle hints of wealth. When a woman could devote infinite attentions to her well-being, it had to show somewhere. In addition to everything external, she possessed the unassuming confidence that old money conferred.

I had always liked Silja. She was friendly and had a good sense of humour and a mind of her own.

Eli's well-bred children Ethel and Leo, my godson, also came out to greet us.

Eli introduced Max to our uncle.

"You remember Max Oxbaum, don't you, Uncle Dennis?"

"Do you think I'm losing my memory?"

"Of course not."

I knew that my uncle didn't care for Max. I wasn't sure why, maybe for the simple reason that Max was arrogant, smug and loud. Any one of those traits would annoy most people, and Max had them all in one package. The combination, especially when bolstered by considerable financial success, was tough to stomach.

Max was so wound up that his tiny wife Ruth found it almost impossible to step out from behind her husband.

I considered Ruth a freak of nature. Nothing else could explain her unstinting admiration for Max, no matter what he did. Ruth treated Max like a mother would a son, not like a wife would a husband. Even if Max had been caught at the scene of a murder holding a smoking gun, Ruth would instantly believe that sweet little Max had been framed. Or if she had surprised him on top of a whore, she would have insisted that Max had simply slipped and fallen with his zipper down.

Eli poured us all a drink and then walked up to me.

"Would you come here for a minute?"

He took me by the shoulder and dragged me into his office.

"As your older brother, I'd like to give you some advice. You probably don't understand how much bad blood your behaviour has aroused."

"What do you mean?"

"Silberstein was so outraged that he's going to write about you in the congregation newspaper... according to him, by refusing to cooperate and withholding information, you've endangered the entire synagogue. In addition, the Israeli ambassador has lodged an unofficial complaint with us about the behaviour of the Finnish police, and by that he means you."

I could only imagine the kind of article Silberstein would hack out in his fury. He was not known for his diplomacy. That didn't bother me in the least. But it did bother me that Eli was dressing me down as if he were my boss.

"Silberstein and the ambassador can think whatever they want. I'm just doing my job."

"Don't underestimate them. They can cause you a lot of trouble."

Eli's expression was so full of concern that you would have imagined he was talking about himself. He looked to see what kind of impression his words had made and seemed a little disappointed when I simply stated: "Could be."

"I think I could set up a meeting where we could settle your differences of opinion. They don't have anything against you, just your bull-headed way of handling things without taking realities into account."

"I'm not a politician, just a fucking poorly paid cop who's never going to make it onto the list of Finland's richest people. For me, the only reality is what my work happens to demand at any given moment."

The F-word on Yom Kippur Eve in Eli's elegant home was as big an offence as bringing a ham hock as a hostess gift. I wanted Eli to understand how insulting I found his offer of reconciliation.

He got the message and melted into misery.

"It wouldn't hurt. Come on."

"I'll think about it."

"Promise?"

"I promise to think about it." I had no intention of meeting Silberstein and the ambassador. I didn't have anything to settle, at least not with them. I just didn't want Eli to be after me all night. I knew what a nag he could be.

I still decided to give him a little more than the challah to chew on.

"By the way, I ran across yours and Max's loan business. You brokered a loan for Ali Hamid, who was shot at the body shop and is the cousin of terrorist suspect Tagi."

It was if Eli had taken a blow to the gut.

He took a deep breath.

"It was... you can be sure that it's a one hundred per cent honest business loan. The body shop and its contents are the collateral. I didn't tell you about it because I didn't want you to be worried for no reason."

"I would have been less worried if you had told me. How was it that Hamid just happened to end up as your client?"

"The application came through the main bank in Tallinn. The loan had already been approved, I just handled the formalities. Believe me... there's nothing shady about it."

"Then why were you scared enough to come ask me about Hamid's death the night before last?"

"Isn't it natural that my client's death interested me? Especially when you're investigating the case?"

"It interested some other people, too. Silberstein has a Volvo hatchback, doesn't he?"

"Two birds with one stone. He was interested on the congregation's behalf. The reason has become obvious enough, I presume."

When we got back to the living room, I could hear Max explaining to my uncle: "It's an international investment company that's looking for a foothold in the Nordic countries. We locked down representation in Finland. If everything goes well, the company has limitless opportunities for growth."

My uncle's response was tepid.

"Here and at this interest level? There's already too much money being shoved onto the market. Who wants to borrow money from a completely unknown company in times like these?"

My uncle laughed.

"Or of course there are people who will take the money, but if you want clients who will pay it back…"

The conversation was interrupted when Silja asked us to the table. Even though she hadn't converted to Judaism, she had set a half-traditional table in honour of the majority of her guests.

Eli asked my uncle to bless the bread.

I was almost envious of the dignity with which my uncle read the blessing:

"*Barukh ata Adonai Eloheinu melekh ha'olam, hamotzi lechem min ha'aretz.*"

"Blessed art Thou, Lord our God, King of the universe who brings forth bread from the earth."

I hung around for an hour after dinner, leaving at the same time as my uncle. He looked tired and remained silent during the taxi ride. It wasn't until we got to Etu-Töölö that he blurted out: "If I were your brother, I'd split the sheets with Max and fast. It's just a matter of time before he makes an utter mess of his affairs and drags Eli down with him."

I almost started. Did my uncle know more than he was letting on, or could he really be that perceptive?

"Don't ask me what I mean. If I were still a bank manager, Max would never get a loan from me. It's not a matter of not liking him, it's a matter of understanding human nature."

20

I had a photo of Hanna at home that had been taken five years before she died. She had been about twenty then. In it, she is smiling so broadly that it brightens her face and her eyes.

At her neck there's a gold chain that I had bought her as a birthday present.

Hanna had also been wearing the necklace when she killed herself with barbiturates.

I hadn't heard from Hanna in over a week, and she hadn't returned any of my calls. On Yom Kippur Eve I had gone over to her place in Tapiola and forced the super to open the door. She had already been dead for two days.

Next to her on the bed was a goodbye note and photographs from her childhood. She had spread them out like a photo-essay of her truncated life.

Along with Hanna, Eli and Dad and I appeared in the photos. Mum wasn't in a single one.

There was no one at the new Jewish cemetery but me.

The place radiated an austere melancholy. The gravestones were for the most part dark and looked like they had been cut in the same mould. Paving stones and crushed gravel took the place of lawns and plantings.

The austerity was appropriate, considering that every Jew – lord and labourer alike – is buried in a coffin made of unsanded planks as a reminder that we are all equal before death.

A tall stone wall insulated the cemetery from the rest of the world. The sounds of the city carried over it in a steady hum.

Hanna's grave was near the wall, under an old bird cherry. In the spring it was white with blossoms; now the leaves were starting to yellow. In contrast to the usual sombre tone, her gravestone was red granite. The stone bore a gold Star of David, the name, the dates of birth and death in Hebrew, and that was it.

I placed a flower on the grave and a small stone I had collected from Hanna's favourite place to play, Hietaniemenranta Beach, on the gravestone.

Whenever I went to the cemetery, I was compelled to imagine what Hanna might have become if she had had the will to live. Something important, I was sure, because she was exceptionally talented in so many ways. Maybe that's exactly why she couldn't take it; she was too far removed from everything normal. A long life filled with mundane worries was meant for mediocrities like Eli and me.

When I found Hanna dead, a handwritten note had been lying next to her on the bed. It read: "Ari, don't be sad and don't blame yourself. Live for me, too. That small star near the sun is me, your loving sister Hannah."

I realized I was wiping away tears, my own. I turned and walked off under the rustling trees. Once I reached the gate, I yanked the yarmulke from my head. My mind had cleared, and I felt strong and sure.

It was time to quit sentimentalizing and wrap this case up.

And Yom Kippur was the best possible day to do it.

Because before I was finished, a lot of people were going to have a real reason to repent.

Josef Meyer was draping a rich brown mink over a mannequin that had faded to a wan grey. When the door tinkled, Meyer tossed a hopeful glance in my direction: the first customer was always the most important customer of the day.

He recognized me and his hopes flew out the window.

He muttered something, turned his back on Simolin and me, and continued dressing the mannequin.

"Good morning, Mr Meyer," I said in an authoritative voice. "Please get your hat and coat and close up the shop. You're being arrested on suspicion of complicity in a murder."

Meyer turned.

"Just leave an old man in peace, Kafka."

"You decide. You told me that Weiss called from Israel and set up the meeting. We examined the phone logs. We didn't find any such call. That means you were lying to the police officer in charge of the investigation. Now you will tell us everything, or you'll be coming with us to HQ."

"You'd arrest me? Do you really hate me that much?"

I didn't answer. I could feel my dander-tortured nose beginning to run.

Meyer's cheeks twitched. He weighed the situation for a moment and then, in the face of the inevitable, gave in.

"If you have something to ask, ask."

"Who was Ben Weiss?"

"I don't know, but I can put two and two together. He was Mossad."

In a small gesture of conciliation, I adopted a less formal tone.

"So what was your role?"

"Weiss needed a front. All they wanted from me was permission to say that we had negotiated some fur deals – if someone asked, that is. They assured me that no one would. I never even met Weiss. I was given a photo so I would recognize him if it proved necessary."

"Who asked for your help?"

"Kaplan. Or before that, Silberstein called and told me that someone would be in touch… He asked me to assist on behalf of the congregation."

"Dan Kaplan?"

"Yes. Salomon's boy."

"What reason did he give?" Simolin asked.

"That they were tracking some terrorists who were believed to be in Finland, and that's why they needed my help."

"What else did he say?"

"Nothing. They're not a very talkative bunch."

"What about when Weiss died?"

"Kaplan called again and told me what to say if someone asked… that Weiss was a fur merchant and that he was carrying a lot of cash and that maybe he had been robbed. That's all I know… I believed and still believe that they were working for a good cause. I wanted to help."

"Like Oxbaum?"

"Yes. He promised to arrange the car. Then he reported it stolen."

"And who else?"

"I don't know."

"Where's Kaplan staying?"

"Even if you arrested me, there's nothing more I could tell you."

Meyer turned around and began fiddling with the fur on the mannequin.

His back was hunched and his head wobbled.

I thanked him.

I managed to make it into the entryway before sneezing.

I had just turned on my computer when there was a knock at the door. Stenman entered my room.

"Ari, is your phone off?"

I had turned it off at the cemetery and forgotten to turn it back on. I had been in total phone blackout for a couple of hours.

"Vivica Mattsson has been trying to call you. She left her number. She claimed it was urgent."

I called as soon as Stenman had left the room. I barely managed to say my name before Mattsson asked:

"Can you come here right now?"

"Where here?"

"My place."

"Is there something —"

"Please come right now…"

Mattsson gave me her address. I shouted for Stenman to join me and we rushed to the garage.

Mattson lived on Castréninkatu in Kallio. We didn't wait for the elevator; we ran up to the third floor. I loosened my gun in its holster and rang the doorbell. There was movement at the peephole, and the door immediately opened. Mattson hurriedly pulled the door closed behind me.

"Thank God you're here…"

Mattsson looked genuinely afraid, but I began to wonder whether the actor in her had got the upper hand. Or had she connived to lure me there because she was interested in me? Bringing Stenman along might not have been such a great idea after all.

Mattson's apartment was the same kind of mishmash of antique and modern furniture as my own place; some of the pieces were clearly inherited. The apartment was spacious and full of light. Her dog came and sniffed me first and then Stenman.

"I saw him."

"Who?"

"One of the two men who was running on the bridge."

"When and where?"

"Half an hour ago… I tried to call right away but I couldn't get hold of you… he saw me and started following me…"

Stenman lowered a hand onto Mattsson's own.

"Tell us the whole story from the beginning."

Mattsson swallowed a couple of times.

221

"I was out walking Jerry and heading home when a car pulled up next to me on Toinen Linja. I didn't pay any attention to it at first... But the car just kept following me, so I turned to look... that man was sitting in the front seat, staring at me... I remembered him immediately, and when he saw me, I could tell he knew..."

She covered her face with her hands. The timing of the gesture was a little too perfect.

"Go on," I asked.

"I went into a bar and tried to call you... the car stayed outside for a minute, but then it left. When I went out, it was gone."

"Tell me about the car."

"It was grey... I was panicking, it didn't even occur to me to think about the car."

Mattsson went over to the window and fearfully scanned the street from behind the drapes.

"I don't think you need to be afraid any more," Stenman said. "He can't know where you live."

Stenman's words clearly didn't calm Mattsson.

"He can find out."

"Was there anyone else in the car?"

Mattsson thought for a moment.

"There must have been, because he wasn't sitting on the driver's side. But I didn't see who was driving."

"Show her the pictures," I said to Stenman.

"Here are two photographs. Was it either of these men?"

Mattson took the photos and immediately said: "This is him. I'm one hundred per cent sure."

She handed me Kaplan's photograph.

"Was the other man on the bridge too?"

She looked at Weiss's photo for a long time.

"I'm not sure, he was farther back and I didn't get a good look at him. Do you have any other photos?"

"No."

Mattson pointed at Kaplan's photo.

"Who is he?"

Stenman glanced at me.

"We're looking for him. I can't say any more at this point."

"Can't or don't want to? Don't I have the right to know the name of the man who's following me?"

"I'm sorry," I said.

"What if I see him again? I don't even know if I should be afraid of him."

"If that happens, call me immediately."

"Does that mean I have reason to be afraid?"

Mattson grabbed my hand and positioned herself in front of me. I could smell the light scent of her perfume and see the fine down on her face. She raised her blue eyes to mine.

Phoney or not, it was effective.

"Should I be afraid?" she repeated. "Tell me."

"He might be dangerous."

"Because I identified him?"

"I can't think of any other reason."

"I read in the papers that there was an explosion in Vantaa yesterday where a young woman died. The paper said it had to do with what happened at Linnunlaulu. So you suspect that the man I saw was involved in that too?"

The question was cleverly posed. I replied that I didn't know.

"What did the paper mean then?"

"There are certain connections. Do you live alone?"

"Yes, all alone."

Mattsson was clearly beginning to recover.

"The performance begins at seven-thirty. What if he knows who I am and waits for me outside?"

It was conceivable, of course. On the one hand, it was difficult for me to believe that the Dan Kaplan I knew would do anything to a woman. On the other, he seemed to have a dark side that I didn't know. And it could just be a coincidence.

Dan had always had an eye for female beauty, and he might have just been flirting with Mattson by driving alongside her.

The thought distracted me, and somehow it just slipped out: "I can escort you to the theatre."

I thought I could detect a little disapproval in Stenman's gaze.

Mattson immediately latched onto my promise.

"Could you, I'd be so grateful…"

My mobile rang. It was Simolin. I moved a little farther away.

"I got right on Baltic Invest. The NBI has a dossier on them."

"Why are they interested?"

"They started looking into the company after enquiries began rolling in. You have a second?"

"Shoot."

"Amazingly enough, it appears to be a totally legit enterprise, even though it's owned by an investment company called Island Group registered in the Isle of Man, which is in turn owned by a company named Global Invest, headquartered in Israel. The main owner is a Jerusalem-based businessman named Benjamin Hararin."

"Thanks. We'll talk more when I get back."

"Meaning?"

"Half an hour."

Benjamin Hararin?

I returned my phone to my pocket.

I remembered the photo on the wall at my brother's office of the fat man boxed in by Max and Eli. I realized the women were staring at me. I said, "We have to go. What time should I pick you up?"

"Is six-thirty OK?"

"Six-thirty."

"Did I screw up?" I asked Stenman as soon as we were in the corridor.

"Depends on what happens between you two. She may be right about Kaplan hunting her."

"But why?" I wondered. "He knows that we know that he was at Linnunlaulu."

"And maybe she knows more than she's letting on. Or else Kaplan thinks she does and is covering his own back."

I had barely made it to my office before Huovinen came to get me for the evening briefing. In addition to the detectives, Deputy Police Chief Leivo was in attendance.

I reported the latest news on the investigation and the inquiries that were still under way. The shell found near Weiss's body was from a different weapon from the Linnunlaulu bullets or the shells and bullets found at Hamid's body shop. However, Tagi and Ali Hamid and Ali's employee Wasin Mahmed had all been shot with the same gun.

Leivo informed us that he and the police commander had met with the Israeli ambassador and been provided with the latest information on Saijed, Bakr, Weiss and Kaplan. He didn't tell us what information the ambassador had been provided with in return. Leivo was clearly taken by his conference with the ambassador and summarized everything he had absorbed by reminding us that there are criminals in every country.

"If an Israeli kills someone, chances are he's an average criminal, not a Mossad assassin. Weiss and Kaplan are common drug traffickers who just happen to be Israeli citizens."

"And what if an Arab kills? Is he always a terrorist?"

I registered Huovinen knitting his brows in a sign to tread carefully.

"Of course not… but in this case there are also other indications of terrorism," Leivo noted. "Weapons and explosives, in addition to the information we have on the perpetrators' backgrounds."

"So we're supposed to base the investigation on the assumption that we're dealing with a showdown between common Israeli drug traffickers and dangerous Arab terrorists and who's worse? Besides, we still don't know who the perpetrators are, we're just assuming."

"I'm not going to say one way or the other, but in light of the most recent information, it would appear so. The Israelis are certain that the man who got hit by the train was Saijed and the one who's still on the loose is Bakr."

"Weiss and Kaplan are up to their ears in the events at Linnunlaulu," I said. "It's hard to consider them common criminals."

"Common criminals can help terrorists in exchange for payment. There doesn't have to be anything ideological about it. According to the ambassador, this is exactly what this is a question of."

"It would be good if you could share the new information provided by the ambassador with the rest of us."

The deputy chief cleared his throat, and his face took on a concentrated expression.

"Yes, well... he promised to deliver us data gathered by the Israeli police and tax authorities on Kaplan and Weiss. He promised to do all he could to help us apprehend Kaplan. He considered Kaplan a dangerous criminal. In addition, we will receive assistance from Klein, the embassy's head of security, as necessary."

Leivo rose and straightened out the creases in his trousers.

"I believe we're on the right trail. I don't see any reason why we shouldn't take advantage of the ambassador's promise of assistance and the latest know-how."

Leivo nodded and exited. Huovinen waited for a moment and quipped: "Use the latest know-how, boys. We're on the right trail."

When we were out in the corridor, Simolin whispered: "The phone records arrived."

I followed him into his office. Stenman followed at our heels: she could sense the news in Simolin's secretiveness.

Simolin pulled out the prints of phone records from a locked drawer. He peeked out into the corridor, which seemed a little excessive, closed the door behind him, and spread the sheets across his desk.

"Here's the data for one month from the phone belonging to the man considered to be Ismel Saijed and the calls made from it to Hamid's body shop, home and mobile phone, the calls made by Hamid, and location information. The information on Laya's calls hasn't come in yet. The calls that were located were all made from the greater Helsinki area, mostly Helsinki proper. There are no clusters; the calls are spread out all over different parts of town. In other words, the data isn't much use. However…"

Simolin clicked the mouse a couple of times.

"I made a graph of all of the calls. It looks like this."

The image made up of lines, circles and points looked like a lace-making pattern.

"Mr X… in other words, the man suspected of being Hassan Bakr. He's clearly the number-one player, this spider here. This number, with the traffic that's pretty unidirectional, must be his. Bakr has placed calls to both Ali and Tagi Hamid and clearly more often to the man hit by the train, who we suspect is Ismel Saijed. Saijed, on the other hand, has only contacted Bakr twice, in other words on the day that Ali Hamid was killed and then slightly before his death… Because Bakr is most important, his back is protected the best. I'm guessing he has contacted Saijed through accomplices abroad. Saijed received about thirty international calls over the month… from Syria, Israel, England and Pakistan."

Simolin underlined two numbers…

"These here are interesting. Ali Hamid called both of these numbers several times during the month, and he was called from these numbers approximately just as many times, most recently on the night he was killed."

I glanced at the numbers. One was a landline number; the other was a mobile number starting in 040. I recognized the first four digits of the landline number.

"That's the number for SUPO."

Simolin nodded.

"Both of them go to our old friend."

"Sillanpää?"

"Good guess."

At least you couldn't blame Sillanpää for not trying. He was popping up everywhere.

When you added the call data to what we'd heard from the sister-in-law of the dead body-shop employee, there wasn't much that remained unclear: Sillanpää and Ali Hamid knew each other, and Sillanpää was trying to milk Hamid for information, or else Hamid was Sillanpää's snitch.

In either case, the season of mutual openness and trust between Inspector Sillanpää and myself had remained uncommonly brief.

21

I barely had time to drop by my place to shower and change for my escort gig. I took the tram to Hakaniemi and continued from there on foot. The weather was cold and it looked like rain.

Even though I believed that Vivica Mattsson was in no danger, I grew more alert as I approached her apartment. I stopped just short of a hundred yards from her building and looked around. I didn't see anything suspicious; I didn't see much of anything, actually. The cold was keeping everyone inside, and the street was totally dead.

I walked over in front of Mattsson's building and scanned the vicinity again. A couple of young people exited the neighbouring building and a car drove down the hill, passing Mattsson's place before turning towards Hakaniemi.

I pressed the buzzer and waited. Nothing happened. I pressed again. No response.

I had Mattsson's number stored in my phone. I called it. No one answered.

I pressed buzzers at random until I got in. I climbed up to the fourth floor and listened. I couldn't hear anything except the sounds of everyday life; behind Mattsson's door all was silent.

I rang the doorbell. No one came to open it. I peeked in through the mail slot, but all I could see was a strip of the Persian rug in the entryway.

If she had decided to go in to work on her own after all, why hadn't she bothered to call me?

I called information and asked them to connect me to the porter at the City Theatre. Vivica Mattsson hadn't arrived at work yet.

I called Mattsson's number again and pressed my ear to the mail slot. The phone either wasn't in the apartment or it was turned off; otherwise I would have heard it ring.

I went downstairs and found the building manager's number on the bulletin board. He answered immediately. I blew things shamelessly out of proportion to get him to hurry. He promised to be there in ten minutes.

I called Simolin and asked him to come to the apartment.

The manager arrived in eight minutes. We climbed up to the third floor together. I pulled out my gun and asked for the key.

He paled and handed it to me.

"You'd better go now."

The guy backed down the stairs.

I unlocked the door and carefully cracked it open. When the gap was about an inch and a half wide, I peered in. No signs of anything unusual in the entryway. I started to creep farther into the apartment, but then I realized it was pointless. If someone was there, they would have heard me enter.

But I still held my gun at the ready.

I saw Mattsson's dog first. It was lying dead on the plush carpet in the living room. The bedroom door was ajar. I pushed it wide with the tip of my shoe. By now it was no surprise to find Vivica Mattsson sprawled across the double bed. A bloody groove coiled around her neck. She was as dead as the dog in the front room.

I touched her hand. It was cool. I circled the body and saw her face. Her swollen tongue protruded from her mouth like some strange flower. I looked at her and felt at first guilt and then simply rage.

"I was sure there was no danger," I explained, more to myself than the others.

Stenman, Simolin and Huovinen looked at me with sympathy.

"What a fucked-up situation," Huovinen sighed, glancing at the body on the bed.

"Why did she let a stranger in if she was so afraid?" Stenman wondered.

I wondered that, too, and then I remembered something.

"It was a man and a woman who went to Hamid's place. Maybe the woman rang the doorbell and she forgot to stay on her guard."

Some critically relevant thought floated through my mind like a dying ember. I emptied my brain of everything else so I could follow the tiny, feeble trail that it left in its wake. Suddenly I caught hold of it.

"The dog!"

"Yeah, what about it?" Huovinen asked.

"I don't mean Mattsson's dog, I mean a woman I saw in the park."

I told them about the woman who was walking the dog in Sibelius Park and my uncle's warning.

"If the woman who rang the doorbell had a dog, then another dog person would definitely open the door."

"Why didn't you tell us about the woman?" Huovinen scolded.

"I didn't believe my uncle."

The CSI came over.

"The dog was shot with a twenty-two with a silencer; the woman was strangled, as you can see. It looks like there were two perpetrators, because it was all done so tidily."

"Maybe they followed Mattsson and saw that she met you two and then they decided to kill her," Huovinen suggested.

"Who's they?" Simolin asked.

"Kaplan and his accomplice."

"Why didn't he just skip the country? What reason would he have for staying here and chasing down Mattsson? Something here is seriously out of whack," I said.

Everyone looked at me, perplexed.

"What?"

"I know Kaplan and I know how smart he is. Why would he follow me in such a way that he'd be exposed, and then Mattsson in a way that he'd be exposed again."

I remembered Dan's call and how he had riled me up, just like when we were kids. I was better than him at table tennis, but he was the most irritating player I knew. It was like he read my thoughts and guessed my next move. If I rushed over to the right edge during a long rally to return the hit, he'd send it left. If I was expecting a backhand smash, he'd backspin me a drop shot that would barely clear the net. After that, it would take everything I had to keep from smacking the smirk off Dan's face with my paddle.

Suddenly I realized what was going on. I was absolutely sure.

"When Kaplan called me, he reminded me that he had always been sharper than me. He wanted me to get worked up and focus all my attention on chasing him, so the others would have room to manoeuvre – the killers, the man and the woman."

Huovinen started to say something, but changed his mind when the crime-scene investigator stepped into the doorway and raised a forefinger to his lips. We all looked at each other. The investigator gestured for me to come into the bedroom.

Huovinen followed me in. The investigator pointed at something underneath the window sill near the bed. We bent over to look. A small wireless radio transmitter had been attached to the bottom of it.

I would never doubt my uncle's wisdom again.

Someone was listening in on Mattson's apartment.

We went back into the entryway. Huovinen whispered: "What do we do?"

"Just continue as normal. I don't think anyone's listening to the place any more."

"Maybe we could trace the tap."

"Mika, get in touch with the experts at the phone company."

Simolin nodded and exited into the corridor.

"Not your average case," Huovinen said thoughtfully.

"No, even though someone's trying to feed it to us as if it were one."

"Who?" Huovinen asked.

I didn't have time to answer before footsteps could be heard from the corridor. I glanced out and saw Sillanpää bounding towards us.

"I happened to be in the area," he said. "Might be best if we hash things out."

"Again? Is there something you want to tell us about your friendship with Ali Hamid?"

"I get that you're pissed off, but so are we. I heard she's dead."

Sillanpää glanced around. The old lady who lived next door was snooping on us through her cracked-open front door.

"Let's find a better spot," Sillanpää said.

Sillanpää's idea of a better spot was a van with tinted windows parked out in front of the building. The back of the van was filled with all kinds of equipment, tape recorders and laptops. There were two men in the vehicle. They were sitting in front of a monitor that looked like a GPS navigator; it was showing a map. Both men had headsets on, and one was talking into his: "*The target is turning from Tuusulantie onto Ring Road III and moving west…*"

Sillanpää looked at us and said: "The target is a van. We're following it."

"What's in it?" Huovinen pressed.

"Two men and a woman and a plywood crate. I believe you'd be pretty interested to meet them."

"Are Mattsson's killers in the van?"

"So it would seem, and Hamid's and his employee's. We also believe that they rigged the Koivukylä bomb."

"I know that Ali Hamid was your snitch," I said.

"Source. It was thanks to him we picked up those guys' trail."

"A little too late."

"What do you mean?"

"Ali Hamid called you shortly before he was killed. You went to the body shop and found the bodies."

Sillanpää looked at me, assessing how much I knew.

"We have eyewitness and security-camera footage of the van."

Sillanpää knew that I knew too much. He couldn't play dumb, so he decided to meet me halfway.

"The operation would have been endangered if the bodies had been found that night. I can't tell you any more than that."

"No need to. You mean that Tagi might have called off the meeting on the bridge, and you and the Israelis wouldn't have got the opportunity to bag Bakr and Saijed."

Sillanpää didn't respond.

"From the police's perspective, that means that you're suspected of aiding and abetting four murders and two homicides," Huovinen stated coldly.

"Sometimes there's a pretty goddamn huge gap between theory and practice. We live in a world where the intelligence agencies of democratic countries cooperate with each other as long as there's a common enemy."

"Your cooperation killed six people," Huovinen continued.

"We realized too late that we were playing according to different rules, and we didn't have time to stop them. Besides, we initially thought that Bakr and Saijed killed the Hamid cousins. We broke off cooperation as soon as we found out the truth, and now we'll help you in every way possible."

"Is Dan Kaplan in the vehicle?"

"No. We don't know where he is, but we know he's part of the same group."

"Do you know where the van is headed?"

"I'm guessing the airport."

"*The target is turning onto Airport Road...*"

"Pretty good guess, huh?"

"Why don't you guess the rest while you're at it," Huovinen growled angrily.

"You'll hear the whole story. But we'll have to agree how things are going to be communicated. This stuff is international-level."

"The lead investigator is responsible for communicating about the case," Huovinen said.

"We have a few requests to make," Sillanpää said.

"You can always make requests."

Sillanpää's story lasted about five minutes.

"The vehicle is outside the cargo terminal," announced one of the men manning the phones.

"Want to head out there with us?" Sillanpää asked.

We didn't turn him down.

Auschwitz and Treblinka. I had visited both as a young Inter-Railer. A million Jews had been killed like slaughter animals infected with a contagious disease. Something like that breeds an incomprehensible amount of agony, rage and fear, the combination of which had conditioned Jews to sensitivity in sniffing out hostility behind, before and within words. At times, anti-Semitism is detected where it doesn't exist. It's monitored like the weather: sometimes it's sunny, sometimes conditions seem to be getting worse. Absolute zero is the winter backlash of the Holocaust, which is never reached but occasionally approached. That's why you always had to be awake and alert. *Never again* was tattooed on the shoulder of every Jew.

One's attitude towards the state of Israel was another eternally ticklish topic. Were all actions of the state of Israel acceptable simply because they were carried out by Israel and its politicians, leaders and soldiers?

By no means did all Jews approve of Israel's power politics in the occupied territories, but on the other hand...

Many of us balanced like the milkman Tevye between traditions and patriotism. On the one hand... on the other hand...

When the Israeli army killed two Hamas leaders with missile strikes, a few colleagues asked what I thought about it. I had been forced to join that band of Jews who wavered between views.

But you always had to draw a line somewhere. A number of Israeli citizens had participated in a string of crimes that had already resulted in the deaths of eight people. Even though I was a Jew, I felt the line had been crossed, and it was easy for me to pick sides.

"Here they come!" Simolin said.

Simolin, Sillanpää and I were sitting in the international transit hall at Helsinki-Vantaa airport, trying to look inconspicuous. We gave a pretty credible impression of three mid-level businessmen travelling abroad to make mid-size deals.

I recognized the woman immediately, even though she was wearing an El Al flight attendant's uniform. She was the same woman I had seen walking a dog in Sibelius Park.

She was accompanied by a thirty-year-old man in an El Al co-pilot's uniform. He was carrying a black leather satchel. I closed my eyes, covered my face with my hand, and played the role of a dozing businessman. I could hear the woman's heels click past. I waited for a second and cracked one eye open. They stopped at the gate to the El Al flight.

"Now," Sillanpää said, and we jumped up. I could see the man trying to open the glass door giving onto the jetway, but it was locked. He said something to an airport attendant and noticed us at the same time.

He grabbed the door again and jerked ferociously. The door shuddered but didn't open. The woman tried to help, but it was too late.

Sillanpää showed his police ID and informed them that they were both under arrest. The woman attempted a smile and asked what was going on.

"Please come with us. You'll find out."

"The plane's about to leave."

"Come with us. It won't take long to clear this up."

A member of the El Al ground personnel rushed up, loudly demanding an explanation. An airport police officer grabbed him and half-forcibly dragged him off.

"I'm just going to inform the captain," said the man in the co-pilot's uniform, pulling out his phone. I snatched it from his hand.

"I want you to call the Israeli embassy immediately," the woman demanded sharply.

We guided both of them into the customs officers' room, where they and their belongings were searched. After that, Sillanpää ordered that they be taken to the airport jail and detained in such a way that they couldn't speak to each other.

The crate was waiting for us at the air-freight office. It was a solid plywood box, a good three feet long, about thirty inches wide, and eighteen inches deep. The contents had been noted as computer equipment on the airway bill.

The clerk brought Sillanpää a crowbar. Sillanpää shooed him off before twisting the lock open. The lock bore the diplomatic mail seal of the Israeli embassy.

The interior of the crate was lined with cellular shipping plastic. A tightly bound, grey-haired man lay there, legs bent and mouth gagged. He was secured at the hands and feet to hooks in the sides of the crate so he couldn't budge. He appeared to be unconscious.

"And now we'll find out who the hell you are," Sillanpää said.

The man's eyes remained closed. I felt his pulse. His heart was beating slowly but steadily. Sillanpää gave me a self-satisfied smile and held out his hand.

"Are we square?"

I shook.

Simolin examined the man and his confined quarters.

"So this is going to turn into an international incident, isn't it?"

We both looked at Sillanpää.

"No, not necessarily."

"What do you mean, no?" I asked, surprised.

"We're not going to broadcast this one to the world yet. Every move has to be considered carefully. If we play our cards right, we have a gold mine on our hands."

"What do you mean, play?" I asked. I was getting a bad feeling. Whenever black or white started being tinted with grey, I feared the worst. I was a police officer, and a police officer didn't play or cut deals, except in the traditional sense.

"So what's the plan, squeezing a special price on oranges out of them?"

Sillanpää could immediately tell that he needed to choose his words more carefully. We knew far too much, so it was in his best interests to maintain a working relationship with us. I was the lead investigator and I answered for communications about the case. All the trumps were in my hand, if we started playing for real.

"I mean that that investigation is still under way. At least your friend Kaplan is still missing."

"If you've been shadowing the Israelis the whole time, maybe you have some idea of where he might be."

"Not the whole time, only since yesterday."

Sillanpää's phone rang. He glanced at the screen and pressed the speakerphone so we could hear the conversation.

"Hello, Mr Klein."

Sillanpää smirked.

"We received a call that the police have arrested two Israeli citizens who are El Al employees."

"Your sources are accurate and fast."

"What's it all about?"

"Routine criminal investigation."

"What type of crime is in question?"

"A very serious one."

"How can a flight attendant and a co-pilot be involved in a serious crime?"

"Anyone can. Even a police officer."

"The flight will be late if they're not released."

"Unfortunately that can't be avoided. You'll have to find new personnel to replace them or cancel the flight."

"What if I arrange to have a representative of your police force accompany them on the flight?"

"The Finnish police don't interrogate suspects in aeroplanes, they do it in jail. And anyways, I don't make those decisions."

"Have you taken into account the possibility that this might simply be a misunderstanding? Do you understand that this incident could have extremely grave consequences for relations between our countries?"

"I understand the gravity of the situation all too well. It's part of my job."

"Would it help at all if our ambassador contacted someone?"

"I don't think so. Besides, if the media discovers that you've tried to exert pressure and prevent the police from investigating a serious crime, then..."

"I'm not talking about exerting pressure... this just happens to come at a very delicate time. Our foreign minister will be visiting Finland, and at the same time citizens of our country, who are in

the service of the state no less, are arrested during the Jewish New Year, and on Yom Kippur of all days. You know how sensitive we are in Israel about things like this."

"At the moment they're only simply in detention."

"Who's investigating the case?"

"I hear it's Detective Kafka's."

"Why? He's also the one investigating the Linnunlaulu case, isn't he?"

"I don't know yet. I haven't spoken with Kafka, and it's not my jurisdiction, at least not yet, not as long as it's a matter of a common crime. But unfortunately, I have to go now."

"Could you keep me in the loop? Please understand my position. This could not have happened at a worse moment, with the foreign minister's visit and Yom Kippur."

"Of course I understand, but Kafka can be touchy. He won't tell us anything, and he'll tell you even less."

"We need to meet as soon as possible to discuss the minister's visit. You do understand, don't you, that I will be forced to report this matter to the ambassador, and that won't be the end of it, either. From there it will go to the Ministry of Foreign Affairs and who knows where."

"Of course. You're just doing your job, but I'm not worried. Luckily, Israel is a democratic country, and everyone there understands how things work in a democracy."

The airport doctor arrived five minutes later and examined the man, who had been lifted from the crate onto a sofa.

"He's been given a powerful sedative. He'll probably still sleep for hours."

"Is he in any danger?" I asked.

"I don't think so. His heart is beating steadily, but it would be wisest to move him without delay to a place where he can be monitored safely as he comes to."

I asked the doctor to order an ambulance and choose a suitable hospital.

Sillanpää stood off to the side, talking into his mobile and glancing at me intermittently. He hung up and walked over.

"I spoke with the commander. He feels that due to the delicacy of the situation, it will be to everyone's advantage for the Security Police to take over communication responsibility for this. We'll also handle the interrogation of the suspects and the man from the crate. All information necessary from the perspective of the criminal investigation will be delivered to you immediately."

"So you'll decide what's necessary?"

"Sorry, but that's how this one's going to go. The higher-ups called it."

I had forgotten Simolin, but he hadn't forgotten me. When Sillanpää went over to consult with the doctor, Simolin walked up and pulled me aside.

"Did you get information on the listening device?" I asked.

"The guys from the phone company went and retrieved it. It was probably being monitored from a vehicle in front of the house. The range is about a hundred yards... And the fingerprints of the man who got hit by the train came in from French Interpol. Looks like we're on the wrong track when it comes to him, and the other guy too."

"What other guy?"

"Weiss's killer, the Focus man. The fingerprints found in Laya's Focus have also been identified."

By the time Simolin finished, I knew I'd sleep just as poorly that night as I had the night before.

22

Although I had wriggled my way free of many traditions, there were a few I still clung to. Yom Kippur was one. I knew I would never completely free myself of it, nor did I want to. Even though working as a cop could harden just about anyone, Yom Kippur still managed to rouse memories in me that were both poignant and as tender as an open wound.

Yom Kippur was like the mournful melody of the *Kol Nidre* that welled up inside you and brought you so close to tears that the only way to avoid them was to close your eyes. It was also loved ones remembering their dead with the *Yizkor* prayer, downcast faces, and the synagogue growing dim as the *Al Chet* prayer drew near.

On Yom Kippur, Dad was always at home and there was no arguing. When I was a child, Dad read Eli, Hanna and me a blessing that every Jewish father read to his children before leaving for the synagogue. During the blessing, he asked God that we would become like Ephraim, Rachel and Leah. As he finished, he would smile at us and read his personal addition: "If at all possible." Eli, Hanna and I would look at each other and giggle.

Those four extraneous words were like Dad's secret gift to us, a gift that Mum knew nothing about. If I ever have a child someday, I'll continue this tradition and complete the blessing by adding, "If at all possible."

* * *

My uncle must have been waiting for me in his entryway, because he opened his door as soon as I stepped out of the elevator. The clank of the elevator carried into the apartment, so he knew I was approaching. He was wearing a dark suit with barely discernible pinstripes. He held the door wide and let me in. We looked at each other, and my uncle, brows knitted, clapped me lightly on the shoulder.

My uncle muttered something in Hebrew but so softly I couldn't hear what it was.

He noticed my puzzlement and said: "It seems as if God and I understand each other better and better every year. When you're as old as I am, you don't have the time or the energy to commit much concrete evil, but you commit all the more in your thoughts. You'd never believe the nasty, ugly things that go through my head. Only a scribe or a lawyer could ever imagine that listing your sins one by one will earn you forgiveness. And God is neither a scribe nor a lawyer."

"Or a policeman," I said.

My uncle laughed.

"And yet God has granted the powers that be a sword so that it might be used wisely and for the good of all."

It was as if my uncle had once again read my mind. I explained briefly what we had discovered during the investigation and what I intended. He lowered a hand onto my shoulder.

"I don't envy you, Ari, but as I said, you have been given a sword so that you might use it. I know you will do the right thing, and that it would be impossible for you to do otherwise."

It was as if my uncle's words had swept away all my doubts and fears. I was in the right, and it was impossible for me to do otherwise.

Both floors of the synagogue were full, the women bareheaded above and the yarmulke-capped men below. In addition to my uncle and me, the Kafka family was represented by my brother Eli. Next to him sat Max Oxbaum and his teenage son.

Dan entered in the middle of the service and sat at his father's left side, his eyes nailed to the floor. Suddenly he turned and looked at me. We were about six yards apart. At first Dan sized me up, then he smiled.

I stood and moved sideways towards the exit. Dan stood too. I made it into the foyer before he did and retreated towards the main doors.

"I'm here to pray, but it looks like you're here to work. What would our old religion teacher Rabbi Motzkind say?"

"Put your gun on the floor," I ordered.

"No, that's not what he would say," Dan sneered. "You don't think I'd come to the synagogue armed, do you? I'm among friends here."

"A lovely gesture. Are you sure you had enough time to ask forgiveness for all your sins?"

"Looks like for once you outsmarted me. You knew I would come here on Yom Kippur. What are you planning on doing now?" Dan asked casually.

"We're going to get into the car that's waiting outside and drive to Pasila. You're under arrest."

"It's that simple for you?"

"Yes. Out."

I opened the door and let him pass.

We stood in the glistening, rain-washed courtyard, eyeing each other.

"Aren't you going to give me a chance to defend myself?" Dan asked.

"There's no time, and it wouldn't change anything."

"It wouldn't? Maybe I'm just a common murderer to you, but to plenty of other people I'm a lifesaver."

"A lifesaver saves lives, he doesn't end them."

"What do you know about me? I've saved the lives of dozens, maybe hundreds of Jews, adults and children. Saijed and Bakr had murdered dozens and would have murdered more if we hadn't stopped them. And believe me, many local Jews helped us in that effort voluntarily."

"Without knowing what they were involved in," I pointed out. "Did you find Bakr?"

"You can forget him. He's already on his way to Israel. We believe he'll be able to provide us with a lot of useful information."

"So you're working for Mossad these days?"

"Good pay, long holidays, get to see the world."

"The only downer being that you have to kill now and again."

"It's not always such a downer."

"It was for Weiss."

"He was always over-confident. I wouldn't have given them a chance."

"Like you didn't give Tagi Hamid either."

"Don't blame us for things we didn't do. We wanted Saijed, but the bastard went and fell under a train. Hamid was one of ours; we were paying him to organize contacts with Arabs and give us information about them. He was useful to us, but then Saijed and Bakr began to suspect him, and Saijed killed him."

"But you finished the job and mutilated his face."

"That was improvisation, but we've been trained in it. He would have died anyways. If you want to play for time, you have to muddy and confuse your tracks."

"Ali Hamid was one of your men too, but you killed him. Mossad's not a very nice employer."

"He was starting to choke, and he and his cousin were plotting against us. See how much I trust you?"

"What about Laya and the kid in the car?"

"Unfortunate accidents. We suspected that Laya had found out about us from Tagi. The plan was to use a remote detonator, but then you found the car and screwed everything up. Our men had to get out of there and activate the detonator. Laya shouldn't have put his woman up to it. The kid's death was just bad luck. Weiss was carrying an incendiary device that we were going to use to destroy Oxbaum's minivan when we were done with it. The kid must have played around with it and set it off."

"How did you find Bakr?"

"By the dog. I saw the woman walking it at Linnunlaulu. But don't think for a minute she was just there taking it for a piss. Bakr must have suspected that the meeting was a trap and she was watching his back. She surprised Weiss – in other words, for all practical purposes, she killed him."

"And that's why you killed her?"

"I thought I sensed something developing between you two. A beautiful woman, I must admit. We didn't kill her."

"Who did then?"

"Bakr knew that we were right on his heels and eventually lost his nerve. He began suspecting she would talk as soon as he left, so he strangled her. We have it all on tape. It doesn't make for pleasant listening. And she loved him, too, or at least she claimed to."

We looked at each other in the light of the street lamp. The drizzle had soaked my hair, and drops were trickling down my face and collecting at my chin. I wiped them away. Dan looked at me. He wasn't smiling any more.

"Can you guess why I trust you?" he asked.

"Because I'm a good Jew?"

"Wrong."

"Because I'm your friend?"

"Are you?"

"Not any more."

"That's what I was afraid of. I trust you because Bakr is the one who planned the bombing at the restaurant where your sister Hanna was. I heard she never recovered from it. That's too bad, Hanna was a lovely girl."

I could feel a buzzing between my ears.

"Do you think that's all it's going to take?"

"What about this: do you know about your brother Eli's and his partner Max's business dealings? They've brokered loans on behalf of a company named Baltic Invest to the tune of at least ten million euros. Baltic Invest is owned by an Israeli businessman, Benjamin Hararin. His affairs are under investigation in Israel, because Baltic Invest launders a hell of a lot of drug money for the Russian mob. We have copies of all the money transfers. They look really ugly. We also have photographs, videotapes and audio tapes."

Dan smiled as if he were remembering a funny story.

"It's strange how you think you know people but you really don't. I was under the impression that Eli and Max were faithful family men, but when I saw a couple of videotapes, I had to adjust my views. It's so easy to stray when you're far from home."

I clenched my teeth so hard they ground.

"Does Eli know where the money comes from?"

"Probably not. He was just greedy, like the rest of us. But that won't have much bearing if this all goes public."

My shoulder-muscles tensed, rock-hard.

"But it doesn't have to," Dan continued. "It would be easy for us to arrange to have one branch of a larger investigation left uninvestigated if..."

If I had felt a momentary empathy for Dan, all I wanted to do now was wipe the self-satisfied smirk from his face.

"Let's go for a little walk," I said.

Dan looked skywards and spread out his arms.

"I've always liked the Helsinki rain, there's something special about it."

The guard sitting in the hut buzzed open the gate and we turned towards Malminrinne.

247

"One more thing," I said. "There wasn't any terrorist attack being planned, was there?"

Dan stopped.

"Do you think Bakr and Saijed had changed their ways and started loving Jews? The attack was just a matter of time. But I know what you mean. No, there was no attack being planned. Yet."

"What about the visit of the foreign minister?"

Dan smiled.

"Don't you get it yet?"

"Not everything. Tell me."

"The most important thing was to get Bakr and Saijed dead or alive, preferably alive, because they knew a lot. We also wanted to send out a message that Israel does not forget, that the killers of Israeli citizens never escape vengeance. Thirdly, we wanted to wake you up from your daydreams. Can't you see how you and your leaders are being fooled? Everyone feels sorry for the Palestinian children being killed by cruel Israeli soldiers. In the Nordic countries, Israel is a dirty word. Your leaders don't even want to meet with ours, but when a Palestinian terrorist shows up here, the same men embrace him with open arms and expressions of sympathy. You've offered safe haven to the terrorists who kill our citizens."

The Dan I saw in front of me was someone I didn't know. This Dan wasn't the least bit funny; he was a fanatic whose opinion there was no point trying to change.

"Our children are killed too," Dan went on. "They're blown up on their school buses, they're shot and stabbed. The only reason people hate us is because Israel has decided that its citizens will never be slaughtered like sheep again."

"That's the only reason?" I replied.

"It's time you opened your eyes. Some day your children and your decision-makers may be the victims. Then you'll be begging for our help. No, our foreign minister was definitely not coming here."

"Why the whole charade, then?"

"It gave our men a good excuse to come help with the operation. Plus, we wanted to get some real fireworks while we were at it. Thanks to the visit, we'll get some show-stopping headlines: 'Israeli foreign minister cancels visit due to terrorist threat', 'Terrorists plan attack on synagogue', 'Terrorist strike thwarted in the nick of time'. Lots of headlines, lots of controversy."

"You planted weapons and explosives in Tagi Hamid's basement and Laya's apartment and framed them as terrorists," I said.

"Of course. The whole is made up of parts, and all the parts have to fit together."

Dan took a step towards me and held out his hand.

"You're a Jew, in your heart you have to understand. I protect my citizens the way you do yours."

I looked at the extended hand, but I didn't shake it.

"Say hello to everyone for me."

"Have you forgotten that you're under arrest?"

Dan had already managed to take a step away from me. He stopped and turned. There was a gun in his hand.

"A gun in the synagogue, very naughty," I said. "And one more thing: you guys got screwed. The brilliant Mossad has been royally duped."

Dan's carefree expression warped into a strained smile.

"Do you think I believe you?"

"Your colleagues were apprehended near the airport. At the time of arrest, the woman was wearing an El Al flight attendant's uniform and the man was posing as a co-pilot."

Dan was momentarily silent. He realized that something had gone wrong.

"So what? They're both prepared to live, die and suffer for Israel. They've been raised and trained for it."

"In this case they won't suffer for Israel, but because of your stupidity. We also found the package you were mailing.

The man you thought was Bakr is not Bakr, and the man who fell from the bridge was not Saijed."

Dan's face was like a mask. I had said something he couldn't take in. He snapped, almost angrily: "You're lying!"

"In reality your Bakr is an Algerian-born drug trafficker named Abbas Musaw. The man you thought was Saijed is his compatriot Salah Madri, also a drug trafficker. Both have been identified. They were in Finland negotiating drug deals with Tagi and Ali Hamid. Laya was in on it too."

I could feel the rain start to trickle down my back from the collar of my coat. I didn't let it bother me; Dan had it worse.

"The Hamid cousins needed money to start up their narcotics business. One of them came up with the idea that they could get it from Mossad, as long as the bait was big enough. They sold you a bill of goods, claimed that Bakr and Saijed were hiding out in Finland. Your helper Tagi knew that the men were suspected of having left Denmark. Finland was a good match for the scenario. After that, there was no shortage of funds. Unfortunately for him, someone from Mossad got a little too excited and decided to put on a real show."

Dan was listening, but he was also scanning around in disbelief.

"Plus, Ali Hamid went and used the drug money to buy an auto-body shop. After that, they didn't have the money to pay their French contacts for the drugs. When the cousins realized that their lives were in danger, they came up with a brilliant idea. They offered their business partners to you as terrorists. That turned out to be easy, because Mossad got all fired up when they saw an opportunity for an act of heroism that would stun the world."

You're not supposed to take pleasure in others' misfortunes, even your enemy's, but I was only human.

"You know there aren't many photos of Bakr and Saijed, and those that exist are old. That's why Musaw and Madri were perfect for the part."

Dan's defences momentarily crumbled. I could see fear in his eyes. He glanced rapidly around.

"Believe me," I said. "The game's over. You lost."

Dan raised his gun and aimed at my chest.

"My father and mother loved you like a son. We were like brothers."

I looked Dan in the eye.

"That was then. Before you went off the deep end."

The mournful rising and falling of the shofar could be heard from the synagogue. It was the sound of joy and sorrow, victory and destruction from bygone millennia.

I took a step towards Dan. He was aiming at me, and his hand wasn't trembling.

"This really sucks, Ari, but…"

A shot cracked through the sound of the shofar, and Dan shuddered from the hit. I thought it came from the van parked on the other side of the street, when several men in dark suits jumped out. Then I realized that my uncle was standing behind me with a gun in his hand. I didn't see how he had approached us without our noticing.

My uncle dropped the gun and looked at me.

"I couldn't let him kill you, and I didn't want you to kill him. It's too heavy a burden. You're still young…"

I bent over at Dan's side. I raised his head from the wet ground. I could see that the shot had been lethal.

"This really sucks, Dan."

Dan looked at me and tried to smile. His rigid face softened and his eyes closed. My friend Dan Kaplan had died a long time ago. Now it was just Dan Kaplan who died.

The police officers gathered around me, and Huovinen placed a hand on my shoulder. Ignoring the wet asphalt, my uncle dropped down at my side. The prayer accompanied every Jew at death. We uttered it together: "*Barukh atah Adonai Eloheinu melekh ha'olam, dayan ha'emet...*"

"Blessed art thou, Lord our God, King of the universe, the one true judge."

The sound of the shofar rose from the depths of despair and died out.